The
Cranberry
Inn

BOOKS BY BARBARA JOSSELSOHN

The Lilac House
The Bluebell Girls
The Lily Garden

The Cranberry Inn

BARBARA JOSSELSOHN

bookouture

Published by Bookouture in 2021

An imprint of Storyfire Ltd.
Carmelite House
50 Victoria Embankment
London EC4Y 0DZ

www.bookouture.com

ISBN: 978-1-80019-933-0
eBook ISBN: 978-1-80019-932-3

ONE

The kitchen was so breathtaking, it should have been real. Laurel stepped into the featured display at Italian appliance maker Samposiera's new Manhattan showroom. Everything worked together so beautifully. The gray marble countertop was a perfect complement to the sleek, high-tech refrigerator, and the checkered backsplash offered a touch of whimsy alongside the ultra-modern cooktop. The black stainless sink looked inventive, paired with an angled faucet. And then there was the unexpected lighting—two hanging glass cubes, each with a bare bulb atop a brushed copper socket. The only thing missing, Laurel thought, was a family. She wondered what kind of family would own a kitchen this sophisticated. What kind of dishes would be stacked in the cabinets? What style of silverware in the drawers? What gourmet dish would be on the menu for Christmas? Who would be coming and what would they talk about?

That was the trouble with model kitchens, she mused as she leaned on the center island and ran her finger along the acrylic cube with "Joanna Miller Interiors" etched in silver letters. They didn't give your imagination much to work with. They didn't tell enough of a story. Of course, she could never tell Joanna, her boss, that this was how she felt. Joanna loved creating showroom displays and was thrilled to have been chosen as Samposiera's newest featured designer. She'd positively glowed a few minutes ago, as she described her choices of colors and finishes to an audience of magazine editors, retail buyers, hosts of home-themed TV shows, and other design professionals, and then proceeded to the showroom lobby for a lavish Christmas-themed cocktail party in her honor.

And Joanna had a right to be proud, Laurel thought. Many designers had vied to create this kitchen, which would appear in all Samposiera's ad campaigns and be celebrated in an upcoming issue of *Elegant Kitchens Magazine*. You couldn't put a price on the publicity and prestige that came with such an honor, Joanna had said—nor on the avalanche of business that would surely follow. And it was the prospect of new clients that had perked up Laurel's ears. She had so many ideas and wanted nothing more than a client of her very own...

"Excuse me? We're about to start, if you wouldn't mind making your way over to the party," a voice behind her said. She turned to see a man carrying two cameras, next to a woman holding a tripod.

"Oh, I'm sorry," Laurel said, snapping to attention, remembering that Joanna had said the photography would start right after the presentation. She straightened up and adjusted the hem of her suit jacket. "I'm not a guest—I work for the designer. I'm here to help if there's anything you need."

"Got it. Well, I think I'm okay for now... Actually, can you take that sign?" he said. She nodded and grabbed the cube. "Man, your boss sure knows how to style a kitchen," he added, glancing around. "This'll look great on the page."

"I know, she's amazing," Laurel agreed, feeling a fresh surge of pride for her boss. "My name's Laurel, just give a shout if you need me."

She smiled and stepped away gingerly, since the marble flooring was slippery and she wasn't used to wearing heels. Thankfully reaching the edge of the raised kitchen platform while still on her feet, she stepped onto the carpet and put the cube on a console table by the wall. It was true, Joanna was so talented. And kind too —maybe more than Laurel would have expected from someone with so much on her plate. How many times in the last few years had Joanna turned a blind eye when Laurel came in late or left early, or took an unexpected day off—the unintended consequences of raising a rambunctious eight-year-old on her own? It wasn't easy balancing Simon's needs with a full-time job, and she sometimes dropped the ball, but Joanna never gave her a hard time. Of course, unlike Joanna's other two assistants, she had yet to be given any design work of her own. Six years into her tenure, she was still mostly a glorified receptionist: fielding calls, greeting clients at the office, following up on orders, and helping at events like today's kitchen reveal.

But maybe change was in the air. If Joanna was busier than ever once the magazine issue with the photographs of this kitchen came out, she'd have no choice but to assign her a client. Hopefully one that she seemed suited to. One that had her same sensibility.

Sensibility. It was one of Joanna's favorite words, and Laurel loved it too. Because she did have her own design sensibility, so different from Joanna's penchant for sharp corners, hard edges, and stark colors. Laurel knew her sensibility had developed over years of watching her mother tend to the twelve-room inn her family owned in Lake Summers, the small town where she'd grown up, tucked into the southwest corner of the Adirondack Mountains. She loved the colors and patterns and shapes that her mom had made a hallmark of the inn: warm winter whites and romantic shades of honey and caramel. Subtle florals and subdued plaids, with pops of colors—tangerine or aqua—as accents. Sofas with thick cushions and plenty of throw pillows, roomy club chairs made of buttery leather that invited you to tuck your feet under you and snuggle in with a good book. Elegant pendant chandeliers or, even better, classic table lamps that spread their light like a billowy blanket.

Her mom used to play a game, asking Laurel and her sisters, "If you were a house, what house would you be?" Tracey and Deb would say Versailles or Buckingham Palace or the Taj Mahal, depending on what they were learning in school. But Laurel would always answer, "I'd be the Cranberry Inn, of course!"

The photographer waved to her, then made a telescope shape with his fist and brought it to his mouth, and she nodded and headed toward the lobby for a bottle of water.

Passing the showroom's tall windows, she paused to steal a quick glance down onto Columbus Circle and savor all the Christmas lights on the buildings, which were glowing brightly now that afternoon was closing upon evening. Shoppers dipped their heads against the wind and plowed forward on the slushy sidewalks, their scarves twisting and dancing behind their necks. There was a touch of electricity in the air, with December having just arrived and the holidays right around the corner. She remembered being part of that energy, the shopping and the anticipation, back when she was growing up. Her mother would take her to New York for a weekend around the holidays, leaving her dad to manage the inn and her sisters to practice for the school's winter sports seasons—basketball for Tracey, indoor track for Deb. But that was a long time ago.

She continued to the bar in the lobby, past a lavish spread of finger sandwiches and petits fours set out on a long table sporting potted poinsettias at either end. Even though it was only the first of December, the guests were already getting into the holiday spirit, with a few swaying and teetering, evidently indulging pretty freely in the eggnog. The editor of *Housing Yes!* looked particularly disheveled, his cheeks bright red and a few strands of gray hair sticking outward from his scalp.

Grabbing two bottles of water—his assistant was probably thirsty too—Laurel started back toward the display area. But then she noticed Joanna—at almost six feet tall, her boss was easy to spot—speaking with Meghan Carle, the young editor of *City Home*, one of the newer industry publications. Taking a few discreet steps in their direction, she tilted her head, hoping to hear a tidbit of their conversation. This was the person Joanna had been discussing last week when the topic of sensibilities came up. Meghan was looking to re-do her beach home on Long Island in a seventies style, with bold paint colors, retro furniture, and even some vintage fabrics. Laurel knew she was the perfect designer to take on the project. She felt so at home with Meghan's artsy, feminine vibe. She loved the outfit Meghan had on today—a gauzy V-neck print dress featuring tiny daisies and roses, and brown wedge ankle boots. Laurel had gone ahead and made a list of some fashion trends from the seventies, in the hope that Meghan Carle could be her first client.

Just then Joanna motioned her over with her chin, which seemed a good sign. Remembering the thirsty photographer she'd left behind, Laurel held up her index finger to say she'd be right back and rushed toward the kitchen display. But before she could get there, she heard the nearby elevator door open and the *clomp-clomp-clomp* of winter boots chugging behind her. A fraction of a second later, a squat, parka-covered bundle tore in the direction of Joanna's kitchen and bounded from the carpet onto the marble platform.

"Simon!" she yelled as the slick floor sent her son stumbling forward, his arms flapping in their padded blue sleeves. She rushed after him as he sideswiped the photographer and lurched toward the tripod, which had a camera perched precariously atop it. Dropping the water bottles onto the floor, she lunged to grasp the tripod and save the camera. Simon flailed a bit more before landing face-down in the middle of the kitchen, his arms and legs extended, as though he were doing the butterfly stroke in a pool.

"Whoa!" he shouted and then rolled onto his back. "Epic fall!"

Laurel let go of the tripod and went to kneel beside him, feeling her pencil skirt resist the position and praying she didn't split a seam. She pulled his arm to sit him up, and when he flopped back down, she pulled again.

"Honey, please," she murmured; the last thing she needed was for the photographer to complain about her, now that *her* first client seemed a real possibility.

This time Simon stayed upright, his wool hat askew, his black-framed glasses tilted on his face and his legs splayed out in front of him. "Whoa, Mom. Now I'm dizzy," he said, making circles with his head.

"Simon, you have to calm down," she told him, thankful that at least they were a good distance from the party and out of Joanna's sight line. "You have to get up off the floor—"

But now Simon was looking past her toward the elevator and chuckling again. She glanced over her shoulder to see his friend, Mason, spreading his arms wide like an umpire judging a close play at the plate.

"Safe!" Mason cried out. "Awesome slide!"

"Home run! The Yankees wiiiiiiiiiiin!" Simon responded, pulling himself to his feet and stumbling off the kitchen platform to knock chests with his buddy.

Laurel followed him as her friend Mara, Mason's mom, lumbered over from the elevator, her face red and her breath heavy, her pregnant belly apparent beneath her coat. Mara reached Mason and corralled him, draping her arms over his shoulders and clasping them together in front of his chest. "Oh God, I'm sorry, Laur," she said. "They got away from me."

"It's okay, don't worry," Laurel said, not wanting her poor, pregnant friend to feel bad. It was nice that she had offered to watch Simon today in the first place. "It looks like they had a blast."

"Oh, we had a great time," Mara said. "We took the train in and had lunch at the Times Square Diner, and then took the subway up here and walked through the holiday market in Central Park. I bought them some fudge, and then they begged me to let them share a Belgian waffle with whipped cream. I didn't realize it would make them so wired."

"It's fine. I just hope they weren't too much for you," Laurel said. "I don't understand why there's no after-school program on Fridays in December."

"And it looks like you're still working," Mara said. "I'm sorry to drop him off now. It's just that it's after four and I should be getting home. I can take Simon back with us..."

"No, no. I'll be done soon." Laurel looked at Simon. "You can sit calmly for a few minutes and wait for me, right, buddy?"

Simon puffed out his cheeks and then pushed the air out, making a squeaking noise that sent the boys into hysterics again.

"Let me get out of your hair," Mara said. "It'll be easier for you with us gone."

"Maybe you're right," Laurel said, reaching over to give her friend a one-armed hug, her other hand grasping Simon's shoulder. Mara was such a good friend—and a lifesaver too. She was a teacher at Simon's and Mason's school, so her schedule was the same as theirs, and she always volunteered to take Simon when Laurel needed coverage. Fortunately, though, she wouldn't need to rely on Mara any more this year, as Joanna was closing up the office starting Monday so she could spend the coming weeks at her ski house in Sun Valley. There wasn't much pressing work around the holidays, and she felt her staff could handle whatever needed to be done from home.

"Thanks again," Laurel added as Mara took Mason's hand and pulled him toward the elevator. "And have a good weeken—"

"Um, excuse me? Could use a mop here," the photographer called. Laurel looked over to see him pointing to Simon's muddy footprints.

"Oh, I'm sorry," she said. "I'll take care of it—and here, by the way," she added, retrieving the water bottles and handing them to him. Then she gave a final wave to Mara and led Simon to the console table by the wall, sitting him down on one of the armchairs flanking it. Simon was quickly losing steam, the sugar rush ending, and his body sank heavily into the tufted chair back. Laurel kneeled beside him, again hoping her skirt stayed intact. "I have to stay a little while longer, okay?" she told him.

"Not too long, Mom," he said. "I'm sweating..."

"I know, it is warm in here," she said, taking off his hat and unzipping his parka. His cheeks were red, obscuring the freckles on his nose, and his dark bangs were plastered to his forehead. She combed them with her fingers. "Just a few minutes, okay?"

He nodded, and she kissed his cheek, then went back toward the photographer, who was scowling, his arms folded across his chest. "Anything you need—oh yeah, the mop, coming," she said, even though she knew she'd never be able to find one, much less someone who could show her where one might be. So she ran back to the showroom lobby and pulled a short stack of green and red cocktail napkins from the food table. Hurrying back, she stepped onto the marble floor—skidded was more like it—and kneeled to wipe the puddles, wondering whether her skirt could possibly continue to hold together.

She gave the floor a few final wipes for good measure, then stood and looked for a trash basket for the muddy napkins. That's when she noticed Joanna walking in her direction. She crushed the napkins into a tiny ball and wrapped her fingers around them.

"What happened to you?" Joanna said as Laurel stepped down to the carpet. "I thought you were coming back so I could introduce you to Meghan."

"I was about to, I... got busy helping here," Laurel said, positioning herself so Joanna's back was to Simon and she wouldn't notice him. "I didn't miss her, did I?"

"Afraid so."

Laurel sighed. "Oh, boy. I really did want to meet her. I just love that seventies project."

"I do, too. And I think she's going to sign with us. We talked about some of the ideas you jotted down, and she was very happy with them."

"Really? She said that?"

Joanna nodded. "It'll be such a fun job. Nora's going to have a blast with it."

"Yes, and— Wait, Nora?" Laurel said, trying to keep her voice steady, even though she could hear it quiver. She didn't want to confront Joanna, especially not now, while the party was still going on. But this was the third project she'd lost out on to Nora since the summer—and the one she'd felt most certain should be hers. What was she doing wrong? How had she spent six years trying to prove herself, only to be passed over again? Was this Joanna's way of telling her she didn't have what it took to be a designer after all?

"What, did you think I was going to handle it myself? Boy, I'd love to," Joanna said. "But I've got those other two projects and now this magazine spread. I don't think I'll even be able to take a minute off while I'm in Sun Valley. Well, maybe Christmas Day, but that's it."

"Yes, well... well, Nora will be great," Laurel said.

Joanna looked toward the kitchen display. "The photographer seems to be finishing up—why don't you head on home? I have a few more people to thank, and then I'm leaving too. I'll be in touch next week after I get settled. Have a great month, and rest up. It's going to be a busy new year!"

"Have a good trip," she said, but her boss was already heading back toward the lobby, waving her fingers in the air to seal her goodbye.

Laurel turned back to Simon, who was now sitting low in the chair, fast asleep, his chest rising rhythmically with his breath. He was such a good kid, and he always made the best of things. Even though he did get shuffled around. Or ended up sitting in random chairs waiting for her. If he were a house, she thought, he'd be a bungalow in the woods: a little lopsided, a little messy, a little rough around the edges. But totally lovable from the very first sight.

Putting her hands on her waist, she watched him sleep. She was glad she didn't have to commute to Manhattan for the rest of the year. It was fun to pick Simon up from school at the normal time, instead of having him stay for the after-school program, which he usually did when she was working at the office. And she could plan some fun holiday adventures for them, just as she did every year.

Of course, it would be nice to go somewhere special for Christmas. Most of Simon's friends traveled to spend the holidays with relatives, even if it was just out to Long Island or up to Connecticut. Mara and her husband were taking Mason to Mexico, where her parents rented a beach villa each year. But she and Simon would make the best of it. This was simply how things were for them, how they'd been for the last four years. Those first Christmases in the inn after her mother died had been miserable, and eventually she, her sisters, and her dad had all decided it was best for her and Simon to stay in New York, and for her sisters to celebrate with their husbands' families. While she missed Christmas back home, it was a relief to escape the sadness of the inn without her mother.

The photographer and his assistant were putting on their coats, and Laurel waved as she walked toward Simon. He looked zonked, so it was going to be hard to get him up and onto the subway to Penn Station, and then onto the commuter train for the twenty-minute ride to their stop in Queens. Maybe tonight would be sandwiches for dinner in front of the TV. Or maybe, if Simon got a second wind, they could get the box of holiday decorations from the storage room in the apartment building and decide how they wanted to arrange things this year.

She was starting for the closet to get her coat and her bag when her phone rang. Pulling it out from her skirt pocket, she looked at the number in surprise. It was her dad calling from his cell phone, which he never did, since service was spotty up in the mountains. She wondered why he wasn't calling from the landline at the inn. Was there some kind of emergency that couldn't wait until he got home?

She brought the phone to her ear. "Dad?" she said. "Is something wrong?"

"Hey, kiddo," he said. "No, not at all."

"Then why aren't you calling me from home?"

"Because something came up, and... do me a favor and come here... a little help here with the inn... few weeks... no more than... few..."

"Dad?" she said. "Dad, you're breaking up. What are you saying? You need me at the inn?"

"... because Joanna... closed and you're off for December, right? So since you don't have to... you can be here... very fast, never expected..."

"Dad, I can't hear you. Can you call me back when you get home?"

"No, kiddo... not home..."

"You're not home?" She raised her palm to her forehead. What was going on? Why couldn't they talk later?

"Explain it all..." he said. "... arrive here tomorrow, okay?"

"What? Dad, you need me at the inn tomorrow?"

"Yes, tomorrow... just a few... all set, kiddo, gotta go..."

"Dad? Dad!" she called, so loudly that the photographer and his assistant looked over from the elevator. She waved to indicate that nothing was wrong, then turned away from them and shouted "Dad!" once more. But there was no response, and when she looked at her phone, she saw that she'd been disconnected.

She called him back but only reached his voicemail. She tried again with no luck, then tried the inn, but all she heard there was the greeting she'd recorded last summer, since Dad felt a female voice was more welcoming: "Hello, you've reached the Cranberry Inn. We can't answer your call right now, but please leave a message..."

Putting her phone back in her pocket, she looked around helplessly, having no idea what to make of that call, that strange request. Her dad had never before asked her at the last minute to come up to the inn. Her trips there were always planned in advance. And he'd never asked her to stay for a few weeks, which he seemed to be asking now. Usually her visits with Simon were for a week, two at the most. She was glad that at least it wasn't an emergency. His words and his tone sounded way too jovial for anything to be wrong. But still, she couldn't imagine what on earth had triggered such a request. What did he need her to do?

She shook her head and headed to the closet, where she pulled her coat off its hanger. The only thing she knew for sure was that she wasn't going to find any clarity just standing and staring into space. Because her father had made his needs clear, despite the spotty phone service, and now he was expecting her and Simon to be at the inn tomorrow. And if she couldn't reach him tonight, then she'd have no choice but to pack up and head to the mountains to stay through Christmas.

And find out exactly what was going on.

TWO

"I thought Grandpa just didn't like Christmas," Simon said as they plowed through the slush on the sidewalk outside their apartment building the next morning, his backpack slung over his shoulders and his arms wrapped around his pillow. It was the only pillow he'd sleep on ever since last year, when someone in his class told him that pillows were made by scraping the feathers off ducks. He'd begged her to buy him a new pillow that night that had POLYESTER in bold letters on the label, and now he wouldn't sleep on anything else.

"That's silly, of course he likes Christmas," Laurel said as they continued to where her car was parked. The tips of her right-hand fingers felt like they were about to snap off under the weight of the three shopping bags filled with Christmas presents for her family that she hadn't yet had a chance to wrap and mail. Her other arm similarly protested as she dragged her rolling suitcase, weighted down by Simon's duffel on top of it. It was at moments like this that she wished she'd sprung for a space in the building's underground garage. Even if they'd have to eat cereal for dinner for the whole winter, it would still be worth it.

"So why didn't we ever go to see him on Christmas?" he asked.

"We used to. You were just too young to remember," she said

as they reached the car, and she studied the back end, trying to determine if she could get the trunk up without putting any of the shopping bags onto the slushy road. "When you were little, we always went to Grandpa's for Christmas. Your aunts and uncles and cousins did, too."

"Why did we stop?"

"Well, Grandma died before you were born, like I told you." She let go of the suitcase and moved the shopping bags to her left hand, then reached into her right pocket for her keys. "And it didn't feel the same because everyone missed her so much. Grandpa especially."

"Doesn't he still miss her?"

"Of course." She pulled the fob out and aimed it at the car. "But I guess he decided he needs us this year, and when someone from your family needs you..." She watched the trunk lid rise and then began loading the bags inside. "Well, did you ever hear the expression, time heals all wounds?"

He shook his head. "Nope."

"It means that things stop hurting after a while," she said. "Like when you scrape your knee and it hurts so bad and then it doesn't hurt anymore? Feelings work the same way."

She put Simon's duffel and her suitcase in, then pushed them further so they wouldn't block the latch. "Now go into the car, okay? If we get on the road fast, we can stop for lunch at the Choo Choo House. And try to keep your feet on the floor. It's a long trip and you don't want the seat to get all wet from your boots."

He sighed, raising his shoulders and dropping them hard, then plodded to the side of the car. She could tell he doubted he was getting the whole picture. And he was right. It wasn't entirely true that time healed all hurts. There were many aspects of her childhood, many memories of growing up as the daughter who never quite fit in, that she'd never be able to brush aside. And yet it was no surprise that when Dad needed a favor having to do with the inn, she was the one he called. Not Tracey, not Deb, but her. Because her sisters had been after him to sell the place, ever since

Mom died ten years ago. She and Dad were the only ones left who truly cared about the place and wanted to keep it.

She closed the trunk, then held Simon's door open as he pushed his pillow and backpack inside and climbed in behind them. Even though it bothered her that she didn't have the whole story about why her father needed her back, a piece of her was happy that she and Simon would be spending Christmas up in Lake Summers once again. Yes, it meant taking him out of school for December and calling on Monday to ask his teacher to forward all his lessons so she could teach him the material herself. But even so, she was hopeful she could make this a great holiday for him.

It wasn't that staying in Queens had been so bad these last few years, she thought. They'd had plenty of fun seeing the huge, dazzling snowflake suspended from wires atop Fifth Avenue, and the light show projected on the façade of the Saks Fifth Avenue department store; visiting Rockefeller Center to marvel at the big Christmas tree and then watch the figure skaters on the ice rink below; buying soft, hot pretzels and roasted chestnuts from food trucks, and then traveling to the Bronx to take in the enchanting holiday train show at the New York Botanical Garden. But the older Simon became, the worse it felt that they had no one special to visit for the holidays. She'd felt so guilty last year when she'd overheard him at school commenting appreciatively as other kids rattled off their plans and the slew of extended family members they'd be seeing: "Sixteen cousins! Wow, Brendan!" "Skiing in Colorado? Good for you, Jackson!"

She wanted more for him than a quiet Christmas week in the city. She wanted him to feel how she'd always felt celebrating the holidays at the inn. Her mother had been Jewish, her dad Protestant, and the guests were mostly graduate students and faculty members from nearby Gorson College whose homes were too far away to travel to for the holidays, and who shared the most fascinating traditions and customs.

Even now, she could remember the linguistics professor from Finland who taught her and her sisters how to make *pepparkakor*, a

Scandinavian Christmas cookie. And the head of the music department, who came from Nigeria and taught everyone a holiday song
in the indigenous language Hausa. A pair of married graduate
students came back year after year to lead a candle-lighting ritual
on the eve of the winter solstice. And there were always instructors
who would dramatize the Christmas and Chanukah stories, or
explain the rituals and symbols of Kwanzaa. Laurel knew her
mother would have expected the family to continue what she'd
created. How horrified she'd be to know that everything had with-
ered away after she died.

And then, over time, they'd all just stopped going to the inn for
Christmas. One year Tracey had canceled her trip home because
she was working on a merger that needed to be completed before
the end of the year, and another time, Deb had decided to bring
her family to visit in the summer instead. Meanwhile, things had
often been hectic for Laurel around the holidays, particularly in
the early years when Joanna was still starting up her firm and
needed everyone to pitch in extra hours year-round.

When the family did get together for Christmas, there were
always arguments, as Tracey and Deb tried to convince their dad to
sell the inn and move on with his life, and Laurel fought against
that. She thought it would be a huge betrayal of their mom, who
had worked so hard all her adult life to keep the inn profitable
while making it into a cherished home for her husband and daughters. Ultimately they'd all realized it would be more peaceful for
everyone if they celebrated Christmas apart.

Laurel knew things never would have turned so ugly if her
mom were alive. Mom had been a bearing wall, holding their
family up, and once she was gone, it seemed the family had disinte-
grated, leaving nothing but sawdust and debris in its wake. But
maybe this would be the year she could finally start to put the past
behind her. She didn't know what her dad had up his sleeve:
Maybe he'd unexpectedly sold out all the rooms at the inn and
needed her help to manage the place. Or maybe he was planning to
do some renovations and wanted her input—it was no secret that

the place had become a little run-down since her mom died and could use a facelift. Or maybe he'd decided to go up north fishing for a few days with his buddies and needed her to hold down the fort. After all, he'd never been a homebody; that had been her mother's terrain. He'd loved traveling with Tracey and Deb back when they were in school and involved in all kinds of sports leagues and regional competitions.

Or maybe he'd decided he wanted to have family around him once again for Christmas, that he wanted to celebrate the holiday with her and Simon. She couldn't help but wish that was the reason for his call. It would be wonderful to have a peaceful holiday with her father and son, especially this year, when she'd been passed over at work—again—and had no choice but to believe she might never be a real designer. Maybe Lake Summers would end up being the perfect place for her to regroup. To figure out whether there was something different she should be doing with her life.

She started the car and glanced into the rear-view window. Simon was digging into his backpack for his rocks book, the hard-cover one he'd begged her to buy him last fall at the school's used-book fair. For some reason, he'd developed a passion for rocks. His collection, which he kept in a shoebox in his bedroom, included nearly every color and shape imaginable—gray, black, reddish, white, grainy, round, oblong, angled. And he was always on the lookout for more.

"Igneous!" he'd exclaim, or "Metamorphic!" whenever a specimen caught his attention at the park or the schoolyard or outside their building. He'd hold it up to his glasses, turning it around and then running his index finger over the surface. Then, back home, he'd record all his data—the date, the place where he'd found it, the shape and color, the circumference—in a blue spiral notebook on his desk. Simon wasn't athletic, and the closest he'd ever come to a sports competition was when the gym teacher let him narrate the gymnastics exhibition last spring. She loved that the rock collection made him feel like a champ.

He pushed his glasses up higher on his nose and started to read, and she headed toward the highway, finding a pop station on the radio and turning the volume low so she wouldn't disturb him. Crossing the Whitestone Bridge, she proceeded north toward the New York Thruway.

She'd been a lot like Simon growing up—always into her own projects and plans. Being the middle child was like being an only child, she'd found, especially since Tracey and Deb were so similar: tall, athletic, gregarious, popular. Sometimes, especially when her sisters were talking about the upcoming basketball or softball or tennis or track season at school, she was convinced that she was adopted. But then she'd remind herself that she was exactly like her mother—small, quiet, imaginative. Someone who loved dreaming up stories and playing pretend games.

Two hours into the drive, she reached the exit for the Red Caboose Pancake Station—or what Simon had affectionately nicknamed the Choo Choo House when he was younger. She parked and looked over her shoulder. Simon was sleeping, his opened book spread across his chest. She reached back and jiggled his knee. "Lunchtime."

He sat up and righted his glasses. "Wow, snow!" he said, looking out the window.

It was true—the slush from home was gone, replaced with clean white snow layered on the earth and sprinkled on the trees and rooftops. The restaurant was decked out for Christmas, with twinkling icicles lining the roof and colored lights swirling around the bushes in front.

Simon kicked open his door and ran to the entrance, and Laurel locked the car and followed him. Inside, red and green cardboard ornaments and white cardboard snowflakes hung down from strings attached to the ceiling. Simon went to the counter and chose his favorite seat, directly opposite a toy wooden building shaped like Grand Central Station, with model train tracks emerging on either side. She took his coat and sat down beside him, noticing how chipped the countertop was. It was too bad; she knew they should have chosen a more durable surface when the owners remodeled the restaurant last year.

Putting their coats on the stool next to her, she grabbed two menus from the metal stand and went to hand Simon one. He pushed it away.

"You know what you want?" she asked. "You remember the menu since last summer?"

He gave a short, firm nod, and when the server came over with two glasses of water, he recited his exact choice: the Red Caboose special with three buttermilk pancakes, two types of syrup—maple and blueberry—two sausage links and two scrambled eggs. "Oh, and orange juice and milk," he added. "Oh, and some blackberry mini donuts with the sugar sprinkles to go."

He folded his hands on the table and grinned, and Laurel did too as the woman chuckled and said he'd done a great job ordering and she'd have it right up. Laurel ordered scrambled eggs, toast, and coffee.

Simon picked up a green train car on the counter by the track and spun its little wheels with his fingertips. "So did I like it there for Christmas when we went?" he asked.

"You loved it," she said.

"Why?"

"Oh, so many reasons. You loved seeing the tiny Christmas lights around the fireplace in the living room and how they glowed when we turned off all the lamps. And you loved Grandma's silver menorah, and the way the wax from the candles would drip down the sides like lava from a volcano. And you loved the big Christmas tree in the corner with the star on top. And you loved Christmas Eve when the carolers came around—"

"The who?"

"Carolers. People who come to the door to sing Christmas songs."

"That's weird."

"No, it's nice. They sang the prettiest harmonies, and then we'd give them cookies or hot cocoa to thank them for the music. And sometimes the firetruck would come around and the firefighters tossed out candy canes. We used to run to get you one, and I always held it while you ate it because I was scared you'd put a big piece in your mouth and choke. And oh boy, did you hate that —you'd scream your head off and try to pull it away from me."

He laughed. "Did we do other stuff for winter? Like sledding or ice skating?"

"You were too young to skate."

"But I can go ice skating this time, right?"

"Sure, we can do that."

He smiled. "Wow, I didn't ice skate since Mason's birthday last winter," he said, his eyes wide. "How far is the rink? Can you walk there?"

She nudged his shoulder. He was such a city kid. "There's no rink, silly! You skate on the lake."

"The *lake?* Really?"

She nodded.

"What's that like?"

The server returned with her coffee and Simon's juice, and Laurel poured some milk into her mug, thinking about how to describe ice skating on a lake. She'd been younger than Simon, maybe five or six, the first time she'd done it. It was her dad who'd brought her out there, and she remembered feeling as though she were doing something magical, gliding on a surface that appeared solid and breakable at the same time, standing on the very same place where she'd been swimming just a few months earlier.

"Well, let's see... there's no Zamboni, right?" she said as Simon unwrapped his straw and put it into his glass. "So the lake isn't as smooth as a rink. It's actually kind of bumpy, I guess because the lake has currents, so that's how it freezes. And it's not like standing on a thin layer of ice, the way you do at the rink. It's more like you're standing on a very tall block. And when you look down, you can see all these layers—the higher ones are clear and then the color changes when you look further down from greenish gray to really dark gray to black..."

She paused, remembering that day, how much she'd loved being with her dad, just the two of them. How safe she felt as he skated backward, holding her hands, and she went forward.

"Nothing to be scared of, kiddo," he'd said. It was one of the only times—maybe *the* only time—when she'd felt that she had his complete attention. She didn't remember ever feeling as close to him as she had that afternoon, feeling his grasp on her mitten-covered fingers, knowing he was skating backward and holding tight because he loved her and didn't want her to fall.

She'd loved that he called her that. Kiddo. Tracey was always Slugger, since she'd been a home-run hitter from the first time she played softball in kindergarten; and Deb was SpeedyDee because, Dad said, she could run before she learned to walk. Laurel remembered how wonderful it was to have a nickname, just like her sisters. It had been a long time since she'd felt that close to her father.

A whistle startled her, and a moment later a toy train came chugging out from the kitchen on the track by the edge of the counter, its cars carrying two oval plates on their roofs. It stopped at Grand Central Station, and the server set their plates in front of them. She returned a moment later with the syrup pitchers for Simon, and he picked up both—one in each hand—and poured two thick stripes onto his pancakes, swirling the pitchers so the stripes eventually formed a cyclone and then bled to the edge of the stack and dripped down the sides.

They started to eat, Simon using his knife to saw off wedges of his pancake and chunks of his sausage. "Will Katie come over?" he asked. "With the chicken nuggets?"

Laurel nodded. Katie Mitchell owned a prepared-foods shop on Main Street, which she'd opened a few years ago, after retiring as a chef at a hotel in Boston and moving to Lake Summers. She and her eight-person staff supplied the inn and local restaurants with breakfast breads and treats, and Simon couldn't get enough of the home-made chicken nuggets she sold at her store. Everyone in the family loved her.

She finished her eggs and looked at Simon, who had done a pretty good job with his breakfast and was now running his index finger along the blade of his knife. "Oh, honey, don't do that," she said.

"Why?"

"You'll cut yourself."

"It's not near the sharp part. See?" He lifted the knife to show her. "The sharp part isn't even that sharp. It was hardly cutting the pancakes. I could run it on my arm and it wouldn't hurt." He pushed up his shirt sleeve. "Not sharp at all," he added, using his TV host voice. "Surprisingly gentle."

"Oh, honey, stop," she said, taking it away from him. "It's a knife, it's sharp—yuck, and it's sticky too." She handed him a napkin, and he laughed as it stayed glued to his fingers, even as he shook his hands over his plate.

"Okay, time to go," she said. "Go ahead into the bathroom and wash your hands while I get the check. Wash them well, okay?"

He nodded, still laughing, and jumped off his chair, and she finished her last bite of toast and signaled for the check. Alone at the counter, she couldn't help but think again about her dad's phone call. It was funny that they had something in common— their love for the inn—since he'd always had so much more in common with her sisters when she was growing up. Tracey and Deb were both outgoing and athletic—so much more like him than she was. But then again, he probably called her simply because he thought she was the only one who could drop everything at a moment's notice. Tracey couldn't, he must have thought, since she was a high-powered corporate attorney in Philadelphia; same for Deb, who was vice president of sales for a tech start-up out in Boston.

Unlike their careers, Dad had never taken hers seriously. That much was clear from his phone call—he'd said she could come right up since she was "off" for December, even though she'd specifically told him last week that she wasn't off; she was simply working from home for the month.

And he hadn't even mentioned Simon's school; how could he just assume there'd be no problem with her pulling him out for so long?

Back in the car, with the bag of mini donuts that Simon had ordered in the seat beside her, she started to pull out of the parking space. Her eyes met Simon's in the rear-view mirror.

"Do all people do that?" he asked.

"Do what, honey?"

"Stop being together when someone dies?"

She took a breath. "Well... no," she said. "But sometimes people feel... well..."

She hesitated because she didn't know how to continue. She was always advising Simon to resolve his disagreements with his own friends. How could she now explain that sometimes grown-ups couldn't move on? That when someone dies, it can expose the problems that nobody wants to talk about? Like finding a tiny moth hole in a favorite sweater and thinking you'll repair it—then noticing all the snags and pulls you never saw before. And sometimes the sight of those imperfections is exhausting. Sometimes it seems the best thing to do is leave the sweater in the back of the closet and wear something else.

"It takes some families longer, sometimes," she finally said.

THREE

A little over an hour later, Laurel crossed the Jason Drawbridge and entered Lake Summers, the town that would always be home.

"Sweetie, look!" she called back to Simon. "Are you awake?"

"I'm reading," he said.

She smiled and left him alone. He didn't feel the same way she did about this town, although she hoped by next week, he might start to have stronger feelings. But his indifference couldn't diminish her delight at taking in this first winter view in so long.

And a gorgeous view it was! The snow coated the trees on Main Street, and the sun shone down, and the twinkling lights and ribbon-decked wreaths adorning the Victorian-style storefronts made her feel as though she were driving through a familiar story-book. Groups of kids bundled in boots and coats and wool hats ran toward the Sweet Shop, while families and couples huddled close as they made their way from store to store. There was an aura of comfort and security and familiarity blanketing the town, and suddenly she was even more hopeful about this trip home than she'd expected. Even though her family was not as close as it should be, even though her mom was gone, it still felt right to be here again.

She reached the corner of Birch Street and drove up the hill, passing the houses of old friends she'd gone to school with: Mindy Samms, Amy Rochester, Chuck Decker, Trevor O'Reilly—the names sounded tuneful, like favorite pop songs she'd played over and over when she was a teenager, the words fixed in her mind. To her right was Meadow Street, where Joel Hutcherson had lived with his mom. Although technically, she thought, he really wasn't a friend. Just someone she had spent some time with long ago. It hadn't meant anything. She'd been wrong to once think that it did.

A few short moments later she reached the top of the hill, and she breathed in deeply as she turned by the wooden sign that read "The Cranberry Inn." And there it was, set back from the road, a grand white Colonial with tall windows flanked by black shutters, the entrance heralded by majestic, fluted pillars, the red front door sporting a wreath around the brass knocker.

Laurel remembered that back when she was a child, she knew that travelers making their way up this winding driveway for their first Christmas here were in for a treat they could never have imagined. Her parents had had so much fun together back then, and their spirit was contagious, especially around the holidays. They acted like teenagers playing house when they welcomed people in. Every breakfast had been a one-of-a-kind experience as they moved from the kitchen to the heated sunroom, harmonizing old show tunes while they served pancakes and muffins and poured cocoa and coffee.

The driveway formed a circle at the top of the hill, and she pulled to the front of the house and parked by the door. The grounds looked different, since she hadn't been there in winter since Simon was three. She'd become used to seeing the place only during the warm weather, when the grass was lush and green, and the white bannisters and railings lining the front porch were wrapped in blue morning glories, and the canopies from the red maples dappled the vast, sunny lawn with patches of cool, alluring shade.

But it was more than just the snow and bare branches that looked unfamiliar. The three evergreen trees on the front hill were decorated in plain white twinkle lights, as opposed to the chain of red, lavender, yellow, green, and blue she remembered. She used to love helping her dad string those multicolored teardrop-shaped bulbs as he moved the ladder around each tree—it was always something she looked forward to as soon as December arrived. The white ones were pretty, for sure, in a cool, elegant kind of way. But the old way was more festive, and she wondered why Dad had changed it.

She pushed the trees out of her mind, not wanting to wait a moment longer to be back inside the house.

"Come on, let's go in and say hi to Grandpa," she said to Simon. "We can come out later for the bags."

She left the car and went to the front door. It was locked, which was strange as well. She couldn't even remember the last time she'd found the door this way. Mom always thought that unlocked doors were the most welcoming sign an inn could offer. It meant that life was going on, that people were around, that conversation and connection were always just a few steps away. Dad would never lock up until midnight, and Mom would always unlock the door by 6 a.m. so guests who liked to take early-morning runs didn't have to worry about bringing along a key. And by six thirty, the place was steeped in the aroma of fresh coffee and muffins or cinnamon rolls or something equally sweet and breakfast-y baking in the kitchen.

Laurel reached into her pocket and pulled out her keys, glad that she always kept the key to the inn on her key ring. It hadn't even occurred to her that she might arrive to find a locked door.

She opened it and stepped inside. The house smelled like cinnamon and chocolate, and she assumed that Katie had been by recently to drop off some desserts from her shop—which would mean that the inn had plenty of guests this week. So it made sense that Dad would want her to help out.

The scent of delicious baked goods was layered atop the subtle balsam fragrance of the Christmas tree in the corner, and the combination was joyful and intoxicating, as it had always been when she was growing up. But this tree, she saw, also had white lights only, like the outdoor ones. She wondered again what had happened to the colorful lights they'd always used.

"Dad?" she called, stamping her boots on the welcome mat. "Dad? We're here!"

There was no answer, and she paused for a moment. She couldn't remember a time when the place had been silent like this. When she and Simon came up in the summers, the inn always had guests and activity. Of course, the inn had been far busier when both of her parents were in charge. Her mom had been so good at designing ads for vacation magazines and getting travel writers to visit so they could publish reviews. Dad had let all those tasks slide after Mom died. He'd never been particularly strategic or detail oriented about the business. He much preferred tending to guests once they made their way here. He loved orienting them to nearby trails for hiking or cross-country skiing, or recounting the history of Lake Summers—something he knew inside and out, since he'd been on the team that had helped incorporate the town many years ago.

She walked past the cherrywood reception desk and toward the sun-filled living room. Opposite the fireplace and next to the tree was her father's blue armchair. No matter the season, it was his favorite spot. How many times had she arrived in the last few years to find him dozing there? He'd always been such a good-looking man, even as he'd grown older, with thick salt-and-pepper hair and a short beard covering his firm, square chin. He'd jump up when he saw her and straighten his clothes—blue or red sweaters over jeans in the winter, and T-shirts in bright colors in the summer that showed off his broad shoulders and slim waist. He prided himself on being a snappy dresser, on always looking fashionable and youthful. Last summer, she'd noticed that he didn't quite have the same energy that she'd always taken for granted. But she didn't let herself dwell on that. Her dad would have hated if she'd said something. He never wanted to admit that he was getting older.

Simon came up behind her. "Where's Grandpa?" he asked.

She shook her head. "I don't know."

He stamped his boots on the mat a few times, then stood beside her. "It's really quiet," he said after a moment, his voice barely louder than a whisper. "And no lights on. It's creepy. Like it's just zombies. Like Grandpa decided to be a zombie or something."

"Stop, don't be silly," she said. She agreed with him—it *was* creepy. But she didn't want to admit it and make him nervous. He was right, there were no lights on, which she hadn't noticed before, since the living room had large windows and got so much sunlight. But now she saw that the staircase leading up to the second floor was dark—and that was as strange as the silence and the locked front door.

"What's going on?" he said.

She shook her head and went upstairs, hearing him following behind her.

"Dad?" she called as she reached the second-floor landing.

She walked down the dark hallway, the closed doors of the guest rooms on either side. Halfway down the hall, she noticed a long, deep scratch in the wooden floor. Dad had told her about it—some workers cleaning out the air ducts had dropped a dresser they'd moved out of one of the suites. He'd told her he would get it fixed, but evidently he'd never got around to it.

She thought now of how mortified her mother would be if she knew guests were walking down this hall and seeing that deep, ugly gouge. Her mom had liked things to be in tip-top shape, and she always saw flaws as opportunities to make things look even better. Her dad, though, sounded hurt when Laurel pointed out problems to him—like the rips in the outdoor furniture, or the hole in the wall in the living room where the drapery rod was coming loose, or the closet doors on the first floor that had swelled and no longer closed, or the rug in the living room that was looking worn, the color faded in spots. It was as though she were telling him he'd let her mother down in some way.

"Kiddo, why are you ragging on me so much?" he'd say. "Have

I really done such a bad job?" It had seemed kinder to turn a blind eye than to continue to torment him.

"Dad!" she called again and went down to his room at the end of the hall. The door was ajar, but when she peeked in, she saw the bed was made and the surfaces of all the furniture were cleared. It didn't look as though anyone had been there in days, maybe longer. This was the bedroom her parents had lived in when they got married, before Tracey was born and they decided to renovate the cottage out back into a private home. It had a four-poster bed and a pretty gold rug, and the wooden furniture was stained in a golden-brown shade that her mother had chosen because it made her think of fall sweaters and autumn leaves. Dad had moved back here after Mom died, although he returned to the cottage when the inn had guests. Which was happening less and less often, Laurel knew. The number of guests had been dwindling.

She led Simon up to the top floor, which was as quiet and empty as the others. Then they went back down the two flights.

"I don't know what's going on," she told him. It was so strange that her dad wouldn't be here, when he'd told her he needed her to come right away. Even if he'd gone out to grab a beer at the bar at the Lake Summers Grill with his pals, she thought he'd have surely left some lights on and the front door unlocked. She didn't know what to think as she'd never encountered a situation like this before. It was as though the inn were a museum or something, not the home she'd grown up in.

Although the truth was, there'd been several times in the past when it hadn't felt so much like a home. Certainly the first time she'd come back after her mother had died. And then again on those Christmases after her mother was gone, when she found herself so at odds with her sisters that they all stopped returning. But she'd never wanted to believe it would no longer be home, the wonderful home where she'd played make-believe games and read novels by the fire and had the most amazing heart-to-hearts with her mother. Those memories were what kept her believing it would feel more like home by and by. That if she kept coming back, if she kept trying, it might feel almost as wonderful as it had when her mother was alive.

She looked around again when she returned to the reception desk, wondering if she'd missed anything. She didn't want Simon to worry or get upset, but now she was getting scared.

She took out her cell phone, but she had no messages, and when she called her dad's number, he once again didn't answer.

"Come on, honey," she said and led Simon toward the kitchen. Maybe he was down in the basement. Her dad had never been especially handy, but he sometimes tried. Growing up, she would occasionally find him in the basement at the workbench, trying to fix an appliance or bathroom fixture or element from the boiler or hot-water heater before finally throwing up his hands and calling in a repairman. It was part of the entertainment, the banter, between her parents that had always entertained the guests: her dad trying to fix things and her mom begging him to call someone or—more often—to give her a few minutes to fix it herself.

She walked through the living room and into the kitchen, looking around to see if there were any clues. But it was as empty as the rest of the house and looked just as spotless—even the table, which had always been full of food and dishes and platters when she was growing up.

The kitchen had been her favorite room, and her mother's, too. Not so much her dad—he thought it was too small for an inn. He was always crashing his chair into the wall that backed the dining room—and when someone else was in that chair, he'd warn them repeatedly to get up carefully. Laurel didn't know why her dad had never gotten around to expanding the kitchen, since that wall both-ered him so much. Maybe he thought it would be too much trou-ble. He probably had no idea what was involved in moving walls or expanding rooms—that was likely as much of a mystery to him as appliances that needed fixing. He had grown up always intending to work in an office as a lawyer. But he'd given the law up when he fell in love with her mom.

She started again for the basement door when her eye caught

some kind of card standing upright on the kitchen counter, leaning against the coffeemaker. A note. It was so unexpected, as their family had rarely needed handwritten notes when she was growing up, since her mother was always around. And when she did have to leave a note—like that one time a guest had broken his leg ice skating on the lake and Mom took him to the hospital—she'd taped it on the front door, so Laurel and her sisters would know right away not to worry.

Of course, in the last few years, there'd been no need for notes at all, since Dad was perfectly comfortable with texts. But here was a note, on one of her mother's old notecards, which he must have found in the reception desk. Maybe he'd thought she'd park behind the house and come straight in through the kitchen. Maybe he'd forgotten that whenever she came home, she liked to enter through the front door and take in the beautiful living room the same way a guest would. She switched on the overhead light and read:

Hey kiddo,

Sorry we got disconnected on the phone yesterday, and sorry not to be here to welcome you. But a lot's been happening, and it looks like I won't be around to give you a proper explanation. Not sure there'll be cell service where I'm going, and anyway, this isn't the kind of thing best said in a text or phone call. But everything's fine, so don't worry. And thanks for keeping an eye on the inn for a few weeks. I hate to close it up in case any last-minute reservations come in, although it's empty now and I don't expect anyone. So have a relaxing few weeks, enjoy yourselves, and give Simon a big hug for me. There are some goodies from Katie in the refrigerator, and I'll be coming home late Christmas Eve with a special surprise!

Love,

Dad

"What's it say?" Simon said, picking up the note when she put it back on the counter. "I can't even read this. What kind of language is this anyway?"

"It's English, silly. It's just his handwriting," she said.

"So what's it say?" he repeated, giving it back to her.

She sighed and took it. This was so typical of her dad. So typical of *her*, actually. Here she'd been hoping for a nice Christmas with him, hoping that he was calling her back to do something special together. She should have known better. Her dad was never like that. He'd attempted a few Christmases with her and her sisters, after Mom had died, and then he'd called it quits. He was never the type to keep hoping and trying to make something work. Her mother had been the one to hold onto hope. The queen of lost causes, her dad used to call her. Laurel thought it probably should be her own nickname too.

"Well?" Simon asked.

She looked at him, her hands on her waist. "It says we have the whole place to ourselves for a month."

"Grandpa left?" he said. "Was he kidnapped? Is that a ransom note? How much do they want?"

Laurel laughed. "No, he wasn't—Simon, come on," she said. "It says he had to go away and that he needs us to stay here and take care of things until he gets back."

"But where is he?"

"He didn't say," she said. "He just says we should enjoy ourselves, and he's coming back with a big surprise on Christmas Eve."

"What? Awesome!" Simon shouted, raising his fists in the air. "I can sleep wherever I want? In any room at all? I can sleep in a different room every night? And we can go sledding and ice skating and everything?"

"I guess—we'll see..."

"I call Blue Mountain Room like last summer!" Simon said. "But backsies, I call backsies—I can take it back later if I change my mind, okay?"

"Relax—"

"And no school? Wait 'til Mason hears! This will be the best Christmas ever!"

"Well, no, you do have school," she told him. "I'm going to call your teacher on Monday and get all your lessons..."

But he was already running toward the living room. "No school! Epic! Nooooooo schoooooool!"

"Okay, okay," she said. "Let's start with getting settled. We'll get our things and bring them upstairs and then we should figure out what we want to do for dinner."

They went back to the car and pulled out their bags and started to drag them upstairs.

"The Blue Mountain Room?" Simon asked.

"Sure."

"But I can switch later?"

"Yes, yes, you can switch. Let's just get a little settled for tonight, okay?"

She led him to the Blue Mountain Room, then smiled as he pulled his duffel up onto the suitcase rack. She liked that he was used to the inn, that he understood what things like suitcase racks were for.

He started to work the zipper, then let it go and climbed onto the bed. "I love this bed!" he shouted, jumping up and down. "A big bed! All to myself! A whole month!"

"Please come down and start to unpack," she said. "I don't know how late the places in town are open, and if we have to go back to the highway, I don't want to have to drive in the dark."

She watched him climb off the bed and then left him to his unpacking, even though she didn't think he was going to get much done. But she needed to distract him so she could have a moment to process everything. What on earth had her dad been thinking? How could he saddle her with this favor, without even giving her a real explanation? And knowing she had a son and her own life in New York? She hadn't looked in the refrigerator or cupboards yet, but expected he'd have left her with an empty refrigerator, other than whatever treats Katie had dropped off. It was just like Dad. Thinking she didn't need him. That she could handle whatever came her way when she was here.

Just like Mom had always done.

Except she wasn't her mother, she thought as she rolled her suitcase down the hallway. She didn't have her mom's coping skills or organizational abilities. There were things her dad had avoided fixing, and she wasn't as good at running things as her mother had been. Would she be able to handle taking care of this place and of Simon—who was now away from school—for a whole month by herself? Would she be able to handle anything that might occur—snow or ice storms, power outages, fallen trees, or even her car breaking down in the cold? She wished she had Simon's enthusiasm. But she knew how hard winters in this part of the country could be and how much work it could take to manage a house this old and big.

She went back to the hallway and looked again at the gouge in the floor. Then she crossed her arms over her chest. People had always told her that she was her mother's daughter.

She was about to find out if it was really true.

FOUR

Joel breathed in the mouth-watering scent, garlicky with hints of ginger and orange. He watched Meg dip her face toward the roasting pan, her eyes closed, and smile as the aromatic steam rose. People amazed him all the time—the unlikely things they did, the unexpected qualities they revealed—but it was his cousin who amazed him the most. High strung as she was when it came to business, Meg was the most patient of cooks. She devoted far more time to kitchen tasks than anyone else he knew. Who could spend three hours on a chicken? But that's what she'd chosen to do today as he was walking along Fifth Avenue, picking up some spy thrillers to give to Doug, the owner of the Cranberry Inn, back in Lake Summers, as a Christmas gift. She'd been preparing the marinade and washing the chicken and parboiling the potatoes and blanching the vegetables and doing all these things he didn't even know were things to be done.

"It's impossible," Meg said, putting the lid back on the pan and turning to continue chopping a thick carrot with forceful strokes, her broad knife sounding a decisive blow every time it met the cutting board. She slid the knife blade under the disks and tossed them into the salad bowl. "Just impossible," she repeated as she used the back of her wrist to brush her feathery black bangs from her eyes, the knife blade slicing through the air. Then she grabbed a red pepper, and Joel watched from the stool opposite her, amused but also a little nervous, as she continued to take out her frustration on vegetables. The alarm on her phone sounded, but she was evidently too preoccupied to hear it.

"He called again this morning, and I told him I'm figuring it out," she said. "But the truth is, I have no idea what to do. He wants to go here, he wants to go there, he wants to go to the other side of the planet"—she waved the knife left, then right, and then in a circle—"and when I tell him to be practical, he tells me I'm the only person he can count on. I mean, come on," she added, now aiming the knife forward. "I'm his agent, not his fairy godmother—"

"Maybe I should finish the salad," Joel said, rising from the stool. "The chicken smells great, by the way," he added. "You know, you didn't have to do all this."

"It's the only thing that's keeping me sane." She handed him the knife and then dropped her arms by her sides. "I'm really upset."

He smiled. "No. Really upset?"

She scowled. "Are you mocking me?"

"Just trying to help." He grabbed a tomato and started to slice. "Meg, you get too worked up over this stuff."

"You don't know what it's like, dealing with people for a living. Actors. You picked the right field to go into. Sitting in front of a computer all day worrying about numbers—"

"Every job has its pros and cons—"

"Yeah, I'd like to see a client of yours threaten to break your contract if you don't find him a place to hide out for a month. Anyway, bring the wine and come out to the table. I don't think I've had a quiet dinner like this since my kids were born. Let's eat."

She transferred the savory dish from the roasting pan to a platter and carried it out to the dining room. The table looked even larger than normal to Joel, with just two place settings at the far corner. But they were the only ones here tonight. Meg's husband,

Reed, had left a few days ago for St. Thomas, where she'd be joining him tomorrow to stay through Christmas at their favorite beach resort. Their college-age kids would be joining them as soon as they finished their finals.

Meg had called Joel after Reed left to see if he'd like to come into the city for a getaway, and he'd been grateful for the invitation. Even though Meg was older by ten years, she was still the closest thing he'd ever had to a sibling. And now she was the only family he had left, with his mom having died so suddenly.

He sat down facing the room's huge windows, which looked out onto New York from their enviable thirtieth-floor vantage point. The vertical blinds were pulled back, and while the black sky made the ordinarily breathtaking view of Central Park invisible, it did showcase the twinkling holiday lights on the rooftop gardens of other luxury apartment buildings.

It was sometimes hard for Joel to believe that he and Meg were related. Their moms had been sisters, and they'd both grown up in Lake Summers in the Adirondacks, and they'd both left the region after finishing high school, but after that, their lives had moved in very different directions. Meg had settled for good in New York right after college, married a Broadway producer, and become one of the city's most powerful theatrical agents, while Joel had graduated from Yale and then spent the last fifteen years as a nomad, hopping from city to city at the whim of his employer, a consulting firm that specialized in analyzing emerging and maturing companies. She was the doer; he was the thinker. Although lately, he'd been wondering if he'd taken the wrong route. If he'd have been happier as a doer, too.

"The thing is, I can't lose this guy as a client," Meg said, continuing her story as she passed the serving platter toward to Joel. "He's very talented and so charming. He has an amazing future."

"So why does he want to hide out?" Joel took a forkful of chicken, feeling glad he was here. Meg was entertaining and funny, in that super-caffeinated way of hers. It was fun to get the inside track on show business, to hear her stories about famous and soon-to-be famous actors. But more than that, he wanted to be around family, now that he was back from abroad, temporary as his stay was going to be. He wanted to be around someone who reminded him of growing up, and how Lake Summers once felt like home.

"The short answer is that his fashion-model girlfriend cheated on him and he can't deal with it," she answered, eating with gusto. "Boy this is good, isn't it? Anyway, I don't even know if he liked her much, I think he's just embarrassed about being dumped. I don't mean to sound heartless, but some actors can be the worst narcissists. Think of it—you're on the brink of your breakout role, your career is about to take off, and suddenly you're falling to pieces about some girl you barely knew? Because she damaged your ego a little? Grow up! This is the big leagues. He just landed the lead in *Orange Nightsongs*. Have you heard of it?"

Joel shook his head as he put some more potatoes and salad on his plate.

"No?" she said. "It's a new musical, and they're announcing the cast on New Year's Day. So he wants to stay out of sight through December. Huge production, lots of money, lots of buzz. They already have their eye on him out in L.A., so I know we're going to start getting scripts by the truckload. And suddenly he tells me he can't be in New York right now—he needs to get away so he can focus on getting into his character. He's playing the part of a young teacher who's grieving because his sister was murdered..."

"Doesn't sound like much of a musical—"

"No, actually, it's very upbeat. But that's not the point," she said, shaking her hands as though erasing his distracting comment. "The point is he wants me to find him a place where he can escape and see how it feels to play the role of a teacher. So he needs to be somewhere there's no chance anyone will know he's headed for Broadway—not that anyone knows him now, but he doesn't want to take a chance. So he doesn't want to go to a hotel or anything with a lot of people, and he also doesn't want me to rent him a house because he doesn't want to take care of it. He wants to be taken care of. He comes from money, this guy—he's willing to pay."

"Sounds like your other client," Joel said. "The one who wanted to see if he could convince people he was a real chiropractor for the TV show you got him?" He shook his head. "God, Meg, this chicken is good—"

"Oh, I'm glad you like it... yeah, he was a headache, too," Meg said. "Yeah, he was even worse. This guy, I think he'll be okay. I think he mostly just feels scared of moving to the big leagues and he doesn't want to admit it. I just have to get him through the next few weeks. Then the announcement will be made, and rehearsals will start, and I'm sure he'll settle down.

"Anyway, enough of my problems," she said, pouring them both some more wine and taking another piece of chicken. "How are you doing?"

He nodded. "I'm okay. Fine."

"But you're all alone up there. Is there anyone in town you know?"

"Well, yeah. Doug Hanover—you remember him, don't you? He owns the Cranberry Inn on Birch Street? He's the one who called to tell me about my mom."

"Oh, I remember that place. Wasn't it a very sweet family that owned it—three daughters, really pretty wife?"

"That's it. I went to school with the middle daughter, Laurel. Anyway, the wife died a few years ago and the place needs some work, even though Doug doesn't think any of it is a big deal. I've been spending some time there helping to fix it up."

Meg paused. "Speaking of houses..." Looking at her plate, she speared a bit of chicken and tightened the fork's hold on it with the blade of her knife. "Speaking of houses, what did you decide to do about your mother's?"

He put his elbow on the table and stroked his chin. "Well, I'm living there for now," he said. "I'll sell it, once I finish cleaning it out."

"When do they want you back in Singapore?"

"The week after New Year's."

Meg looked up at him. "You know, you don't have to do it yourself," she said. "You can hire people for that. These companies come in and haul everything away. They donate stuff, too, the stuff that's in good condition. So it's a nice thing, the stuff can go to people who need it."

He shook his head. "No. No, I want to do it. I owe it to her—you know, to look through it. Anyway, the house is so small, and she didn't have a lot of stuff. It was the shop that was more like home to her."

Meg bit her lower lip and nodded. "Have you been over there yet?"

He shook his head. "It's just crazy, you know?" he said. "She had to have known something was wrong. She had to have been in pain. She never told me anything."

"Because she loved you. Oh, Joel, you should have heard her go on and on about you whenever I called. She was so proud of you." Meg smiled. "Oh boy, I remember that pretty shop of hers back when I was growing up. What was it called—The Heart of Lake Summers, right?"

He nodded.

"God, I loved it there," she continued. "She used to let me choose stuff sometimes from the catalogs—felt pens and the embroidered pillowcases with the sweet sayings and all the pretty-smelling soaps and lotions. I loved when she let me use the cash register. It was such a wonderful little store."

He sighed and put his plate to the side, then folded his arms on the table.

Meg pursed her lips. "I would have called you if I knew," she said. "I had no idea either. I thought I'd be seeing her this Christmas. I wish I had heard something in her voice. I wanted her to come here for Thanksgiving, but she said she had someone coming over—a young girl who owns the dress shop next door. She said she couldn't leave her alone. I feel terrible that she was up there so sick and I was here going about my business." She shook her head. "Maybe she was in denial. Or maybe she was scared."

"Whatever it was, she should have told me," he said. "I could have done something. She didn't have to die alone."

Meg tilted her head. "She'd be glad you're going back to Singapore, you know. She'd want you to keep doing what you were doing."

"I intend to," he said. "As soon as I can."

He sighed. "You know, it's strange—you get this call in the middle of the night and you gotta get back. And it sucks, you know, but you're thinking, I'll be home. At least I'll be home. At least I'll have that. But then it turns out, that's not what it feels like at all. That's the last thing it feels like. I mean, I grew up in that town. And it feels... like I never even lived there." He chuckled. "Does that make any sense at all?"

"Actually it does. A lot," Meg said. "I haven't been alone in this apartment in years. I mean, I've traveled, I've been alone in other cities. But never in New York. And I was thinking with Reed gone and the kids at college... I was thinking how strange it is, being alone in the city. It's weird, isn't it? Feeling like you're not home when you're right there in your own house. I mean, I know what you're going through is very different. But I think I do sort of understand."

She stood, putting her napkin on the table. "Well, the good news is, I did channel those negative feelings into making the most delicious chocolate cake in the world for dessert."

"Aha! I noticed that in the kitchen, and I was hoping that was for me," he said. "Now *that's* the kind of thing that can put a smile on someone's face."

"Then let's get on with it," Meg said. "Go relax, it'll take me just a moment to clean all this up."

Joel insisted on helping, so they cleared the table and then brought the cake, dishes, and wine out into the living room. Meg served the cake with a generous hand, and Joel took his plate and sat on one of the two slim white sofas, with Meg on the other one across from him. He'd always been impressed with how Meg's apartment was so well organized: the knick-knacks perfectly spaced along the shelves, the table lamps and track lighting designed to provide the perfect glow with no glare, the paintings on the walls featuring warm gold and orange tones that blended perfectly with the gold-and-white rug. But the room also made him a bit uncomfortable, especially with a plate of chocolate cake in his hands. He much preferred an easy-going style. He wondered how Meg's kids managed it, growing up surrounded by this intensity. He suspected they avoided the white furniture, if not this whole room.

Meg picked up her fork. "Aren't you dating someone in Singapore?" she asked. "She didn't want to come back with you?"

"That's over. It wasn't working out. They'll probably send me somewhere else soon anyway." Joel ate a forkful of cake and shook his head. "Amazing," he told her. "Wow. So good."

"But why wasn't it working out?" she said. "You guys looked adorable in those pictures she posted."

He rolled his eyes. "You know as well as anyone that if you want the truth, you shouldn't go looking on social media."

She laughed. "So what are you doing for the holidays?"

He shook his head. "Nothing. Staying up in town. Going through my mom's stuff."

"What? But it's Christmastime! You shouldn't be alone. And... hey! I have an idea," she said. "Why don't you join us in St. Thomas for Christmas? I bet you can still get a flight. Even if you have to make a connection."

He shook his head. "No, no."

"But why not? Just come! We know a ton of people who'll be down there. It'll be fun."

"I've got a lot to do," he said. "The house and the store. And I've got to finish up some projects I started at the inn. I don't want to leave that unfinished when... when there's so much going on there."

"But there's still time before Christmas. And nobody works Christmas week."

"No, it's okay. I want to stay near the inn while I'm here. I'm..." He hesitated, then shrugged. "To be honest, I'm a little worried about the owner. Doug. He's been stressed lately, and he's going to be alone all month. I can work on the place, and then we can hang out a bit in the evenings."

He took another forkful of cake, hoping to leave it at that. He didn't want to say any more because he didn't want to betray Doug's confidence. Doug had a lot on his mind. He'd opened up to Joel last week about his doctor's appointment and the possibility of surgery, before swearing Joel to secrecy. Joel was hoping he could convince Doug to tell his daughters what was going on. Coming home to the news that his mom had been sick, he knew how it felt when a parent hid important information. He didn't want Doug's daughters to have to go through the same thing.

Especially not Laurel.

"And that's how you want to spend the holidays?" Meg said, sounding incredulous.

"I'm fine with it," he told her. "He's a good guy."

"But he's old. You should be having fun, getting drunk, kissing a girl on New Year's Eve... As a matter of fact, we know a lot of single women who'll be in St. Thomas—"

"Stop. Meg." He put up his hand. "Look, it's fine. It's what I want to do. Doug's daughters don't come back for the holidays, and there are no guests at the inn this month at all. And you know, he was there for my mom at the end," he added. "He was the one who picked me up from the airport when I got back to town."

"Sounds like he should be coming to St. Thomas too," she said. "God, this sounds so sad. Just the two of you stranded in that empty inn, that quiet town."

Joel chuckled. "Come on, it's not that bad. Lake Summers is great. And quiet can be nice. Just ask your actor guy. Sounds exactly like the kind of town he'd like to spend the winter in..."

He paused, and then saw Meg's eyes widen.

"Do you think...?" she said.

He nodded, realizing they were both thinking the same thing. "I can't believe I didn't come up with this before," he said. "It's just what he wants. Quiet. Pretty. And there are no other guests—he'll be totally alone. And it'll keep Doug busy, and make him a little money, which I know he can use. And hey, I'll be around doing some repairs. I can keep an eye on him and make sure he's happy."

Meg licked her top lip. "Hmm," she said. "Interesting. But I don't know," she added. "Christopher—that's his name—he wants a nice place. Fancy. You said this place needs repairs..."

"Nothing terrible. It's still beautiful—the whole town is beautiful. You know that."

"Well," she said as she rose and began taking the dishes to the kitchen. "I suppose I have no other ideas. If you're sure this is what you want, I'll run it by him. And if he's okay with it, I'll call up there and make the reservation."

"Okay then," Joel said as he followed with the cake. He started back for the wine bottle, but then stopped and turned back toward Meg.

"Just one other thing," he said. "I don't want Doug to know I did this. I don't want him to feel like I'm pitying him or this is charity or anything. So when you make the reservation, don't tell him that you're my cousin or anything about how you found the place. Say you're a travel agent or something."

"Same here," Meg said. "Christopher wants to be anonymous. If he knows that someone in town knows his story, he's going to be furious. You can't let on that you know me."

She shook her head. "I hope this doesn't turn out to be a huge headache for your friend. Like I said, my guy's a little high mainte-nance. And he's a bit of a flirt too, by the way. Probably worse now that he's been dumped. You better figure out a way to warn any pretty women in town to be on their guard."

"Well, if he's hiding out, then he probably isn't looking to start up with anyone," Joel said.

"I guess. I guess you're right." Meg smiled. "Okay then. If you're sure we should do this..."

"I'm sure. And I think it will work out great for both of them. For all of us."

They finished cleaning up, and then Joel said goodnight and headed into the guest bedroom. He couldn't believe how hopeful he felt—more so than at any time since he'd come home. He understood how surprised Meg must have been to hear him suggest this idea. He wasn't usually the guy who made plans like this. He wasn't secretive. And he wasn't calculating. But everything had come together. The pieces fit.

At least if there was a guest, Doug would be busy again. Maybe the inn would feel more like it used to, when his wife and daughters were around. Maybe it would feel like home to him again. Because that's what everyone wanted, wasn't it? To walk into their house and feel at home?

It sure was what he wanted. And maybe if he fixed things for Doug, Lake Summers would start to feel like home to him again, too.

It was worth a shot.

FIVE

In bed that night, Laurel stared at the ceiling of the Cranberry Room, with its dark-brown furniture and deep-red rug, where she always slept when she was here. She was tired but restless, both at once. It wasn't an unfamiliar feeling though, as sleeping at the inn had been difficult ever since her mother died. She still felt so empty without her.

Turning onto her side, she slid a hand under her pillow, trying to get more comfortable. But the pillowcase felt slick, even slippery —not at all what she was used to. She couldn't imagine what had spurred Dad to buy this type of bedding. Had some overly persuasive salesperson talked him into it?

She pulled herself out of bed, knowing she'd never be able to sleep unless she had a regular, cotton pillowcase.

In the hallway she tiptoed, needing no light to know exactly when to stop, when to reach for the small knobs on the closet's accordion doors, when she needed to tug on them slightly to maneuver the doors silently past the sticky spots in the tracks. It was after midnight, and she didn't want to turn on the light and risk waking Simon, whose room was right across from the closet. Although, she reminded herself, he was a very deep sleeper.

And he loved his room, which her mother had dubbed the Blue

Mountain Room because it looked out on the blue hydrangea bushes lining the back porch each summer and, beyond that, the southern peak of Mount Marcy in the distance. Simon always went straight for this room when he got here, and she suspected he'd stay here, even though he had reserved the right to switch. He loved that the room was much bigger than his room back home, with two beds that were both available to him. And that both beds were full-size, so much larger to him than his regular twin-size one.

She pulled open the closet, and in the dim light from her room, she noticed that the bottom three shelves had collapsed and were now piled haphazardly on the floor.

She stooped and ran her fingers over the gouges where the shelves used to rest, which were just as deep as the one in the hallway floor. She couldn't imagine what would have caused the shelves to rip out like that. Maybe her dad had tried to put something heavy on them. They were thin and meant only for sheets and linens. Maybe he'd tried to straighten up one of the rooms and had shoved some heavy items into the closet. Or maybe a guest had needed more shelf space, so he'd cleared out some books and put them in the closet. Her father wasn't detail oriented and didn't have a sense of where things belonged, as her mother had. He would have tried to stick anything in the closet to get it out of sight. And then when the shelves had crashed down, he would have kept the closet door closed, so he wouldn't have to see and think about the damage.

The sight of those gouges now reminded her of other things she'd noticed last night but hadn't wanted to think about—like the dimmer switch in the dining room and the row of under-counter lights in the kitchen, both of which no longer worked. And the crack in Simon's window, which they'd pressed pillows against so no cold air would get inside. She supposed her father might not have noticed the crack—but her mother would have seen it and had the window replaced right away. Her mom had been aware of every inch of every room at the inn, and her eyes zeroed in on anything that was amiss. And Dad evidently hadn't noticed the leak in the ceiling above the showerhead in her bathroom, where a water stain was forming. Or the tile in her bathroom, which badly needed regrouting.

She wondered what similar problems—or, for that matter, what additional ones—she'd find if she examined all the other guest rooms. The whole inn was apparently in more serious need of repairs and upgrades than she'd ever imagined. How had her father let so many things go?

Grabbing a cotton pillowcase from the top shelf of the closet, she tiptoed back to her room, telling herself she'd have to examine the inn closely tomorrow and make a list of all the things that needed fixing. Maybe she and Simon would stop by the Grill—Maxine and Gull, the owners, knew everyone in town and could surely recommend an electrician and a plumber, maybe a carpenter as well. She was glad that Simon hadn't noticed any of these problems. To him, the inn was exactly as it always was, and new flaws—like the crack in the window that needed to be blocked with pillows—were simply fun and intriguing eccentricities that didn't diminish his delight in the least.

Back when she was his age, she'd also viewed the inn with nothing but love. Even now, she remembered the fun of seeing people from all over the world make themselves at home in the inn's sunroom as they ate one of her mother's hearty breakfasts or chatted with other guests over afternoon lemonade or sparkling wine on the front porch in the summers, or a toasty-warm drink in the living room in the winter. Her mother had created a special winter cocktail known as the Lake Summers Spiked Cappuccino, while Dad had invented the Cranberry Inn Hot Toddy. Laurel never knew what was in them, but she remembered how much the guests all enjoyed them.

And she remembered, too, how the inn had had a whole staff of interesting and unusual people: Frank, the front-desk manager, who could juggle four plates without ever dropping one; Charlie, the night manager, who had the longest ponytail Laurel had ever seen; Garcelle and Paula, the part-time cooks, who spoke at least five languages each; and a stream of housekeepers, waiters, land-scapers, interns and maintenance staff who always had a smile and a nice word for her. There was even a flower designer, a young woman who came in twice a week to take care of the indoor and outdoor flowers, and would carry on the most animated conversa-tions with them as she gave them a good watering and gently pulled off the dead blossoms.

In those days, the place was like a fairy-tale castle to her, with its grand stairway and always-gleaming banister, and its commer-cial kitchen, the appliances looking like they were built for giants. Laurel and her sisters would beg to be allowed to sleep in the inn, and in the winter when there was a night with no guests, their parents let them. They usually slept in the room Laurel now occu-pied, the Cranberry Room, the wallpaper back then dotted with cranberries. She and Deb would sleep in one bed, with Tracey getting the other one for herself since she was the oldest. Even though the room was big, it still felt so cozy to Laurel as she snug-gled under the red comforter that enveloped her and her younger sister. She'd always loved the peaceful sound of her sisters breathing softly, and she'd listen for a few moments just before she drifted off to sleep.

Sometimes she'd awaken in the middle of the night to the sound of the heat kicking in, the pipes knocking quickly at first and then slower and slower until the sound faded away. She didn't know why they knocked like that, but she loved that sound. It told her that the house would stay warm while she was asleep. The rhythmic thump was like the beat of a lullaby.

She replaced her pillowcase, and then climbed back into bed, turning again to gaze at the ceiling. How she missed those sounds, those homey feelings. Now she felt like she was dreaming, one of those disturbing dreams where you wander around looking for something familiar, believing that if you could find even one familiar thing, everything would fall into place and you'd realize you were home. But you never found that familiar thing.

She supposed it made sense that she'd feel this way. The inn

right now didn't match up with all her wonderful memories.
Maybe she was especially bothered by all the problems and flaws
because she was the sole grown-up in charge. And that was a
frightening notion. She didn't feel secure at all, despite the
pinging that now rang out from the pipes, and she wondered if
her dad had asked her to come back because too much was going
wrong. Yes, he'd sounded happy on the phone, and his note—
with the mention of the Christmas Eve surprise—was practically
joyful. But that was her dad—cheerful no matter what was going
on. Even bad winter forecasts when she was young, with threats
of trees down and extended power outages, had never changed
his tone. At least not in a way she had noticed. But she
wondered now what might be going on beneath his unflappable
exterior. Maybe the tone in his note masked his awareness that
the inn was crumbling before his eyes. Maybe he was asking for
help.

Because it had always been her mom's job to take care of every
detail, big or small. Her mom had been the one to make the guests'
dinner reservations or purchase their ski-lift tickets or book the car
service to bring them to the airport at the end of their stay. She
managed the housekeeping and kitchen staffs, and contacted
plumbers or electricians when things were broken, and pitched in
to scrub bathrooms or change dirty linens when the inn was full
and more hands were needed. Then, after being out all day with
Tracey or Deb or one of his fishing buddies, Dad would stroll in at
cocktail hour to charm the guests with his banter and his stories
and that broad, handsome smile, and soon everyone would be
laughing. And if her mom had felt burdened, it no longer mattered;
he'd found a way to make her forget.

That was the way Dad always was, she thought. Disarming
people with his smile and his wit. Even she'd had a hard time
staying mad at him, and she never let him know when he inadver-
tently hurt her feelings or made her feel she wasn't as important to
him as her sisters were because she wasn't an athlete or sports star.
It was easier to return his smile, to listen for him to use her nick-

name—*kiddo*—and to believe that everything was right in the world, and he loved her.

She didn't know how long she stayed awake, but the next time she opened her eyes, the sun was streaming in below the red window toppers and through the gap between the partially closed white curtains.

She checked her phone—7 a.m. Kind of early, but she liked getting an early start when she was here. Her mom had adored the dawn, and Laurel felt the power of that joy every time she returned.

She slipped her feet into her slippers and wrapped the red knitted throw at the foot of her bed around her. Tiptoeing into the hallway, she peeked into Simon's room, and when she saw that he was still asleep, she headed downstairs.

Opening the front door, she stepped onto the front porch and looked at the thermometer mounted near the porch swing. She'd forgotten how cold it got up here in the mountains in December—eight degrees, two below zero with the windchill!

Scurrying back inside, she grasped the blanket tighter around her and went into the kitchen to make a pot of coffee. Waiting for it to brew, she turned and leaned against the countertop. She loved everything about this kitchen: the wide windows from which you could see the whole backyard; the sheer white curtains; the big farmhouse table and wooden chairs her mother had painted in light yellow. Maybe her dad was right, and it was a little too cramped for an inn. Still, the ultra-modern kitchen Joanna had designed for the Samposiera showroom couldn't hold a candle to this one. Joanna's choices were eye-catching and would look good in a magazine, as the photographer had said. But this was the kind of kitchen that Laurel would design if given half a chance.

She turned back and looked out at the patio through the window. Her mother's only regret about the inn was that it didn't have a ballroom—not a huge, fancy one, but a pretty room where she could host small weddings or showers, or special-occasion parties. She'd always intended to break out the back wall of the kitchen and sunroom and create a beautiful room that would look out onto the woods and catch the last of the setting sun. It was the only thing she'd planned to accomplish but never did. Last summer, Laurel had been looking in the junk drawer by the refrigerator for an eyeglass repair kit—Simon had lost one of his eyeglass screws at the lake that day—and she'd come upon a small floral notebook filled with her mom's ideas for the ballroom: floor-to-ceiling windows in a curved arrangement; recessed lighting; solid-wood floors with a cherry finish; skylights; tan window shades that could block the glare without diminishing the view of the setting sun; beautiful glass-topped round tables and elegant banquet chairs; French doors that opened onto a magnificent garden...

She sighed and took a sip of coffee, then wrapped her hands around her mug and let the fragrant steam bathe her face as she walked into the living room and sat down on the big sofa. With the throw still around her shoulders, she pulled a knee up to her chin and raised her mug again to her lips. How many times had she sat here early on a Saturday morning in the winter with her mom, working out whatever problem was bothering her? Sometimes it was a hard homework assignment or upcoming test, sometimes a boy she cared about, like Joel Hutcherson, whose street she had passed when she arrived in town yesterday. But mostly it was that awful feeling that had always plagued her, that she didn't fit in anywhere. That she wasn't pretty—her hair wasn't honey-gold like her sisters' but a dull copper-red, and it wasn't silky and straight like her sisters' but kind of limp and stringy. And her face was too wide, her eyes way too round, her complexion too pale. She wasn't popular, and she wasn't interesting—she wasn't someone that other people noticed. She liked being in the drama club more than on the softball or soccer or track team. And even in the drama club, she was only good at backstage stuff, not acting.

Then, when she was in high school, the talks with her mom always centered around the pressure she felt to leave Lake Summers after high school—pressure Dad was putting on her. She didn't want to leave Lake Summers; she wanted to stay and work at the inn and go to college locally. It was the constant struggle in her life, the push and pull between leaving and staying, and she had no idea why her sisters didn't struggle the same way. Tracey and Deb were both anxious to leave town as soon as they could—the further away, the better.

Of course it didn't help that on those mornings, Dad had usually already left to take Tracey or Deb, or both, to whatever multi-school sports competition or regional travel-team try-out was on the calendar. But being with Mom, and knowing she had Mom's full attention, had always made her feel better. Mom had been so certain that Laurel would find her way, that her special-ness would make itself evident before long, that she'd find the life that would fulfill her and the people she was meant to surround herself with. That her green eyes were beautiful, that her pale complexion was lovely, that the reddish shade of her hair was capti-vating. Those Saturday mornings were when Laurel could say what was in her heart and take comfort in her mother's love. And somehow, there was always enough time to get what she needed from her mom before there'd be stirring upstairs, the sound of showers running, sometimes even someone coming down in a bathrobe for coffee to bring back up. That was when she and Mom would head to the kitchen to begin to fix the inn's renowned country breakfast. Laurel had loved helping when Dad was away.

She went back to the kitchen now and looked out the window again. In the summer it was impossible to see the lake, the big oaks and maples in the back so full and leafy that they blocked the view. But now the lake was visible, the trees wrapped only in a thin layer of snow.

She took a last sip of her coffee and wondered if her mom would be proud of her. She wasn't a success like her sisters were, although it wasn't for a lack of trying. She'd left home too, the way Dad had wanted her to, and she'd gone to a good college a few hours away, like her sisters had. But she had never made it out of the state. She had floundered in New York City for a while, not knowing what she wanted to do, starting jobs and quitting them, starting on additional degrees and then changing her mind. She'd thought about being a teacher and went back to college for her certificate but never finished. It wasn't her style to stand at the head of a classroom. Year after year, she longed to come home and help run the inn. But she knew she'd be a disappointment to Dad yet again if she did, and she couldn't bear the thought of that.

What would he say when he found out she still hadn't landed a client? That Joanna still didn't trust her? That she had missed out on her dream job again?

Sighing, she rinsed out her mug and went back upstairs to check on Simon. He was still sound sleep. Watching him now, with his glasses off, she saw how much he resembled her father. Yes, Simon was young and his face was round, while Dad's was longer and thinner. But they had the same wide eyes and high cheekbones, the same thin, wide lips. And suddenly she felt bad for her dad. Even if he had taken off like a child because he couldn't handle everything, it didn't mean he was irresponsible or selfish. He had always hated to be seen as incapable—just like she did. It must have been horrible for him, she thought, to see all the problems with the inn surfacing. And to know he should have prevented them but never did.

Closing Simon's door, she went back downstairs, stopping at the reception desk. Curious, she turned on the computer and searched "The Cranberry Inn, Lake Summers, reviews." As she suspected, the results weren't good:

"Used to be nice but looking a little seedy."

"Our shower leaked all night."

"I am so sorry to see what's happening to this place. It used to be magical. Looks like there was a change in ownership and the lovely lady who ran things isn't there anymore. Definitely needs a facelift."

Laurel looked away from the computer. She couldn't deny it—her dad was in over his head. But things didn't have to keep spiraling downward. She wasn't a real designer, at least not yet, but she'd learned a lot from Joanna—and one of the most important things was that when it came to a room, a suite, or a complete home, nearly all problems were reversible. Reinvention and renovation were always options. And even if the so-called facelift would take a little money, Laurel knew her parents had been good about saving for repairs. As Joanna always said, investment in real estate paid off.

Sitting at the desk looking toward the living room—toward the Christmas tree in the corner and her dad's blue armchair—she knew what she had to do. She needed to make her father proud, to help him and to leave the inn in a better state for when he returned. And she could do it. Even if Joanna hadn't given her a client, that didn't mean she didn't deserve one. That didn't mean she wasn't capable of handling a big and wonderful project.

She hadn't expected to be here, but her dad needed help, and she knew she had no choice. Fixing the inn was something she needed to do for him.

It was something she needed for herself as well.

SIX

Joel walked along Main Street, his head down to block the wind, his coffee from Mrs. Pearl's clenched in his gloved hand, the steam warming his face as he lifted the lid to take a good, hot gulp. It was the same walk he'd taken millions of times when he was growing up, from home or from school, but he hadn't been down this way since he'd returned to Lake Summers, so the trip occupied that strange space between the familiar and the foreign.

He hadn't planned to go to his mother's store today. He'd been avoiding going there ever since he got back to town, and he hadn't been in any hurry to change course. But his conversation with Meg the other evening had made him realize it was time to stop delaying. He wanted to have time to spend with Doug, to help convince him to talk to his daughters about everything that was going on. He'd realized on the ride back home last night that time was moving quickly, and he had a lot to do before he needed to be back in Singapore. So it was time to rip the bandage off and face whatever was awaiting him at his mother's store.

He finished his coffee, tossed the cup into a nearby trash can, and made his way to the middle of the block. There it was, the little gift store, with "The Heart of Lake Summers" in light-blue letters imprinted in a crescent shape on the window.

He stepped up to the entrance, pulled off a glove, then reached into the front pocket of his jeans for the key. He turned it in the lock and pushed with his shoulder, harder and harder until the door came unstuck from the frame, sending him stumbling inside. He looked at the door and then closed it, wondering how long it had been like that. His mother had had an eagle eye when it came to the store; some would even call her a control freak. She must have hated having a door that stuck, and he was surprised that she hadn't had it fixed. He could have fixed it in a heartbeat, if only he'd been there to do it.

And other things felt wrong too, he thought as he walked inside. The ring of the entranceway bell sounded out of place in the empty store. And the air smelled sharp, a little bit like sawdust, but not entirely woodsy. It was more of a stale smell, almost chemical. Not particularly strong, just different from the sweet, flowery scent he remembered, the kind of smell that would make him frown and hold his nose when he was a kid. Walking with friends through town, getting a hot dog from Lonny's hot-dog shop or a milkshake from the Ice Creamery, he always went right past the store, ignoring it. It had been embarrassing, this store, when he was growing up. Too pink and flowery. Too girly.

He stepped further inside, the intense chill penetrating his coat. Well, that was something he could fix. He blew into his hands to warm them and then looked around to locate the thermostat. He'd never touched it when he was growing up. His mom had always kept the place at the perfect temperature.

Spotting the box on the wall, he went over and tapped the button a few times, then went to the front windows to raise the shades and let some sun in. One rose easily, but the other came crashing down, and he covered his head to block the shower of paint chips that followed. Then he put his hands into his coat pockets and looked around.

The store was depressing. Well, maybe that was an exaggeration. It wasn't as though it was a shambles. Despite the film of dust in the air and the window shade that was now wedged between the windowsill and the casement, it looked well stocked and organized. There were items stacked neatly in the three large display cases arranged around the perimeter of the store: tablecloths and embroidered napkins and bins of napkin holders; bowls and mugs and platters painted in sunset colors; jewelry and little soaps and lotions. And there were four-sided glass shelving units in the center of the store with all kinds of trinkets neatly arranged— picture frames and padded clothes hangers and sculptures and paintings, boxed notecards. So much stuff.

And yet the shop looked abandoned, he thought. Like a ghost town or an illicit speakeasy from the 1920s, a place where the specter of past revelries floated in the stale air.

In the middle of the shop were two open shipping cartons, waiting to be unpacked. Joel could tell his mom must have thought she'd be back, that day she closed up for the last time. He could almost see her lowering the window shades, turning down the heat, and locking the door for the night, the bell jingling on the other side as she walked home. She'd no doubt planned to unload the boxes when she returned, and make room for the new items on the glass shelves, so they'd be visible when the first customers walked in.

He unbuttoned his coat as the heat started to kick in. His mom had loved this place. Much more than the little two-bedroom house they'd shared. She'd wanted it to be the kind of place where you never knew what you'd find, where there'd be new discoveries to explore even if you came back every day. She'd studied catalogs from vendors all over the country and spoke to distributors who brought in merchandise from far-off places. But it was the local artists and craftspeople she loved working with the most.

He smiled, remembering some of the quirkier items she'd shown him the last time he'd visited, six years ago this spring. Collages made of metal scraps from an autobody shop, crafted by an artist in Syracuse. Framed replicas of landmark buildings from around the world, constructed from twigs and stones and dried flowers by a florist out in Old Forge. Sweaters and scarves made of natural materials like sea algae, bamboo, and jute, by a weaver in Ayelin Point. They felt uncomfortable and didn't sell well, but his mom wanted to support the weaver, so she carried them anyway.

And she was constantly coming up with new ideas for the store too. That last time he was here, she'd been so proud to show him the tea shop she'd created in the back of the store, just four little tables, where she'd serve cookies and herbal teas in china cups in the dead of winter. She'd told him she'd designed it for mothers and young daughters who were tired of snow and wanted to pretend they were far away in some exotic location. She kept a few picture books back there so they could share some stories while they drank their tea.

The place was continuing to warm up, so he took off his coat and, walking to the back corner, threw it over one of the tea-shop chairs, which were less dusty than the display counters. Then he headed toward the closet across the floor, although he wasn't quite sure what he was looking for. A mop, dust cloths, a vacuum, cleaning sprays? He knew he needed to spruce the place up, so he could open it back up, get customers in, and start to move merchandise. And his time was short, because he wanted to help out at the inn a lot too.

There was a tapping on the glass storefront, and then the door opened, the bell jingled, and a young woman in snow boots and a red parka peeked in. Her head was covered by a green wool beanie, her face dominated by large, brown eyes and a huge, white smile.

"Hello?" she said. "Are you the son?"

"I... uh," he started, surprised at how casual she sounded. Was he supposed to know her? "Yeah, I guess, I am the son. Jeannie's son. And you are...?"

"I'm the neighbor," she said, coming in and closing the door with her back. "Or, at least, the business neighbor. I'm Lexy Stone, I own the dress shop next door. Well, my husband and I do."

She pulled a glove off with her teeth and walked over to shake hands. "You're Joel, right? I've heard so much about you, I feel like I know you. You're the really smart guy who does something with finance that nobody understands and has lived all over the world. Sydney, Tokyo, Ankara—I'm not even sure where that one is. But now somewhere in Singapore, right? See, she told me everything. She must be so happy to have you home. She told me you weren't coming until April."

She looked past his shoulder toward the back of the store. "Where is she anyway? Downstairs? She usually gets in much earlier than I do. I wanted to tell her that I accepted some of her boxes from the UPS guy, so she doesn't think they've gone missing. Did she end up going away? We were both talking about doing something impulsive, going to Florida or the Caribbean for Christmas. Did she actually do it?"

"What?" Joel asked. "Wait, what?" She was talking so fast, and nothing was making sense. Did she not know what had happened?

"No, I guess she wouldn't have, not if she knew you were coming home," she said. "Or did you surprise her for Christmas? Is she in the basement? Because I should tell her I have a few boxes..."

She started to walk past him, and he stepped sideways to block her. "My mother... she's not downstairs," he said.

"So she did go away. I knew she would!"

"No, she..." He hesitated. He hadn't had to break the news to anyone. Everyone had known when he came home. He'd been one of the last to find out, since it had taken Doug a few hours to track down his number and call him.

"Lexy—that's your name, right? Lexy?" he said. Suddenly he felt very protective of her, this young woman who seemed to have liked his mom so much. "Look, my mom... I hate to have to tell you this... but you see, my mother passed away."

"What?" she said. He saw her eyes widen and her jaw sink. She had such an expressive face, and she didn't look just sad; she also looked shocked. And terrified. "She... died?"

"I'm sorry," he said, realizing how crazy it was, that he was consoling her. But he thought she needed it. "It happened suddenly. A friend called me. I came home right away. I was surprised too."

She walked toward the back of the store, and as she passed him, he noticed she was pregnant. Significantly pregnant, since it was apparent through her parka. She reached the tea shop and sank down into one of the chairs. Then she took off her hat and held it by the pom-pom, leaning forward, her elbows on her thighs, her long blond hair falling forward toward her face. "Oh man. I can't believe it."

"It was... um. It was in the paper," he said.

"I didn't see it," she said. "I went away right after Thanksgiving. I just came back a couple of days ago. I really thought... I really thought she went on... vacation..."

"Hey, do you need something—some water or something?" he said. "I don't know where she keeps everything, but I bet I can find a cup somewhere...."

"No, no," she said. "That's okay. I'm okay. I just never thought..." She shook her head. "I was just hoping that she was okay, you know? When I got home a few days ago and she wasn't around. I was hoping she was like a lot of older people I know— that she went somewhere warm and forgot to leave me a note. I thought she'd be back, maybe show me some new teas or some cool new jewelry she found. And I was saving some clothes for her. She looked so beautiful in purples and deep blues—vibrant colors, you know? They were so beautiful with her skin tone and that white hair. I had a couple of sweaters... for her. And when I looked in just now and saw you, I thought maybe she was back and you were here visiting. I thought she must have been so happy to see you."

She sniffled. "How did she die?"

"Some kind of blood infection, the doctors said," Joel said.

"A blood infection? How did that happen?"

"I don't know," he said. "They said there was some infected wound on her leg. Did she ever cut herself? Anything you remember?"

"No, not that— Oh my God, yes. Oh, I remember it now," she

said. "She fell going down to the basement that time. I came to say goodnight that night and I found her sitting here. It was pretty deep, I told her to get it checked out. But she said she'd put some ointment on it and a bandage. She promised she'd go to the doctor if it got worse. But she never said anything, and I thought she was fine."

She shook her head. "I told her I'd take her to the doctor, but she said I was overreacting and she loved me for caring so much about her. But she wouldn't go. She said she was fine."

He nodded. "She hated doctors. I remember that. She said they always found something else besides what you went there for."

"A lot of people feel that way," she said. "They never want to think something's wrong. I guess they're scared. I'm scared, too—all the time. But I still think it's better to know things, right? Anyway, you know her better than I do. You probably know what she's like. Was... like..."

"I guess," he said. Although he didn't understand what his mom had done at all. It had to have looked terrible, that wound, if the infection got that bad. Why wouldn't she go to the doctor? Or call him even?

"She stayed home a few days," Lexy said. "I brought her dinner. She said she was just a little under the weather. And then she came back. So I just never thought. I don't think she thought anything. Or maybe she did." She looked up at him. "What do you think?"

"I don't know," Joel said. "I hadn't seen her in a long time..."

"I figured she decided to go away," Lexy repeated, rubbing her forehead with her fingertips. "Like we talked about on Thanksgiving. I was going to be alone, and she invited me to her house. We had a really nice time. Then I went up to Maine to visit Gary's parents—that's my husband. I didn't even want to go because I don't like them very much, and they totally hate me. But Jeannie convinced me to go. She said it was important, because of the baby, that I'd understand better when the baby came. So I went. And it was okay, better than the last time. I was so excited to tell her all about it. And then when I came back into town and saw the store closed, I figured she went away. I thought we'd have so much to catch up on. I was happy for her..." She looked up at him again, and he saw the tears start to run down her face, her eye make-up dripping in thin black lines.

He took a few steps in her direction. "I'm sorry," he said. "She was a really good person. I know. A good mom and a good person."

He paused, hating that he was talking about her in such generic terms. But he hadn't known his mom well, not anymore. He didn't know her the way someone who saw her every day would know her. Someone who mused with her about vacationing somewhere warm. He hadn't talked about things like that with her. All they'd ever talked about when he called was him. What he was doing, who he was dating. He'd asked his mom to visit, many times. She'd said she would. But he'd known she wouldn't. She didn't want to leave the store. They'd video-chatted on Thanksgiving morning, probably before Lexy had arrived. She'd said she was fine, she was happy. He told her he'd visit in the spring, and she'd said she couldn't wait.

He saw Lexy looking at him, her eyebrows raised, as though she was waiting for him to say something. Like maybe it was all a mistake and his mom was downstairs after all.

"I wish I could get you something... I'm just back in the store for the first time in years," he said. "Can I go down the block and get you something from Pearl's to eat or drink or something...?"

"She was such a nice person," Lexy said. "So welcoming. We opened our store last summer, and she brought over a big cake to welcome us. And she sent all her customers over to us. She made us feel so good. We thought we were going to love this town, and she solidified it for us. We knew this was the place we wanted to live."

"We.... meaning you and your husband?" he asked. "Is he here —should I go get him for you?"

She shook her head. "He left in September. He's in the military." She smiled. "Jeannie and I were both alone. Both women business owners, both alone. When the cold weather came, it felt like we were pioneer women taking care of one another. Except I guess she was really taking care of me. She made me think she needed me, but she was really taking care of me."

She sighed. "After Gary left, she was like a mother to me. I lost my mother a long time ago. It was nice to have a mom around when I was getting ready to... you know. To be one."

She ran her fingers through her long hair. "Look at me, being such a baby," she said. "When you're the one who just lost your mom. I mean, she was your *mom*. I just really, really liked her."

"It's okay," he said. It was clear that she wasn't going anywhere, so he went over and sat down on the chair opposite her, moving his coat onto a nearby table. "It's nice to know she made such an impact on you."

"She was really proud of you, you know," she said. "She talked about you all the time. That incredible work you were doing, how smart you were. She said you spoke with diplomats and government people, all kinds of important people. That you advised them even. She followed your career so closely. All those newspaper and magazines you were quoted in? She showed them all to me. She even framed some."

"Did she?" he asked. There had been a few articles in some very specialized magazines. They were just tiny publications. Hardly any readership, maybe a few hundred. He didn't even remember sending them to her.

Lexy nodded and pointed to the wall behind the cash register, where now he noticed a row of framed newspaper and magazine pages.

"You were doing such important research, she said," Lexy added. "She was so happy you were doing work you loved. She said you were going to save the world and end all poverty and hunger and make small countries much richer and more successful."

He laughed and shook his head. "That's not what I was doing. Not at all..."

"She said you were. But I guess that's how moms are. Thinking the sun rises and sets on their kids. She said I would feel that way too. She said I would be surprised by how much I was going to love this baby. She said as much love as you think you have to give—it's only a tiny fraction of what you actually have..."

Lexy's words hung in the air, and they both sat still for a moment. Then she pushed herself up to standing, using the table for leverage. "I think there's something I should show you," she said.

"There is?" he asked. What else could there be? What else could this woman know that he didn't know?

"She said it the last time we were here together, that I should know where it was. She hid it so it would be safe. I think she was scared you might not find it. I just thought she was going through old things. I never thought she meant she really didn't know if she'd ever be back.

"Come," she said and motioned to him to follow her.

They went through a doorway at the back of the store, and she flipped on a light switch and then led him down a steep staircase. It was even dustier here, and particles of who knew what—sand? dirt?—crunched below his feet. And at the bottom of the stairs, he noticed a small pile of mouse droppings on the floor. He grimaced and looked away, wondering if Lexy had noticed it, knowing how his mother would be if she'd known anyone had seen that. How had his mom let the place get this way? She'd always taken such pride in this store, even the dark and remote areas. There never used to be a speck of dust anywhere—and she'd never have tolerated rodents. He wondered how long she'd been feeling ill. She must have felt very bad to have ignored mice, even down here in the basement.

They reached the basement, and the space grew darker as they moved away from the staircase. In the dim light from the top of the stairs, he could make out a row of steel filing cabinets by the back wall. He looked around, then spotted a string hanging from a light bulb fixed to the ceiling. He pulled on it a few times, but nothing happened. He took his phone from his pocket and turned on the flashlight, then gave it to Lexy to lead the way.

She stopped when she reached the cabinets and opened one of the middle drawers. Inside was a thin steel box with a combination lock. She lifted it and dialed the knob, and the latch clicked as the top of the box popped up. She rested the box on her belly, opened the top all the way, and took out an envelope.

"She wanted me to make sure you saw this," she said. Then her face puckered, and she looked away, pressing the backs of her fingers underneath her nose.

Joel didn't know what to do. He wasn't used to women showing emotion around him. At least not tears. Stella, his old girl-friend in Singapore, had been more prone to anger, throwing things. His mother, by contrast, had been stoic when she was scared or sad.

Instinctively, he reached out and touched her elbow. "Hey, you okay?"

She wiped her tears then put the box back into the drawer. "I'm fine. I never was such a crybaby. But these days anything sets me off. Part of being pregnant, I guess."

He started to open the envelope. It was sealed and also taped shut.

"I shouldn't be here, when you're reading this," Lexy said. "And anyway, I should go check on my store. Sorry to have taken so much of your time—"

"No, it's fine, you don't have to rush out—" But she was already lumbering back to the staircase.

"Do you need help or—" he added, but she waved him off and headed upstairs.

He ripped open the envelope and unfolded the piece of paper inside. There were only a few words, and while he recognized her handwriting, the words looked shaky, as though her hand were trembling as she wrote them.

Joel, my sweet boy. Don't stay here. Go back.

Don't believe him. Go back.

He stared at the sentences. She'd clearly known she was dying when she wrote this. And she'd expected that he would come home. And he'd always intended to go back to Singapore after he took care of his mother's affairs. He'd never intended to stay in Lake Summers.

But still, why would his mom be so worried about him staying? Why would this be the final message she had for him? And who shouldn't he believe? What was that all about?

He folded the paper, put it back in the envelope, and then put the envelope into in his back pocket as he headed upstairs. When he reached the top of the staircase, he looked around the store again. Now it didn't merely look abandoned. Now it looked confusing as well. Who shouldn't he believe? What was she talking about? He would have to, somehow, figure out what had been on her mind.

He'd never be able to put this store and this town behind him if he left without understanding what she was saying—and why.

SEVEN

Laurel spent the rest of Sunday making a list of food and supplies she and Simon would need, and then they went downtown to shop. She'd been right—Dad didn't have much food in the cabinets or the refrigerator. She suspected he went out to the Grill or Sal's Pizza for dinner, or maybe regularly picked up some prepared sandwiches or meals from Katie's shop, since he loved to be out and about. But Simon needed home-cooked meals and a regular routine.

It was nice to be back in town, catching up with the sisters who ran Lake Summers Groceries, where she stocked up on food and condiments, and the couple who owned Maple Street Hardware, where she picked up some nails and hooks and wood glue, for any repairs she could handle, along with containers of salt that might come in handy if the driveway or outdoor steps iced up. Back home, she made roast chicken and potatoes for dinner, and then she and Simon found some holiday decorations in the basement that Dad hadn't yet gotten around to unpacking.

She slept better that night, and the next morning as she lay in bed, she decided it made sense to begin getting the cottage ready for her and Simon. She figured that she was going to have a lot going on at the inn once repairs got underway, so it made sense for her and Simon to move out while the work was being done. She could only hope the cottage was in good enough shape for the two of them to live there until Christmas. She hadn't been there in years so wasn't sure what condition she'd find it in, and she wanted to get started on any necessary clean-up as soon as possible.

Walking downstairs from the Cranberry Room, she still felt different than she had when she was growing up. Her footsteps sounded loud, and all the noises in the kitchen—getting a mug out of the cabinet, scooping the coffee from the canister, pouring the water into the machine, watching the coffee drip down into the carafe—sounded sharper, almost amplified. She also had the sensation that she was being watched—by two different sets of people. One set seemed to be whispering among themselves that she wasn't up to the task, and that a person more senior and responsible should be running things and handling repairs—but the other seemed to be cheering her on, acknowledging that this was her moment and she was ready.

With Simon still asleep, she took her mug to the sunroom— more often known as the breakfast room back in the days when the inn was full—and over to the doors. The view this morning was gorgeous—thick, snowy woods below a vibrant blue sky and a rich yellow sun. Then she turned, and the room looked so dark and lifeless by comparison. It never used to look that way, when she was young.

Right around this time of day, the space would be coming to life. Now would be the time that her dad and mom would be putting out the tablecloths—white in summer, forest green or deep red in the winter—and adding a small vase atop each one with an arrangement of whatever flower was in season—poppies, dahlias, peonies, or snowdrops. Sometimes there'd be a college kid from the culinary school or the community college in Lyons Hill helping, setting the coffee and silverware and napkins, putting out silver milk pitchers and sugar bowls, tiny plates with butter, and little bowls with jam from Corsico's farm, a tiny spoon resting inside each one. And ceramic pitchers with real maple syrup. And tiny metal stands with the little handwritten menus her mom would have prepared the night before, describing the four-course breakfast—fruit or juice, oatmeal or porridge, muffins and scones, and the main dish, a choice of an omelet or breakfast casserole or blueberry and pecan pancakes.

How she used to wish she could peek into the sunroom to see the people tasting their first delicious bites on weekend mornings! Her mom never let her go in there, because, she'd say, the guests were on vacation and didn't need to be reminded that they had kids or pets or chores or other worries waiting for them at home. So Laurel would sit in the kitchen with her sisters, all in their pajamas, and watch Mom cook and Dad pour the juice as he warned them for the hundredth time to please not let the chairs knock into the wall and scrape the paint. And Mom would fill their bowls with oatmeal and place a platter of pancakes in the center of the table, and then follow Dad into the sunroom. The girls would drench their pancakes in syrup as they listened to Dad singing and the guests applauding.

Laurel turned again and looked out the windows, spying the area where her mother's ballroom was to have been built. She'd been so sure she would build it—next year, next year, she'd always say. She'd expected to host her daughters' weddings there—or maybe her grandchildren's weddings. Her mom wanted so little, and everything she wanted was all about celebrating life and love. She'd desperately wanted to build a space that would be all about celebration. And she'd never seen it happen.

Just then the inn's phone rang, and Laurel went through the living room and over to the reception desk to answer it. She hadn't answered that reservation line in years, as so much was done online now. But she hoped it was her dad calling so she could hear from him exactly what was going on. She'd tried to reach him a few times again last night, with no more success than she'd had all weekend.

"Hello?" she said. "The Cranberry Inn, Laurel speaking." It sounded so strange, to hear herself answer this way. When she was a teenager and would answer the phone, she'd always felt so much pride. But it was hard to be upbeat now toward strangers seeking a room when there were so many things at the inn that needed fixing. It didn't look nearly as good as it had when she'd answered the phone years ago.

"Hello," an efficient-sounding voice said on the other end of the line. "I'm looking to make a reservation for a client of mine. From Wednesday, the sixth, through Christmas Eve."

"Yes, we're—wait, *this* Wednesday? Two days from now?" Laurel said. Her dad had said the inn would be empty all month. He hadn't expected any guests at all. And hosting a guest was just about the last thing she wanted, what with helping Simon with his assignments and overseeing the work she wanted to have done.

"He's a teacher in New York City, you see," the woman continued. "But he has a small, part-time teaching job in Lyons Hill for December, so he needs a place to stay. And he's hoping for some place quiet and beautiful. Some place he can be completely alone, except for the staff."

"Oh?"

"Yes, he really wants the place to be empty. And he wants everything taken care of—meals, good food. Full room and board."

"He wants meals?" Laurel said. She didn't know how she could arrange that. Although Katie did have a very nice store downtown. She knew her dad sometimes brought in a cook from there to prepare meals, when he had a guest who requested that. She didn't know how busy Katie's shop would be this month, but she supposed something could be worked out.

"I don't know—I suppose it's possible," she said.

"He's willing to pay extra if you can guarantee he has the place to himself," the woman said.

"Well, I don't know if that would be necessary," Laurel said. "I'm not expecting any other guests this month... but we're doing some renovations here. It might be better if he can come another time—"

"He can't," the woman said. "He has to get away this month.

You see, he's about to begin a very big project after the new year. So he really needs a place where he can recharge and gear up. I think for his own peace of mind, he needs this kind of escape. And honestly, it's hard to find a beautiful place. Many winter resorts are fully booked. We just happened to hear about this one... from a friend..."

Laurel paused. She didn't want to do it. It would be easy to walk away. Her dad had said there'd be no guests. But there was something hard to resist about the woman's pleas. She knew her mom would have wanted to know more.

"You said he's a client?" Laurel said.

"Yes, I'm... a travel agent. He's rather a special client. Someone I want very much to help. He really needs this time away, a small and very quiet town..."

Laurel thought for a moment. She didn't want to take care of someone so needy. But on the other hand, she knew her mom would be drawn to someone who needed to get away, someone who was about to embark on some kind of major life change. Her mother had always seen the inn as more than a place to sleep. It was a place to kick off your shoes, to regroup if that's what you needed. Laurel remembered the graduate students from Gorson College who always spent their Christmases here before starting a difficult new semester. Or the sweet married couple who showed up one winter for a "babymoon"—a last vacation together before their first baby was born. Or the older couple who were starting out on a cross-country trip after dropping their youngest son at college. Her mom had loved helping people get ready for a new adventure, a new chapter in their lives.

She let out a breath. She couldn't say no. Not when she knew that her mother would have opened the inn to this guy, no matter what else was going on in her life. She would have been happy to have him, especially since this travel agent had sought her out. And this way, perhaps she could show her dad—and her sisters too—that they could keep the inn going.

"Okay," she said. "We'll look forward to having him. And

doing everything we can to make his stay exactly as he wants it to be."

"Oh, that's wonderful," the woman said. "Just perfect."

Laurel said she'd prepare an invoice right away and got to work as soon as she hung up the phone. She emailed it to the woman just as Simon came downstairs, still in his pajamas. She went to the kitchen to make a pot of oatmeal for the two of them, thinking that now she had another reason to check out the cottage.

"Come on, buddy," she called. "We have a lot to do. Believe it or not, we have a guest coming."

Simon was full of questions, and as she answered them with as much as she knew, she began to feel better about this unexpected arrival. It would be nice to have someone new in the inn, and it would be fun to host that person all on her own. She knew there was a lot she'd have to get done in the next few days: arrange for housekeeping with her father's regular service, Annie's House-keeping; call Katie's shop to arrange for a part-time cook; choose what room she'd put the guest in, and freshen up the supply of toiletries and linens; get the florist to bring in some plants and cut flowers; and order up more firewood. But it was all exciting. This was what she'd felt was missing when she was in the appliance showroom with Joanna—a real person making use of a beautiful space. She only wished the inn didn't need so many repairs. She wondered if she could find someone who could get a few things fixed before this person even arrived.

When she and Simon were finished with breakfast, she brought down a stack of clean sheets and towels, and they trudged along the winding slate path that led from the kitchen to the cottage's front door. The bushes were overgrown as they approached the cottage, just as they'd always been, and the pine-tree branches—one after the other—blocked their way and doused them with snow as they moved forward. Her mother had wanted the path and cottage to be hidden by foliage, because she felt it was important that the family have a secluded, private home. Even so, Tracey and Deb had found plenty to complain about.

"Why do we have to live in a stupid shack while strangers get our big house?" Deb said after a particularly busy summer week, when Dad had taken Tracey to look at colleges, and Mom had put Laurel and Deb to work stripping beds and emptying trash baskets. "It's embarrassing, having to serve the people who kick us out of our own home."

Laurel had rolled her eyes. "Don't be such a baby," she'd murmured. She hated when her sisters complained to Mom. It sounded like they were attacking her, and she didn't know why Mom tolerated it. And the quieter Mom stayed, the worse the complaining became, as her sisters learned there were no limits to how rude they could be. They'd never talk that way to Dad, Laurel knew, and she wished that just once, Mom would tell them to keep quiet or they'd be sorry. But Mom never asserted her authority or even asked for an apology. For years, Laurel wondered why she had been so passive. But maybe their complaints simply rolled off her shoulders.

The cottage, it turned out, looked pretty good. All that was needed was a little mopping and dusting and sponging of surfaces, and a couple of hours for the heat to kick in and the hot-water heater to rev up.

Simon, who was still entranced by the snow, volunteered to haul most of the clothing and shoes and toiletries from the inn, once they'd brought all the things downstairs and stuffed them into trash bags. He wanted as many opportunities as he could get to be outside. He made at least a dozen trips back and forth, and she watched him through the cottage's upstairs windows as she folded clothes and put them into drawers. She loved how enthralled he was—how he'd push the tree branches forward so they would shoot back and send a shower of white all over him; and how he'd kick the snow into mounds and then pounce on it belly first.

It took until the early afternoon for them to finish cleaning and put the bedrooms into move-in condition, and when they were through, Laurel suggested they head over to the Grill for a late lunch. Simon ordered his favorite dish, the Garbage Plate, and while he dug into the mash-up of burgers, French fries, and maca-roni salad, and baked beans, Laurel caught up with the restaurant's owners, Maxine and Gull.

"So what's keeping the two of you here in Lake Summers, other than my exceptional cuisine?" Gull said, rumpling Simon's hair. His blue eyes smiled beneath sparse gray eyebrows.

Laurel explained about her father's phone call and the note she'd found at the inn. "Did he say anything to you about going away?" she asked.

Maxine shook her head. "Not a word. Although now that you mention it, I did think something was up. He had a.... I don't know, a bit of a spring in his step lately. He was almost giddy at times."

"My dad?" Laurel said. It was such a strange description. She'd never have used that word to describe her father.

"Let's give the man a little privacy, shall we?" Gull said. "I expect he'll speak when he's ready. On to more important things. Does this mean we get to enjoy this young man's company right through to Christmas?" He nodded toward Simon.

"Yes, you do," Laurel said, smiling. She loved how fond Gull and Maxine were of Simon. She went on to tell them about the guest arriving later that week, and Stan and Trey—who owned the smoothie shop across the street and were finishing up their lunch a few tables over—walked over to join in the conversation.

"A teacher, huh?" Stan said, stroking his bushy salt-and-pepper beard.

"That's what the travel agent told me. He's got a part-time job teaching nearby this winter, and he wanted some time away from New York."

"Well, maybe we can do something to welcome the guy," Stan said. "It's kind of a slow time around here, we could use a new project. You know, Trey was almost a teacher, before he became a smoothie genius. Maybe we should make a teacher-themed smoothie."

"Yeah, an educational smoothie," Trey said, his eyebrows lifting—a sure sign he was in invention mode, Stan liked to say.

"Maybe something with a science hook—like, with steam or something lava-ish pouring out when you sip. Or maybe something with a chemical reaction, maybe a smoothie that glows or sparks... not anything that could electrocute you, of course..."

"My goodness, what a thought," Maxine said, shaking her head as she pushed her silvery-gray bangs to the side. "Well, anyway, Laurel, let us know if you need anything."

"Thanks, I will."

She watched Simon sit back in his chair and sigh, puffing out his cheeks to show he was full. Gull laughed and took his plate to box up what he hadn't finished, and Laurel smiled as she watched him saunter toward the kitchen, holding the plate in one hand and twirling a kitchen towel with the other. No matter how she felt about the way she'd ended up here this month, she had to admit that Lake Summers was a wonderful place to spend the winter.

A short time later they walked back home, with Simon stamping his feet in the snow. Making their way up the driveway, Laurel spotted someone kneeling near the side of the inn, inspecting a loose board.

It was Joel Hutcherson.

She hadn't seen him in so long, but she recognized him immediately—tall and broad-shouldered, with that thick black hair. What was he doing at the inn?

She pulled on Simon's arm to slow him down as she figured out how to get Joel's attention. Should she cough, or wave? She decided simply to say hello.

"Joel?" she called.

"Laurel?" he said, looking her way. "What are you doing here?"

He seemed as surprised to see her as she was to see him. She supposed that made sense; she hadn't been back in Lake Summers at wintertime for years. But he hadn't been around either, she knew. The last thing she'd heard, he was traveling all over the world, doing some kind of consulting. Her dad had admired him since he was in high school, certain that he was destined for fame and fortune. And Deb would always tease her for having a crush on him, which she always denied. Although the truth was, all the girls in town had a crush on Joel Hutcherson. Even Tracey, who was a year older.

"I live here," she said, feeling too tongue-tied to say anything more. She hated that his appearance was still so disarming. He looked the same as he always did—but no, she thought; if anything, he was better looking than he'd been as a kid. His body looked more solid, his attractiveness combining so beautifully with a lot of living, a lot of experience. A lot of depth. That was it—his eyes, his expression, looked deeper, more serious, than when he was a classmate, working alongside her backstage. And he had been a pretty deep person to begin with. If he were a house, she thought, he'd be a cabin in the woods. With so many nooks and crannies and intriguing spaces, she could poke around forever and never grow bored.

"Of course you do," he said. "Sorry. I just haven't seen you here in a long time."

"Well, I guess I live in New York now."

"I heard. Your dad told me."

"You've seen my dad?"

"Yeah," he said, walking toward her, his hands in the pockets of his ski jacket.

"But aren't you living someplace far away? Like, Bangkok or something?"

"Singapore," he told her. "But I'm back for a few weeks. My mother died unexpectedly. I came back to put things in order."

"Oh, I'm sorry," she said. "I didn't know." She immediately sympathized with him. It was so hard losing a mom.

"Thanks," he said, nodding. The wind pushed a lock of his hair over his eyes, and he shook his head to send it back. "Anyway, I seem to have gotten friendly with your dad since I came back to town. He's a good guy. He must be glad you're here."

"I guess," she said. "Especially since he's not."

"He's not what?"

"He's not here. He called me to come and run things."

"What?" Joel said. "But I just saw him last week."

"It must have all happened suddenly," she said. "When I got here, there was a note that said he'd be unreachable for a few weeks but would be home on Christmas Eve."

"Is he... is he okay?" Joel asked.

Laurel detected a tone of worry in his voice.

"He sounded fine. He said he's coming back with a big surprise. I honestly have no idea what's going on." She gave a small laugh. "If you saw him last week, then maybe I should be asking you these questions."

"No... no, I don't know either," he said. "I thought he was staying in town. Unless... Is Katie around?"

"Katie?" Laurel said. "Why? Was Katie doing some work here too?"

"No... no," Joel said. "No, I don't know why I even... asked that... "

"Mom, I want to go in," Simon said, tugging on her arm.

"What? Oh, of course, honey," she said. She smiled at Joel. "Sorry, I should have introduced you. This is my son. Simon."

"Hey, Simon," Joel said, stooping over and resting his hands on his thighs so they were eye to eye. "Nice to meet you. Your grandpa talks a lot about you. I went to school with your mom a long time ago."

"How long ago?" Simon asked.

"About a million years ago," Laurel said. "I was a very different person then."

Joel stood. "So... um... what are you all up to while you're in town?" he said.

Laurel heard a strange note of something—uncertainty? Confusion?—in his voice.

"Well, we were supposed to relax... except that now it turns out there's a guest showing up. My dad didn't say anything to you? I wish I knew what was going on with him."

"What? No. He didn't..." Joel said. "And now it's you who's running the place when the guest gets here?"

She nodded. "It's so crazy. I didn't even plan to be here for Christmas, and now I'm taking care of the inn and hosting a guest for the next few weeks. It's a bit more than I expected."

She felt Simon pull her keys out of her coat pocket and then saw him tear toward the front door. She knew she should follow him inside, before he tramped his snowy boots all over the place. But she didn't want to leave just yet. Joel was still so warm and easy to talk to, just like he'd been in high school. She was suddenly very glad for his company.

"Is there anything I can do to help?" he asked.

"That's nice of you," she said. "But it's not so hard, actually. I just have to make a few arrangements, a few phone calls. Although... was there something you were looking at just now? Something wrong on the side of the house?"

"Just a loose board," he said.

"Great, I guess I should add that to my list," she said. "There are a bunch of things that need to be fixed inside. If you know anyone who can handle a bunch of repairs—woodworking, electricity, even plumbing..."

"I have some time," Joel said. "I've been planning to do that kind of stuff for your dad ever since I got back."

"No, I don't want to impose," Laurel said. "I know my dad has a way of getting people to help him even when they don't mean to offer—"

"I'm happy to," he said. "I like doing that stuff. These kinds of old houses do need some attention—"

"But still—"

"Look, I just stopped by for a minute to take a look at that loose board, and there are a couple of other things around the outside that I promised to take care of," he said. "I'll be back tomorrow, and maybe if you have a little time, you can show me what needs fixing. I'll give it a look. I bet it's not all that much trouble."

Laurel paused for a moment. He was so sweet—he made it sound as though she'd be doing him a favor by letting him help out. So she nodded, and a familiar, beautiful wide smile spread across his face. Then he held up an arm, signaling goodbye, and headed back to the side of the house. She waved in return, even though he had already turned away, and she stayed a moment to watch him. He was the last person she'd expected to see here, the last person she'd expected to help her with all the problems she'd noticed in the inn. For a moment she was tempted to tell him to forget it, that she'd get a recommendation for a handyman on her own. After all, she'd opened herself up to him once, and she'd been burned, and she still remembered how bad that felt. She didn't want to take a chance that that would happen again.

But she didn't call to him. She didn't tell him to forget it.

Because she was looking forward so much to seeing him again.

EIGHT

After leaving the inn, Joel walked down the driveway toward Birch Street. He couldn't decide if he was more surprised to find Laurel at the inn or Doug gone. Both were way beyond anything he could have imagined.

He'd gone to the inn this afternoon to see if Doug wanted to share a pizza and some beers, maybe watch some TV together. Doug liked watching classic baseball games, and there was sure to be one on the baseball channel. Then, when he'd found the inn empty, he'd decided to wait—and to check out some boards on the side of the house that caught his attention. The last time he'd spoken to Doug was last Thursday, before he'd gone to visit Meg, and Doug hadn't said a word about leaving town this week.

Still in the mood for pizza, he walked to his house to get his pickup and drive downtown to Sal's, so the pizza would be hot when he arrived home. He'd been all set to watch TV with Doug and then calmly suggest he tell his daughters everything that was going on in his life. He didn't understand why Doug was so hesitant to open up. What was he scared of? Joel had known the three sisters, especially Laurel, since they were all young, and he was sure they'd want to support their dad however he needed them to. But from the short conversation he'd had with Laurel, it was clear that Doug had told her nothing. And that troubled him. He didn't like knowing more about Doug than Laurel did. He'd never believed in keeping secrets from family, and he felt that way even more strongly now, after finding out how much his mother had concealed from him.

He wondered what happened to people as they got older. Why did they insist on telling their kids they were fine when they weren't? He supposed they didn't want to worry or upset them. They didn't want to intrude on their lives. But why would they think so little of their own children? Were they so sure they'd raised selfish people who wouldn't want to know the truth?

And didn't they realize that by letting their kids off the hook, they weren't being considerate and generous? No, they were being selfish—by refusing to give them a chance to deal with the information on their own terms. The chance to say what they wanted to say and do what they wanted to do while their parents were still alive. Shouldn't they give their kids that level of respect?

That was one of the reasons he'd wanted to spend the holidays in Lake Summers instead of going to St. Thomas with Meg. He wanted to work on Doug, all month if necessary, to break down his resistance and convince him to talk to his daughters. Especially Laurel, the daughter he knew, the one he liked so much. He wanted Doug to do what his own mom hadn't done—give his kids a chance to be involved. And to help. And maybe even get ready to say goodbye, if it had to come to that. He couldn't change what had happened with him, but he could change things for Laurel.

And maybe that would make up for how he'd let her down so many years ago.

He found a parking spot a few doors away from Sal's and got out of the truck, lowering his head against the cold wind that was picking up now that dusk was settling in. To his right was Gourmet by Katie, which looked busy inside.

He'd gotten to know Katie a little bit in the past few weeks, since she'd been around the inn a lot lately. She was an appealing person—smart, and with a good head for business. He'd seen her in action sometimes when he'd picked up dinner at her shop—pasta with meat sauce or meatloaf with mashed potatoes or buttermilk fried chicken. The food was good—filling and flavorful. And the store, though small, was run well. The display cases and floor-to-ceiling refrigerators and freezers around the perimeter were filled with prepackaged foods you could grab and pay for, if you knew what you wanted and didn't feel like waiting for counter service.

Katie was different from a lot of people in town, especially the ones who'd grown up here. She ran a tight ship, with employees who stood behind the counter in matching blue aprons with the GBK logo. She was ambitious. A little bit like Meg in her high-octane style.

He went into the pizza shop, then up to the counter. Before he could order, though, he heard someone calling out his name.

"Joel! Hey, Joel! It's me, Chuck Decker. From high school!"

He turned to see a short, bald man with glasses carrying five pizza boxes. He looked older for sure, but his mile-wide smile made him instantly recognizable.

"Oh, sure. Chuck. Nice to see you," he said, reaching out to shake hands.

Chuck shifted his load toward the left so his right hand was free. "Boy, long time no see, huh? You've been living overseas for a while, right?"

"Yeah, that's right."

"Hey, I read about your mother in the paper. I'm awfully sorry about that."

"Thanks," Joel said. "So what brings you to town?" He was anxious to change the subject. He didn't like people talking about his mom's death. He didn't like that he had no good explanation for what had happened.

"Visiting my brother's family," Chuck answered. "Like I do every year. Us accountants can work remotely from anywhere. Makes the holidays a lot easier. All of us are here—my wife, my five kids..."

"Five? No kidding."

"And my brother has three, so it's madness most of the time. But super fun. And everyone wanted pizza tonight. Somehow they all agreed." He lifted the pizza boxes to show him the proof. "You know, there are a bunch of the old gang in town," he added. "Mindy Samms, Amy Rochester, Connor and Dean Hanson—have you run into anyone yet?"

"No, no," he said. "I just got back to the States about a week ago, and I haven't spent a lot of time in town."

"Some of them are visiting too, and some of them live here now. Oh, and guess who else is back? Laurel Hanover. I haven't seen her yet, but I heard she was here. And with a son, too."

"That one I know," Joel said. "I just ran into her. At the inn."

"Yeah? Say, you guys were a couple once, weren't you? You went out for a bit in high school, right?"

"No," Joel said. "No, not us."

"Oh, I could have sworn... after that show senior year? I guess I'm wrong. I guess you went out with more sportsy types, right? Annie Thompkins... and Darcey something too, right?"

"No, I didn't—"

"Or was it Kathy Conroy? You were Mr. Popularity back then, I remember—"

"I wasn't really like that—"

"Anyway, give me a call," Chuck said, reciting his number for Joel to plug into his phone. "Or stop by my brother's house—I'm staying through New Year's. You remember where, right behind the high school, right? And hey, there's a town ice-skating party at the lake on Saturday night. My brother's the town manager now. He's built this thing up to something really big. It's going to be a blast—a lot of the old gang will be there. You should come."

"Sounds good," Joel said. Although he didn't really think he would. He hadn't really been part of the "old gang" Chuck was talking about. He never knew those theater kids all that well. Only Laurel.

"Or let's just get everyone together to hang out one night," Chuck said.

"Sounds good," Joel repeated.

"Look, I should get going," Chuck said. "I got a hungry gang at home, and I fear my wife will soon have a riot on her hands. But give me a call, or stop by. And come to the lake Saturday night, okay?"

Joel nodded and opened the door for him. "Enjoy your pizza."

"You too, pal!"

Joel stood by the door, watching Chuck tuck his chin into his jacket and start down the block. He hadn't known Chuck nearly as well as Chuck had made it sound. But the guy had always been friendly, almost like a mayor. It was no wonder that his brother ran town events. And it was nice too, he thought, that Chuck was married with so many kids. And that he came back to visit his family for the holidays. And ran to get everyone pizza on a cold winter evening.

He walked up to the counter to order. Chuck had sounded surprised, too, that Laurel was back in town. He also sounded surprised that Laurel had a son. Joel had known for a while about Simon. He'd heard about him from Doug—that he was precocious and a handful, and Doug was crazy about him. Joel had also gathered from Doug that Laurel wasn't married, that Simon's dad wasn't in the picture. He wondered how Laurel came to be alone.

The guy behind the counter looked at him, and he ordered and sat down to wait. It was funny that Chuck thought he and Laurel had been a couple. He wondered if everyone from high school thought that. Because they'd never been one. They'd spent time together in the spring of senior year when Laurel was directing the senior play. And they'd talked together that one long night backstage. But they hadn't been a couple. Almost, but never.

For some reason, that made it even harder to think about seeing her again tomorrow.

He remembered, too, how pretty Laurel had been in high school. She'd had that long red hair that she sometimes pulled into a ponytail down her back. Now her hair was softer, more tamed, and she wore it shorter, just below her shoulders. She'd always been small, with a little nose and chin that came to a point—and that was all still the same. But she looked prettier now. More poised and confident. Back in high school, she'd always seemed to be hiding.

She was so quiet back then, too, he thought. But so talented. She was a member of the drama club and spent all her time after school at the school's auditorium. She was usually one of the kids who worked backstage or was in the chorus of the school's productions—an extra, sometimes a character with one or two lines. Then, in senior year, she'd stepped up to direct a show—and that's what had drawn him even more to her. His friends all tended to do things that were fun, or strengthened their chances to get into a top college, or helped them meet girls: playing sports, running for student government, volunteering at after-school programs around the county. But Laurel was someone who did things that deeply mattered to her, and she threw her whole heart into them.

She'd chosen the show herself—something about a family, a play he'd never heard of. Nobody at school had, for that matter. It had to do with a girl who learns she's a superhero. And it was a really sad show, he remembered, because the girl's magic only lasted one night, and she didn't accomplish everything she wanted to. People in the audience cried.

When it was over, the cast had called Laurel out on the stage, and she'd been given a standing ovation. The school paper had said it was the first time a senior-play cast had ever done that.

He'd spent a lot of time backstage with her that spring. It was a tradition—the baseball team always helped to build scenery for the senior play, and he'd been the captain of the team. But while the other guys did it because they had to, he'd loved it. He'd always liked working with wood and nails, building stuff. He stayed way later than any of his teammates every night. And it was on one of those late evenings that he'd run into Laurel backstage. The night they'd had that talk. It started in the early evening and then suddenly it was midnight, the hours passing like seconds. He'd never talked to anyone like that before. But he came to see that their evening was just like the girl's magical power in the play. They'd only had that one night. They never talked to each other that way again.

He thought about Laurel now, and how he'd seen the flash in her eyes as she called to him on the driveway. He didn't quite understand her expression, wasn't sure if she was happy, or unhappy, or just surprised that he was there. He wondered if she still remembered what had happened that night after the play, how he'd let her down, and if she was still mad at him. Was that why she had looked at him just now as though she didn't trust him? Or did her thoughts have nothing to do with him—did they have only to do with the way she'd rushed back here to Lake Summers and suddenly had the burden of a guest to take care of?

A burden, he realized, that he had caused.

He thought now about what she'd said, how her dad had left her to run the inn and wasn't even reachable. He knew Laurel had struggled all her life to get along with her dad—that was one of the things they had talked about that night in high school. She was so confused that spring because she wanted to stay home for college, but her dad wouldn't let her. Joel knew exactly what she was going through, because he was going through the same thing. And he'd felt so sorry for her, and so close to her too, for sharing all that with him, and for listening to him tell her his own story.

And now, she was going to be at the beck and call of someone Meg had called a narcissist. And he felt horrible about that. Why had he interfered in the first place? He'd never meant to toy with Laurel's life. He hadn't meant to hurt her. He was just trying to help her dad.

He got his pizza and drove back to his mom's house, the house he'd grown up in. It was a small place, just two bedrooms, and yet ever since he'd returned, it had felt huge and empty. Not that a lot of people had lived there when he was growing up; it had just been him and his mom for as long as he could remember. But somehow the house had seemed so much busier back then. He always had so much going on. There was school and the baseball team and the student government and homework. And parties and friends. And dating and girls. And planning his future, preparing to apply to Yale. There was so much going on in his head, it had never struck him that the house was always so empty.

In the kitchen, he put the pizza box on the table and took his phone out of his jeans pocket. Unlike Doug, Meg would be reachable, even in St. Thomas. She was never out of touch with her clients. And he needed to get her to change her actor's plans. It was bad enough that he was keeping Doug's secrets from Laurel. It was indefensible that he'd also saddled her with an unwanted guest to take care of.

"Meg?" he said when she answered. "Look, this isn't going to work. You have to get your actor a different place to stay."

"What? Joel, is this you?"

"Yes, it's me, and I'm telling you, we have to change this. Immediately."

"What are you talking about? He can't wait to get there."

"He'll be just as happy somewhere else."

"I don't think so," she said. "He looked at the website, and he thinks it's perfect. I even spoke to a friend of mine and got him a part-time job teaching a drama class at a private school in the next town over, so he can really get into his character. He's not going anywhere else."

"But you don't understand." Joel went on to explain what had happened. "I can't do this to this family. I can't do this to her. I'll find him another place. I'll get to work tonight."

"Another completely empty place in a small jewel-like town? What, is there a listing somewhere of empty inns in the mountains? Forget it, Joel, there's no other place like that. We both know it. This is it."

"But Meg—"

"I told you that I had misgivings," she said. "I warned you. But you wanted to do this."

"I know. And you were right—"

"But my hands are tied," she said. "I'm sorry, cousin. You're going to have to find a way to make this work…"

Joel breathed out heavily, knowing he was not going to change her mind. Meg was tough, and she rarely backed down. And he couldn't even make things right by coming clean and telling Laurel what he'd done. He'd promised Meg he'd keep quiet. Just as he'd promised Doug he'd keep Doug's secrets to himself.

He hung up, hating that he was betraying Laurel again. This time by deceiving her. By letting her believe he knew less than he did. And that's when he decided that he would make it up to her. Somehow, some way, he would make it right. Without her ever knowing that was his plan.

NINE

The next day was Tuesday, and Laurel got an early start making calls to get the inn ready for the guest's arrival the following morning. Before long, she had the housekeeping set up and the flowers and firewood ordered. She called Gourmet by Katie and learned that Katie was out of town for a few weeks. But one of her employees, Mavis, said the store was well-staffed for the holidays, so she could spare the time to prepare meals at the inn.

Hanging up the phone, Laurel noticed an article on the front page of the *Lake Summers Press* announcing that the town's winter day camp was getting underway. She'd forgotten that the schools in Lake Summers closed in early December, since so many people traveled for the holidays. For the kids who remained, the town ran a daily program starting tomorrow, offering tutors and study time interspersed with holiday games and crafts. So she decided to enroll Simon. He'd make friends and would probably learn more than she could teach him in her spare time. Plus, it was a good idea for Simon to have somewhere to go each day, since the travel agent had emphasized that her client wanted a quiet setting.

When Simon came downstairs, he ran to the window in the living room to see the fresh snow that had fallen overnight and begged her to take him sledding. She loved how excited he looked, and since she felt she was in good shape to welcome the teacher the next day, she was happy to indulge him. They found a blue plastic saucer-type sled with rope handles in the storage shed behind the inn—her mom had always kept a supply of sleds on hand for winter guests, along with sand chairs, shovels and pails, sun umbrellas, and even a couple of kayaks for summer ones—and then walked over to the Public Works Building, which had the biggest sledding hill in town.

It was even steeper than Laurel remembered, and Simon's eyes widened behind his glasses as they arrived at the starting point. He'd never faced anything like this back in their own neighborhood, where the only big hill was behind the elementary school, and because the slope was bumpy, sleds didn't slide very well.

Simon watched the kids around him for a while—there were plenty, since school had let out last week and the winter camp didn't begin until tomorrow. Their sleds sailed down the hill, barely skimming the snow and even occasionally lifting off slightly from the ground. He stood with his hands in his pockets, and Laurel kept quiet and let him watch. She didn't think he was frightened, just kind of amazed at how different things could be from what he knew.

"I'm ready," he finally said and climbed onto the saucer, checking the kids around him every few seconds to confirm he was doing it right. When he was settled, she gave a little push, and then laughed as she watched him glide down, knowing the thrill he was surely feeling. That was what she'd always loved about sledding: Anyone could do it. There wasn't any training needed, no lessons and no practices and no awards. You just climbed onto the sled and enjoyed the ride, like everyone else.

Simon reached the flat stretch at the bottom of the hill and coasted to a stop. Then he climbed off the saucer and jumped up and down with excitement a few times, before righting his glasses, pulling the waist of his pants up higher, and charging back up the hill. After a few more runs, she saw him get up off the sled and talk to a few kids his age. He was kind of a loner back home, as she had been, and Mason was his only close friend. It was nice to see him fitting in.

They stayed at the hill for another hour, Simon having too much fun to leave. At one point, Laurel heard someone call out to her, and she turned to see Chuck Decker, an old friend from the drama club at high school and a fellow "aardie," the name the stage crew had given themselves since, like aardvarks, they avoided the spotlight and did their work in the dark. Chuck still had the sweetest, widest smile of anyone she knew, and she was happy to see him. He said he was an accountant living in Vermont but was back in town with his family for the month, visiting his brother. And it turned out that one of his brother's kids, Garrett, was the same age as Simon—and the two boys were now sledding together.

"I'll give a call at the inn—your family still owns it, right?" Chuck said. "There are a few of us here in town this week—we should all get together. And hey, there's a big ice-skating party Saturday night. Everyone will be there. You and Simon should come."

He waved and went to help his little daughter with her sled, and a few minutes later Simon showed up by her side, tired and ready to go back to the inn. He asked if Garrett could come over later to make a snowman, and when Laurel said sure, he waved and gave a thumbs up to his new friend, who was at the bottom of the hill.

Then they started back for the inn, Simon stomping his foot every once in a while and laughing at how high and wide the powder-like snow would spray. At the intersection near Pearl's Café, he stared at the crosswalk where cars had stopped to let pedestrians pass, and he shook his head.

"That's crazy," he said. "Nobody even needs a walk sign here. People just go right into the street."

"Well, they don't just go," she said. "They still have to make sure the driver sees them and stops. You've seen this before. We were here last summer."

"I know," he said. "But I was a lot younger."

She laughed and nudged him with her elbow. "Silly."

"It's just you can sled and not be scared and cross the street and not be scared—you don't have to be scared of anything here," he told her.

"That's not true," she said. "It's like any other place. There are plenty of things to be scared of."

"Like what? Bears?"

"Well, no. I don't remember ever seeing any bears."

"Then what?"

She thought for a moment. "Power outages. There are lots of those. With all the snowstorms."

"Like no internet? That happens at home, too."

"No, more than no internet. All the electricity. That doesn't happen at home because the power lines are underground. But here, the cables are overhead, and they can fall in a storm. So you have to use flashlights for light and the fireplace to stay warm."

He stopped and looked at her. "No way. That is the best thing I ever heard in my life."

"It's not so great. It's hard. Once when I was little, the power went out for almost a week."

"A week? That must have been epic!"

"Well..." Laurel started to object further, then stopped, remembering that it had been fun, that power outage. One of the best weeks of her life. It was the week before Christmas, and the guests had all left because of the threatening forecast, and many families in town also left, heading to Albany or Syracuse to wait out the storm. Laurel remembered she was in fourth grade, so Deb would have been in first grade and Tracey fifth. Fortunately the temperature outside wasn't too cold, and the fireplace kept the living room toasty warm. Mom let the three of them set up sleeping bags near the fireplace and stay up as late as they wanted. And some nights Tracey would tell ghost stories, and other nights the three of them would improvise little skits, pretending to be pioneers or survivors of an apocalypse, foraging for food in the cabinets and searching the inn for other survivors.

Every morning the family would bundle up and walk to the Grill, which had a generator, for a hot meal, and then to the Village Hall, which also had a generator, to watch the news and catch up with neighbors. The house must have been cold, she thought, and food must have been at least a little scarce, with lots of stores closed. But what she most remembered was feeling so close to her sisters. And wanting those long days and nights to never end.

Lake Summers got its power back on Christmas Eve, and Laurel remembered how the town celebrated with a huge bonfire beside the lake. Then, on Christmas Day, the town organized volunteer caravans to bring hot meals to people in surrounding communities who were still without power. Laurel's family had been part of the group that went to New Manorsville, and she remembered how good it had felt to help serve food and hot beverages to the families who'd gathered at the local community center. As the sun went down, the music teachers from the Lake Summers and New Manorsville schools had played their guitars and led everyone in Christmas carols.

When Laurel and Simon reached the inn, there was a black pickup truck in the driveway. At first Laurel thought it was Garrett's mom dropping him off. But then she saw Joel getting out of it. She'd been trying not to think about him all morning, but now she had no choice, and she felt her face get warm. It was almost as if she were in high school again—except that in high school she hadn't been nervous around him. Not at all, at least in the beginning. When he'd started showing up, she'd wanted nothing to do with him. The other girls working on the production were always finding their way over to him, asking him to help nail a plank or steady a ladder. But she didn't like having the baseball players around. They weren't theater people—aardies—and she didn't think any of them cared about the play. They came only because the coach made them.

Soon, though, she noticed that Joel was different. He always stayed through the evening, way later than any of the other players. And he had such a knack with carpentry. He found the most ingenious way to make one of the backdrops pivot seamlessly from a classroom setting to a bedroom—something that not even the veterans on stage crew had been able to figure out. And after a few short weeks, she started to look forward to seeing him. She came to love his smile, which spread so wide across his face when she said something he considered funny or smart or clever. She would try to be clever, just so she could see that smile more often. And she loved how hard he worked, how focused he was when he was crafting a piece of scenery. She never thought she'd be one of those girls who ran after a guy, who tried to find an excuse to show up when the guy was around. But that's who she became. And it was okay. Because she'd never felt as good as she did when she was with him.

He looked up from the bed of the pickup and waved. "Hey!"

"Hi," she answered. "How's it going?"

"Not too bad. Almost done out here. Then I'll come inside and take a look at what needs to be done."

"Pretty cold out here. Can I offer you a cup of coffee?"

"That would be great."

She nodded, just as Garrett's mom pulled up and Garrett hopped out of the car. His mom introduced herself and said she'd be back to get him in a few hours, and the boys ran around to the back of the inn. Simon had already decided that the lawn in the back produced much better packing snow than the front yard did. She'd told him that didn't make any sense, but he insisted that the small experimental mounds he'd made over the weekend proved it, and he believed it had something to do with the angle of the sun and the way the surrounding trees in the back kept the snow colder and moister.

Laurel waved goodbye to Garrett's mother and headed inside, hanging her jacket and hat in the closet and leaving her boots by the door. She started to head to the kitchen in her socks, then changed her mind and went upstairs for a pair of loafers. She knew it was ridiculous but somehow it felt too intimate to be without shoes when Joel came in.

She paused for a minute, and then went to the closet and changed out of her sweatshirt and into her favorite pale-blue sweater. She continued on into the bathroom to brush her hair and put on some fresh mascara and lip gloss.

She came back downstairs and, after bringing the boys some snacks to eat on the covered side patio, started to make coffee. She didn't know what had possessed her to invite Joel in. She hadn't thought about it before she'd called out to him; she'd done it instinctively. It was ingrained in her, after years of watching her mother invite people in all the time—the mail carrier, the UPS driver, the gardeners and tree-care experts who came by regularly to do their jobs, or even a neighbor who showed up to drop off a letter that had been sent to the wrong address. You always invited people in for coffee and a pastry, her mother believed, no matter how busy you were or how unexpected the visitor.

Still, there was something different about this visit, she thought. Joel wasn't merely someone stopping by to drop something off. If he were, she wouldn't have changed her clothes or fixed her hair and make-up just now. Joel wasn't just a guy who did work for the inn, she told herself. He was the guy who'd left town years ago for a huge career. And he was the guy who'd broken her heart. The guy she was nevertheless looking forward to being with.

And she wasn't used to feeling this way, infatuated and starry-eyed. She'd promised herself after Simon's dad left her that she'd never lose herself over a guy again. But she'd appreciated how caring Joel had been yesterday, offering to help with the repairs while her father was away. Maybe she had misjudged him all those years ago. Could it be that she'd overreacted when she was in high school? That her tension with her dad had poisoned her feelings about other things too?

Maybe he'd had a good reason for what happened after the play. She'd never even let him explain.

The coffee was ready, and she was pouring a cup when there was a sudden rap on the kitchen window. Startled, she spilled the coffee all over her hands and quickly put the mug down so she could shake off the hot drops. She looked outside, where Joel was standing, holding a white bakery bag with the Pearl's Café logo. She went to the door and opened it.

"You scared me!" she said. "Why did you come all the way around here?"

"I was knocking out front and then ringing the doorbell for about ten minutes. You didn't hear me?"

She shook her head. "I guess that bell is something that also needs to be fixed."

"I'll add it to the list," he said. "Sorry about scaring you."

"It's fine," she told him, embarrassed that thinking about him had made her so jumpy. "No big deal. Come on in."

He leaned down toward his boots and looked at her, and she knew he was offering to take them off. She shook her head to tell him no need—she didn't want herself without shoes and she didn't want him that way either—so he stomped the snow off on the doorstep and came inside. He was wearing a big ski jacket and an aviator hat, and his nose and cheeks were red from the cold. But she could see those dark eyes and that sweet smile.

She led him toward the table, walking sideways as her mother always used to, so as not to turn her back on a guest.

"Coffee smells good," he said.

"Milk? Cream? Sugar?" she asked, motioning him to the table and then pouring two cups.

"Milk or cream, whatever you've got," he said, taking off his coat and hat. "Whatever your dad usually has. It always tastes good to me."

"My dad makes you coffee?" she asked, handing him a cup. She wondered just how often Joel had been coming around.

"I dropped by a couple of times last week for breakfast." He put the Pearl's bag on the table and took a seat. "And I stopped by Pearl's on my way here today. Blueberry and apple muffins. And croissants, the kind your dad loves."

"You brought him croissants?" she asked as she went to get the cream and some plates and silverware.

"I like your dad. I liked talking to him about the inn, about the things I could fix around here. It gave me something different to think about."

She came back to the table and sat down opposite him to give him her full attention. She'd been so reluctant to seem vulnerable to him, and yet he didn't seem to have the same reluctance. Here he was, referring so clearly to his mother, his grief. It made her feel tender toward him.

"I'm really sorry about your mom," she said.

He nodded.

"My sisters and I adored her store," she said, remembering all the times she'd gone there to look around, sometimes two or three times in one week. "We always found the most beautiful things. She had such a knack for making the space so welcoming. You felt good the moment you stepped inside."

"Thanks," he said. "This place feels that same way to me."

She smiled. "Our moms, right?" she said. "They sure had the magic touch."

He nodded and took a sip of coffee. "And your dad too. He's the one who called me to tell me about my mother. He's the one who picked me up from the airport."

"I'm glad he could help," she said, feeling a little jealous that Joel had spent some time with her dad and had seen that kind, generous side of him. Especially since now that she and Simon were here, her dad wasn't even around.

"So what now? Will you be going back to Singapore soon?" she asked. She was kind of scared of the answer. Suddenly she didn't want him to leave.

He nodded. "I was able to get time off to take care of things here," he said. "I have another four weeks to put the house on the market and clear out the store. Not that the house is that big a deal. It's the store that's harder to deal with. Because she loved it so much."

He chuckled. "Maybe that's why I'm here a lot. There's something really good about fixing things. Building things up instead of tearing them down. Well, anyway, let's see what we've got here," he added, reaching into the Pearl's bag.

Laurel put her elbows on the table and clasped her hands together against her chin as he took out the muffins and croissants, one by one, and put them on one of the plates she had brought over. She couldn't believe it, but she felt as though she was about to cry—for him, for his mother, for the kid he used to be and the time they'd shared when they were both so young. This was the guy she'd been with those long nights in the auditorium, finishing up the sets. She could almost hear his words the night he'd finished the revolving platform, saying pretty much the same thing he'd said just now: how much it meant to him to work with his hands, to craft things and create things, to build something that didn't exist before he imagined it.

And then he'd told her how much he didn't want to go to Yale and major in finance and work in an office for the rest of his life. "But it would kill my mom if I did anything else," he'd said. "After all she sacrificed for me. The last thing she wants is for me to be a carpenter. That's what my dad was before he left her."

She got up from the table, pretending that she needed to put the cream away—but really to get ahold of herself. She remembered that night long ago so well, how they'd been sitting on the floor, the two of them, in the darkened wing of the theater, with only a few lights from the stage glowing, when he'd told her about Yale and his mom. And she'd crawled closer to him and stroked his head, while he bent his knees and dropped his forehead into the heels of his hands. She knew exactly how he felt. Because just like him, she knew how it could destroy you inside, to know you were disappointing a parent. She knew he'd do anything to make his mom proud. She'd struggled the same way with her dad all her life. And it was brutal. Impossible, when you were a kid. If he were a house at that moment, she'd thought, he'd be a castle on the edge of a cliff. Beautiful and well built, but on the brink of disaster. Still somehow standing... but for how long, no one knew.

She returned to the table as he broke a piece off the croissant.

"So I can't believe what happened here," he said. "I mean, I left to go visit my cousin, but I rush back, thinking your dad's all alone and needing company. And now he's gone."

She smiled, ready now to open up. The memory of his pain that evening in the theater had softened her. "I know," she said. "And it's got me a little worried. I mean, he didn't sound like there was any emergency. But the inn isn't in great condition. I know it's a big place and things break all the time. But all the problems I've noticed... it's as though he lost his ability to deal with everything. There's a closet that's falling apart upstairs and a big gouge in the hallway floor, and cracks in windows, plumbing problems, electrical problems."

"And then there's something else strange," she added. It felt good to talk about these things to someone who knew her father and could understand why she'd be concerned. "He did a few things that my mother never would have agreed to. Like, all the Christmas trees have white twinkle lights instead of the colorful ones we always had. And he bought these weird, fancy pillowcases for all the guest rooms that my mom never would have bought. It's like he's forgotten what this place is all about. I keep trying to call him, but he told me he'd be unreachable, so I guess I shouldn't worry that he's not answering. But still."

"Do you have any idea what's going on?" she asked.

She watched him tap his chin with his thumb, and she assumed he was thinking.

"Oh, boy, Laurel," he finally said. "I just wish you could reach him and ask him. He should know how you feel, he should answer your questions. Maybe I'll try to call him too..."

He nodded slightly, then let out a breath and sliced a blueberry muffin with his knife, almost as if he didn't know what else he could do with himself. He took half and pushed the plate her way. She cut a chunk, not because she was hungry, but because she didn't want him to eat alone. He seemed to be looking for connection, or validation, and she wanted to provide it. She'd been concerned about letting him back into her life, back into her heart, from the moment she saw him. But he was making his way there anyway.

They did have a lot in common, both coming home to their childhood homes, now empty—although his situation of course was worse, having just lost his mother. Still, she was confused about her life, with her dad gone and her dreams of being a designer slipping away, and she got the feeling he was confused, too. It struck her that sometimes it wasn't only high school kids who had to figure things out. You could be in your late thirties and still not know what to do with your life.

"So," he said, as though trying to change the subject, lighten the mood. "When does this guest show up?"

"Tomorrow."

"Then show me everything you need done," he said. "Maybe I can knock a few things out before this guy arrives." He pushed his chair away and bumped the wall. "Oh, hey. I'm sorry."

"Don't worry, that happens all the time," she said. "See how scratched the wall is? That's the one thing that drives my dad crazy. He hates how cramped that corner is. But he always thought it would be too much trouble to do anything about it, since the dining room is on the other side. I'd love to surprise him and push that wall back somehow. Although I don't suppose there's any way to change the dimensions of a whole room in three weeks."

"No? Let me see," Joel said.

He walked through the doorway and into the dining room, and she followed him. He pressed his fingers along the wall and then knocked on it a few times.

"You know something?" he said. "I could move this wall just about eight inches. That would make that space by the table larger, and you wouldn't even feel it here, since this is such a big room."

"Moving a wall?" she said. "Isn't that a big job?"

"No, not so much," he said, and she followed him back to the kitchen. "I'll just take it down and rebuild it. It's not a bearing wall so it's fine. I'll move the cabinets and then reinstall them, and I'll move the chandelier in the dining room so it's centered, and then just repaint the wall and the ceiling."

"Oh, but wait," she said. "I have that guest coming. I can't start moving walls."

"Why not? Nobody goes into the dining room. That's your family's private room, according to your dad. So it won't bother this guy at all. And I'll get started today and do the really loud work when he's not around."

"You make it sound so easy," she said.

"It is easy," he told her. "And it will make a big difference. Amazing, how a really small change can mean a big deal. The dining room won't feel any smaller and the kitchen won't feel so cramped. It's making better use of the space. It'll be beautiful."

She smiled. He was right—there was something beautiful about using space well. About creating something that would make someone's home feel even more... like a home should feel.

He started to prepare for the teardown a little while later, hanging a tarp he had in his truck to protect the kitchen and laying plastic down on the dining-room floor. Simon and Garrett stayed outside in the snow most of the afternoon, and when they came in, Joel let them both draw on the wall that was coming down and then take a couple of swings at it with a hammer, which they both said made it the most fun day ever. Garrett left a little while later, and Joel soon after that. Laurel liked that Joel had a project at the inn. She was happy that he'd be around a lot while he was still in town.

At the dinner table that evening, Simon looked restless, claiming he wasn't hungry. Instead of eating, he played with his food, separating the peas from the chicken and lining them up along the rim of the plate. Then he flicked each one with his knife, shouting "Yes!" or "Score!" when they rolled up the opposite rim and onto the table, and "Dang it!" when they made it only partly up the opposite rim and then sank back to the middle of the plate. She suspected he was getting nervous about starting the winter camp the next day. Getting wild was how he handled transitions to unfamiliar places, like the Samposiera showroom last week. She tried not to get annoyed as she watched him playing hockey with the peas, because she knew he didn't have it easy. But when one pea flew across the room and rolled beneath the refrigerator, which made him throw up his arms and burst out laughing, she told him to bring his plate to the sink and go upstairs to get ready for bed.

She used the handle of a broom to retrieve the errant pea and then went up to his room. He was sitting on his bed, studying some rocks he'd brought with him from home.

"How's it going?" she said as she sat on the edge of his bed and stroked his bangs away from his eyes.

He shrugged, still studying the rocks.

"Are you nervous about the camp?"

He shrugged again.

"You know, it's normal to be nervous about starting something new," she said. "But it's like an adventure. And Garrett will be there tomorrow, right? That's good, isn't it?"

He nodded, still looking down. Then he took off his glasses and put them on the night table. He slid down in the bed and turned onto his side, facing the wall. She kissed his cheek and switched off the lamp, then started for the door.

"Mom?" he said.

She turned back toward him, her hand on the doorknob.

"You know I thought I liked this big room with the big beds," he said. "But now, I don't know if I like big stuff after all."

"Well, the bed in the cottage is a twin size," she said. "So it'll be just like your bed at home, when we move over there."

"I guess it's all the same," he said. "I worry about bigness back home too."

She went back and kissed him again. "Honey, it's been a busy week, with a lot of changes. But hang in there. It will all look better in the morning. I promise."

She left the room and closed the door. She knew just how he

felt. Disoriented and alone. An outsider, even in a place where you were with family and knew you were safe. She remembered having that feeling so often when she was growing up. If you didn't feel at home in your own skin, everywhere felt overwhelming. And Simon's world was far more complicated than hers had ever been, with a single mom who worked a lot, a dad he'd never met, and a grandfather and aunts who usually stayed apart because they didn't know how to deal with the loss of the only person who had kept them all together. And now he had a new home and a new schedule for the month—and he'd be changing beds again tomorrow, when they relocated to the cottage. The only thing he could rely on was her—and he knew, he had to know, she was just as alone as he was. No wonder he was nervous. No wonder he had bigness on his mind tonight.

She went into the kitchen and over to the wine refrigerator. Her dad fancied himself a connoisseur and he used to like to pore over wine catalogs and call distributors from all over the country. Then he'd bring out the bottles with huge fanfare during cocktail hour at the inn, describing to guests why the label or the variety or the vineyard had caught his attention, recounting the conversation he'd had with the buyer.

She pulled out one of her dad's old favorites, a Shiraz from Australia, and was about to pour herself a glass when she heard a sound outside. She went to the front door and opened it, hugging herself to stay warm. Joel was there, his truck at the far end of the driveway facing the garage, his lights on full blast. He was carrying paint cans and tools from the back of his truck toward the garage. She was glad to see him. In the last thirty hours, he'd become a grounding presence in her life.

"Joel!" she called over to him.

He raised a hand in her direction, still holding a paint can by its wire handle. "Sorry if I disturbed you. I was up and just thought I'd drop some supplies over. I rented this pickup over in Ayelin Point. These babies can sure hold a lot of stuff. Anyway, I'll see you tomorrow. Have a nice night!"

She nodded and watched him carry more things into the garage. It was kind of wonderful, how much he'd perked up once he'd decided to move the wall. And it was funny, too, that the two men in her life right now were focused on space, but in very different ways: Simon was worried about bigness, while Joel was taking joy in shifting a wall a few inches over. A short distance, but it was something he could control. Something little that could make a big difference.

She thought there had to be a lesson in that.

The next morning, the crew from Annie's Housekeeping showed up, and she let them in and then left with Simon for camp. They stopped in at the main office of the elementary school, where the camp was being held, and she signed some paperwork. Pushing his glasses up higher on his nose, Simon instructed her to stay at the office because he didn't want to look like a baby by having his mom walk him down the hall, and that at no point should she even try to kiss him. She complied and merely waved, even though her heart broke as she saw him marching off in the same direction as the other kids, looking like he was heading for a firing squad. She worried about subjecting him to so much change. She hoped so much that he'd have a good day.

Back at the inn, she took a look around the first floor. The housekeepers were doing a good job, and the front hall, living room, and sunroom were spotless. She could hear them finishing up upstairs, and then they would be heading to the kitchen to work their magic. Mavis from Katie's shop had stopped by while she'd been with Simon at school, with some sample menus to show Christopher when he arrived. She'd left them in the mailbox, along with a note saying he could change anything and she'd be happy to accommodate.

She went behind the reception desk, the polished cherrywood surface and tiny antique grandfather clock on top gleaming. Sitting down, she reached beneath the desk for the latest issue of the *Lake*

Summers Press, to pass the time until her guest showed up. She started to read a story with interviews from local merchants who were hoping for a busy winter. There were a couple of quotes from the owner of a newish store, Lexy's Dresses. The owner, Lexy, sounded sweet, and Laurel decided she'd stop in soon and introduce herself.

She was glancing at some of the dresses pictured when she heard the front door open. She looked up and saw a man standing right before her.

"Hey," he said. "I'm Christopher Charles. Checking in. How's it going?"

TEN

He was gorgeous. Not at all what she'd imagined when she heard a teacher looking for peace and quiet was coming to town.

"Hi. Welcome," she said, transfixed. It wasn't anything in particular that struck her as gorgeous. Just the whole picture. He was a slender guy, looking sporty and hip in a slate-colored sweater. His hair was short and golden brown, and his eyes were blue—a romantic soft blue, the color of a denim jacket just worn in enough to be comfortable. And although they were on the narrow side, they fit perfectly with his other features: his straight nose, his smallish mouth and ears. And he also stood so straight—his shoulders back, his chest open. It wasn't something she often thought about, posture. But now she did, as she saw how attractive it made him.

"Welcome to the Cranberry Inn," she said.

"Thank you very much... um?" he said, his eyebrows raised.

"Laurel," she said, feeling herself blush. "I'm sorry. I'm Laurel. I'm the owner. Well, the owner's daughter."

"Well, hello, Laurel, the owner's daughter," he said, his tone cute and teasing. He didn't seem at all like someone who'd want to be alone in an inn. He seemed the kind of guy who liked to make people smile along with him, the kind of person someone would smile at if for no other reason than to see *his* smile last a few seconds longer. If he were a house, she thought, he'd be a beach house, full of windows, with a great view of the ocean. Maybe a touch dangerous too, the way the ocean could be when a storm rose and thunder cracked right above you.

"Sorry, did I catch you off guard?" he said. "You're expecting me, right?"

"Of course. Oh, of course, I don't know what's wrong with me. I'm all ready for you," she said, then wondered if she'd sounded too flirty. *I'm all ready for you*—it was an innocent comment, but with someone so handsome, it felt kind of suggestive. She tried to think what her mother would say at this moment. "How was your drive?" she asked.

"Long," he said, with a little scowl. "Tons of traffic. This is not an easy ride from the city."

"No, it's not—I've done it myself more than a few times," she said. And suddenly she understood anew why her mom loved hosting guests so much. Life had become so much about work and Simon these last few years, and she was always focused on things that had to be done. She'd forgotten how nice it was to meet and chat with someone new. Her mom had been so approachable, and probably had enjoyed having a little banter with guests. There was something nice about making a connection and being noticed, about knowing you'd made others feel seen. Her mother had had that ability to make others feel important, and that's why people adored her. It was why they came back year after year.

"Well... you're all checked in, everything's been taken care of," she said. "So come on in and get settled. Do you have any bags? I'm happy to help you with them."

"Yep, in the car," he said. "I'll be right back," he added and jogged back outside to get them.

She walked to the door and watched as he went to his car—a white Mercedes sedan, way more upscale than what she thought a teacher would drive. And it was not at all a good choice for December in Lake Summers.

He came back with a couple of rolling suitcases and rubbed his sneakers on the outside mat before walking inside. "Boy, it sure gets cold here," he said. "And wet."

"Especially if you're not dressed for it," she said, assuming by his appearance that he hadn't spent a lot of time in the mountains in winter before now. "I hope you brought boots and a coat. And I hope you don't plan to do a lot of driving up here. If we get a storm, you better plan on staying put."

"Don't worry—I'm not going anywhere," he said.

She took one of his suitcases, lowered the handle, and carried it upstairs. Her mom had always helped guests carry suitcases upstairs too. It was all part of the job, and it felt good to be assertive. She led him to the third floor, then lowered the suitcase and rolled it down to the end of the hall.

"So this is the Hemlock Suite," she said, pushing open the door and then stepping back to let him walk through. "It's the largest suite in the inn, and it looks out on those beautiful evergreens at the edge of the woods. The bathroom is fully stocked, and there should be plenty of towels and extra blankets, but if you need anything or run out of anything, just let me know. There's firewood there by the fireplace, but if you run out, I can restock that as well."

He circled the perimeter of the room, nodding. "Nice," he said, looking out the wide window. "Wow."

"Now, I have a chef from town all set up to take care of you," she said. "Her name is Mavis, and I think you'll be very happy with her delicious food. Of course, if you'd like me to stock anything special in the refrigerator downstairs, just let me know. And it would be good to know where and when you'd like your meals—I can have the sunroom downstairs set up for you, or if you'd like them brought upstairs, we can do that too."

"What service," he said. "I'm super impressed."

"We've got a nice welcome lunch waiting for you whenever

you're ready," she continued. "And I also have some sample menus Mavis drew up for your stay. Now, if you need anything, I've left my number on the desk. I'll be living over in the cottage there"—she pointed in the direction of the lake—"so I'm just a stone's throw away. We have a great housekeeping crew, but feel free to let me know if you'd like your linens changed more frequently or anything else you'd like done differently. The Wi-Fi password is on the little card by the TV, and I can also help you with anything you want as far as recreation goes. We heard you have a part-time teaching job over in Lyons Hill, but there are a couple of gyms nearby that I can call for you, and there's skiing not too far away, too. Downhill and cross country."

"Thank you," he said. "Very thorough."

She looked down at her feet, a little embarrassed at sounding like a brochure or a press release. "Yes, well, I guess I've covered it," she said. "Anything else I can answer now?"

"Just one question," he said. "Do you ever eat?"

"Well, yes, I was just saying..." she said. "I mean there's plenty of food, and a welcome lunch ready for you today, and we have a wonderful chef—"

"No, I'm asking if *you* ever eat," he said. "Would you join me for lunch? I've been alone in the car all morning. I could sure use the company."

She thought at first she'd heard him wrong. "What? No, you don't have to ask me to join you. I'm just the innkeeper—you're the guest. I'm here to make sure you're satisfied and then to disappear."

"Well, I'm not a big one for standing on ceremony," he said with a wink. "All I know is that I'm super hungry. And if you are too, then nothing would make me more satisfied than to have lunch today with the owner's daughter."

Before long, they were sitting in the kitchen, a big bowl of fruit salad, a basket of chips, some cans of soda, and a platter of club sandwiches and wraps in between them. He gestured that she should go first, so she put a mozzarella wrap and some fruit salad on her plate, then watched as he took a brisket club and some chips.

It was outrageous, she knew, that she was sitting here with him. As warm as her mom was, she'd never have done such a thing. She'd wanted the guests to feel pampered, and not obligated to make small talk or even be polite if they weren't in the mood. And Laurel was sure her mom would have frowned on having a guest eat lunch in the kitchen—especially with that tarp hanging down to hide the wall Joel was building. Guests were always served in the sunroom or the guest dining room or, in warmer months, out on the porch. But Christopher had walked straight into the kitchen when he came downstairs, and she didn't feel comfortable correcting him.

"So, tell me—how exactly did you come to be running this place?" Christopher said as he got up and walked to the refrigerator to fill his glass with ice. She started to offer to do it for him, or apologize for not having brought ice to the table, but then sat back down. He'd said he didn't stand on ceremony, and he seemed to like making himself at home, even when he was as out of his element as he was right now, having driven from New York in a car that didn't seem built for the snow, and wearing sneakers and a sweater but no coat.

"Well, it's my dad's, like I said," she told him. It was strange that he was so upbeat, considering that he was looking for a place to escape from his life, according to what the travel agent had said. But people handled things differently, she knew. Her dad had been upbeat the week following her mom's funeral—so much so that people kept commenting on how well he was managing. But she could tell he was trying not to feel anything. She knew he didn't want to let the grief in.

"And he's usually the one here," she continued. "But he's away right now." She tried with her tone to make the situation sound normal. But talking about her dad reminded her that she had no idea where he was. It was frustrating to be so in the dark, and she wondered why he'd done that to her.

Christopher nodded and Laurel watched him take a bite of his brisket sandwich. "Oh, boy, you were right, this is amazing." He swallowed and took a gulp of soda. "So, where's your mom?"

"Oh, well, she... she died. A few years ago."

"Oh, hey," he said, swallowing quickly and wiping his mouth with a napkin. "Hey, I'm sorry. I didn't know, I didn't mean to—"

"No, it's fine," she said. He was asking personal questions, but she didn't feel he was prying. His tone was casual and friendly, and his eyes were warm and attentive. It seemed that he simply found her interesting. It was nice that someone she'd just met felt that way.

"It was a long time ago. They had a great marriage. Many great years. My mother's family owned this place. My dad's law firm was helping the town incorporate, and my dad was part of the team. They wanted to stay at the Lake Summers Resort on the hill, the fancy place, but it was booked for some convention. So they stayed here."

"So he came here as a lawyer and fell in love with the inn?"

"I think it was my mom he fell in love with," she said. "She was friendly and warm and funny, and she loved people. And he wanted to be with her, that's what he always said. But she wasn't going to leave. His only choice was to stay."

"So he just stopped being a lawyer to be with her?"

"Pretty much. He kept up his license, did some work on the side once in a while. But mostly he just put it behind him."

"Wow," he said. "That's love, huh?"

She thought for a moment. "Yeah, he really did love her a lot. She was the only one he sacrificed anything for. He's not the kind of guy who gives in or compromises. Although she sacrificed too."

"Oh? How did she sacrifice?"

"She flew under the radar sometimes, I guess. My dad liked to be the center of attention. He's a complicated guy."

"But he's the one that gave up his life for hers," he said.

"Well, it wasn't always like that— Anyway, you don't want to hear about my crazy family," she said. "How about some coffee?"

She put her sandwich down and went to start a fresh pot. It was interesting, what this guy had just said, this person who didn't know her parents at all. Because he was right, her dad had given up a lot for love. His whole life, in fact. She remembered the night before her mom's funeral, when Tracey had mused about their parents' relationship as the three sisters sat in front of the fireplace. "If there's one good thing, it's that Mom went first," she'd said. "Dad's so strong, he'll be fine. But I don't think Mom could have carried on without Dad."

She and Deb had agreed, but now she wondered if Tracey had gotten it wrong. Because Dad hadn't done so well all these years. He hadn't been able to keep the inn up, as her mother would have.

"And what about you?" Christopher said, walking over to the countertop where he lifted the glass cover off the pastry dish and picked out a cupcake for himself. The best one they made at Katie's store, she noticed. With the cannoli-cream frosting drizzled with raspberry coulis.

"What about me, what?" she said.

He came back to the table and took a big bite of the cupcake, nearly three-quarters of the whole thing. Then he took another napkin from the stand in the center of the table and wiped his mouth thoroughly. As casual as he was, he evidently cared a lot about his appearance and wasn't going to let his face be marred by a wayward crumb.

"What about you and the inn?" he asked. "Are you going to inherit the family business? Or are there other family members vying for that honor?"

"What? No. Oh, no," she said, shaking her head. His tone was kind of sarcastic, but he was very good-natured about it. "I'm just here to help my dad out. I have a whole life"—she waved her hand in the direction of the living room—"elsewhere."

"Yeah? Where's elsewhere?"

"New York."

"No kidding," he said. "You're a New Yorker? Me too. I thought I recognized a kindred spirit. So what is it that you do"—he smiled teasingly and imitated her, waving toward the living room —"out there? You know, your whole life?"

She laughed and looked at him sideways, acknowledging his teasing. "I'm an interior designer," she said. She knew she was overstating her role. She didn't even have any clients of her own. But she didn't want to come across as a failure. She wanted to impress him. "I work for another designer right now. But I hope to have my own firm one day."

"Is that so? And what is it you want to design?"

"Well, homes. Classic homes, period homes. Any kind of home actually."

"And you like that kind of work?"

"I love it. I love the idea of creating places that started out only in my own head."

"Very cool," he said and got up for another cupcake. "And what else do you do... out there in your whole other life?"

"Well... I raise my son."

He turned to look at her, the cupcake in his hand and his back against the countertop. "You have a son?"

She nodded. "He's eight. Keeps me very busy. You'll meet him later—he's at a kids' program right now."

"Oh, so he left his whole life, too?"

"He did. We're a package deal. Where I go, he goes."

"Is his dad here too?"

"His dad?" Laurel pressed her lips together. She wasn't used to being asked so directly about Thomas. "No. No, he's not in the picture. Never was. But it's fine. We do okay, Simon and me." She smiled, surprised at how nice it felt to talk about her life this way. Without embarrassment. Without facing judgment. Her family always stayed quiet about Thomas. As though Simon's origins were shameful.

"Well, good for you then," he said. "I'll look forward to meeting him." He arched his back, throwing his head back and squeezing his eyes. "Boy, five hours of driving can really do a number on your body. I could use a hot shower and a good massage. Remind me to never do that trip again by myself."

"If I ever have the opportunity, I will be happy to remind you," she said.

He laughed and finished the second cupcake, then went to pick up his plate, and she reached over and took it from him. "No, please. You don't have to clear the table. You're the guest."

"So what?" he said. "I can help out a bit."

"No—absolutely not," she said. "It's not how we do things here."

"You're the boss." He winked again. "And the cutest innkeeper I've ever seen."

She looked down, embarrassed, and heard him chuckle. "It is a pleasure to meet you and have lunch in your fine establishment, Ms. Hanover," he said. "I am looking forward to being at your inn this month and to taking advantage of all this fine hospitality."

"And I'm pleased to do whatever I can to make your stay more pleasant, Mr. Charles," she said, lifting her head and trying to match his tone. "And if there's anything you ever think of that I can do—"

Just then the kitchen door opened, and Joel walked in, bundled up in his heavy parka, aviator hat, and thick black boots, a plaid scarf wrapped around his neck. He looked up, surprised, as though he hadn't expected anyone to be there.

"Wow, a real-life mountain man," Christopher murmured.

"What? No," Laurel said, walking over to the door. She was glad it seemed that Joel hadn't heard Christopher's comment. She wasn't sure Joel would find him funny.

"Joel, hi," she said. "I wasn't sure when you'd be coming back over."

"I thought I could get some work done before your guest came. But I guess he's here earlier than I expected." He walked over to

Christopher and extended his hand. "Hi, nice to meet you. I'm Joel Hutcherson."

"Hi. Christopher Charles. You work for her?"

"No," Laurel said. "No. He's a friend."

"I'm doing some repairs," he said. "I'll try not to disturb you."

"Appreciate it," Christopher said. Then he turned to Laurel. "Thanks again for having lunch with me, Laurel," he said. "I'll be back to you with that shopping list and some things I'd like to do while I'm in town." He squeezed her elbow before leaving the kitchen.

When he was gone, Joel looked at her. "You had lunch with him?"

She nodded. "He wanted me to. He's a very nice guy. A teacher, actually." She paused. "Something wrong?"

"No, no. No, it's fine."

"Want some coffee? Some lunch?"

He shook his head. "I'm just going to get started on that closet upstairs."

"Okay. But I think the guy is tired," she said. "He had a long trip. I really want to make this place nice for him. Can you maybe wait a little before you do any loud stuff? Maybe he'll take a walk later."

Joel looked where Christopher had gone. "Yeah. Sure. I'll keep it down." He stamped his feet on the mat by the door and then walked through the kitchen toward the living room. She saw him pause, walk again, then stop and turn toward her.

"Hey, Laurel?" he said.

She nodded.

"I ran into Chuck Decker the other day. He told me there's an ice-skating party at the lake this Saturday night. And I was wondering if maybe you and Simon would like to go with me."

She smiled. Chuck had told her about the party too, and she'd been thinking she might take Simon. It could be a great way to cheer him up, after this upheaval of a week he'd had. But she was touched by Joel's gentle, shy invitation, and she wanted very much for them to all go together.

"Sure," she said. "We'd like that."

He nodded and she watched him continue out of the kitchen, then cleared the table and walked outside and onto the back porch, folding her arms across her chest against the cold. It was a nice story, the story she'd told Christopher about her parents. About her father giving up his whole life because he fell in love. About changing his whole life plans because he'd found what he was looking for. She'd never really thought of her dad as romantic; he'd certainly never been a romantic when it came to raising her and her sisters. But he really had been in love, back then.

She walked to the railing and looked out toward the lake. This was where her dad had proposed—her mom had told her all about it. Right here on the porch.

"I told him about my dreams for the inn," her mom had said. "How I thought I could build it up into something famous and beautiful. And I told him how the only thing missing was a ballroom, where people could have weddings and all kinds of wonderful parties. And there would be big windows and sparkling lights and a view of the sunset and the mountains. And he said we'd build it together. And then asked me to marry him."

Of course, they'd never built the ballroom—there'd always been other uses for the money they were able to save. Her mom's parents had left them with a lot of debt. And then she and her sisters were born, and there were all the expenses with running the inn and saving for college. Dad wanted all three girls to go to the best school possible.

But her mother hadn't minded that they didn't get around to it. That's what she'd told Laurel shortly before she died. What she'd loved was that he'd taken her idea seriously, when her own parents never had. And that he'd given up his job at the law firm in Syracuse and married her and run the inn with her—that he'd turned her dream into his. He'd loved her that much.

In the end, she'd never quite achieved the world-renowned inn she'd imagined. She'd never even gotten her ballroom—not the big one she'd envisioned when she was young and not even the smaller one she'd settled on as the years passed. But through it all, until her mom's last day, her parents had stuck together. Making a home together was ultimately more important than building something big or world-famous.

She wondered if she'd ever know a love like that.

ELEVEN

Saturday night arrived, and Joel wound a scarf around his neck and slung his old high-school ice skates over his shoulder. Then he left the house, the door sounding a definitive thump that echoed in the still air. He stayed still for a moment, lulled by the quiet that allowed the echo to be heard. Pulling the collar of his jacket closer around him, he walked down the front steps and over toward Birch Street, his hands deep in his pockets, his breath visible in the cold atmosphere.

Surprisingly enough, he was glad to be going ice skating.

He hadn't expected to feel this way, back when Chuck first mentioned the party. It had been so long since he'd been out on the ice. His visits home these last several years had always been in the spring, when there was little chance of weather problems that could delay his flight there or back. And when he could help his mom get ready for summer by fertilizing the lawn and replacing the storm doors with screens; by reassembling the outdoor furniture and carrying bags of topsoil over to her garden. It had been a long time since he'd thought about how much he'd liked tearing across the ice at breakneck speeds, feeling the snap of the cold wind against his face as he raced his pals, until the officials on duty told them to slow down or be kicked off for the rest of the afternoon. Everyone used to go skating on Sunday afternoons in the winter.

Even Laurel, although she usually stayed off to the side, practicing some move or skill. He'd known before they started working on the play together how determined she was, how much she wanted to be perfect. Sometimes he'd thought about going over to her and encouraging her to ease up, maybe get a cup of hot cocoa with him. But he hadn't been sure she'd say yes.

He started down Birch Street, taking in the vast black sky and the chilly air, the way the snow snapped and crunched under his boots. This was how he'd always remembered Christmastime, all these years when he was away on the other side of the world. These were the feelings that stayed with him. Nothing big ever changed back home—that's what he'd always thought. Maybe a new shop came into town, maybe a house was sold. Maybe a mayor was challenged for the office and lost reelection, maybe a teacher retired. But he'd always expected this was the place he could count on to stay the same. To be a steady foundation, a bedrock, waiting in stillness for him to return.

And then his mother had died, so suddenly. And now Doug was off who knows where and Laurel was back home. He'd tried several times to call Doug on his cell phone these last couple of days, but there'd been no answer. He still didn't understand why he'd left so suddenly without saying anything to him, let alone Laurel. Doug knew Joel was expecting to see him, hang out with him. They'd talked about it—the pizza and beers, the baseball games they'd watch on TV. They'd grown close so quickly. Doug had even asked him to recommend a jeweler where he could buy an engagement ring for Katie; he hadn't bought jewelry since his wife died ten years ago, he'd said, and the store he'd always gone to was out of business. Joel had been happy to give him the business card from his mother's favorite place, which he'd found in her desk at the house.

Now, though, he didn't know anything—not what was going on with Doug's health, and not where Doug was, although he suspected he was with Katie. He could only wait and trust that Laurel was right to think her dad was fine and would show up on Christmas Eve as promised. But Laurel didn't know as much about her dad as he did. And that felt so wrong.

He reached the entrance to the inn, the winding driveway lit by wooden lamp posts, and saw Laurel and Simon heading his way. Laurel looked riveting—that was the only word he could think of—in her jeans and a red ski jacket, and a blue knit hat with a pom-pom on top, her wavy hair cascading past her shoulders. Her walk was as it had always been, confident and assertive, as if she'd never let anyone stop her from doing what she needed to do, even something as benign as ice skating. That was the attitude he'd always loved about her, the attitude that had driven her as she'd directed the senior-class play, her vision for the production clear and unwavering.

"Hey," he said, gesturing toward their skates, their laces knotted as his were and slung over their shoulders. "I guess you're ready for the lake."

"Ice... skaaaaaating!" Simon shouted, raising his fists in triumph as he stamped his feet, one and then the other, into the crunchy snow. "Lake skaaaaating!"

"Simon, be careful," Laurel said. "Those skates have sharp blades—you know that."

"I can't help it!" he said. "I can't help it, I can't help it, I can't help it, I can't help—"

"Yes, you can," she said. "Or maybe you want me to carry your skates?"

"No, it's fine, I'm fine, I'm— Look it's Garrett! Hey, Garrett!" he said and began running and stumbling in the snow to catch up to a group of kids in silhouette turning onto the street ahead of them.

Joel watched Laurel stare ahead, holding her breath, as Simon caught up with the kids and slowed down. Then she sighed. "He's going to give me a heart attack one day," she said.

"He's a great kid. Just like your dad told me."

"He's a handful," she said, and he could tell from her smile how much she adored him, despite her complaints. "But he's a happy kid too."

"So he liked that camp program?" Joel said.

"So far so good—although it's only been three days," she told him. "The teacher is lovely. She called and said I should send over his assignments from his school, and she'll make sure he works on them, so he won't be too far behind when we get back. I think he's really been looking forward to tonight. It was so nice of you to ask us to come with you. I might have let it go if you hadn't said something."

"So I see you're skating too," he said.

She nodded. "It's been a long time. But I couldn't find any skates that fit Simon in the storage shed, so we went to the skate shop in Lyons Hill this morning to rent some, and I figured I'd get some too."

"I remember you skating. I remember you were pretty good."

"No, I never got good. But I tried. My dad taught me when I was little, and all I wanted was for him to see me improve."

Joel looked ahead, thinking this might be a good segue to find out anything new about Doug. "I tried to call your dad a few times, but he didn't answer," he said. "Have you heard anything from him?"

She shook her head. "No, but that's my father. He said he'll be home Christmas Eve, and as much as I'd like to hear from him, I don't think I will unless something changes. Now, if it were my mom, she'd be checking in every day." She looked at him. "Why? Is there something you're worried about? You seem more concerned than I am."

"What? No, no," he said. "Just making conversation." Although the truth was he'd been hoping maybe Doug had checked in and given her some news. So he didn't have to hold onto all his secrets anymore.

He paused, then asked the other question on his mind, trying to sound casual. "And how's... how's the schoolteacher?"

She laughed. "He's actually quite a character. Not at all what I expected, from what the travel agent said. I thought he was going to be all quiet and hermit-like, but he's outgoing and kind of funny and... and kind of outrageous, in a way. Simon's enjoying him too. It's like he's an old friend. He fits in so easily."

"No kidding," Joel said. "Great. I mean... great. That could have gone a lot worse." He nodded to emphasize his approval and hoped he was masking his real feelings. He could hear Meg's words in his head: *He's a bit of flirt.* He didn't want Laurel to fall for his story and possibly get hurt.

He didn't want Laurel to fall for him at all.

They reached the lake, which looked like some kind of huge, clear gem, glittering thanks to the line of large spotlights along the shore. There were tons of families there, and before long he realized Chuck hadn't been exaggerating—many people from high school were there as well. They were mainly Laurel's old gang, the theater crew, and while he shook hands in greeting, he was moved by how strongly they all embraced her, and how glad—emotional even—she was to see them.

"Mindy! Amy! Connor! Dean!" she said as she hugged them one by one, her voice breaking a little as she went on to share memories—the way Amy was so great at making costumes, the way the twins, Connor and Dean, were such daredevils, always climbing along the scaffolding to fix the stage lights, even though they were supposed to wait for a teacher.

Joel didn't know what it was like to feel so strongly about old classmates, the way she did. He'd had pals in high school, friends who were as equally focused on college and their futures as he was. She'd had... well, it was clear how this whole group all felt. The theater crowd had been a family.

Just then Simon came up beside her. "Mom, come on—I need help with my skates!"

"Okay, I'm coming," she told him. "Everyone, this is my son, Simon. I'll introduce him around later. Let's go, honey. Anyone else coming?"

Joel walked down the slope with the others and sat on a bench to put on his skates. When he was done, he went to where Laurel was launching Simon from the edge of the lake, among all the other children and adults. Simon started out gingerly, his skates chopping into the ice, his arms floating upward by his sides and his ankles caving inward. Although he was shuffling his feet quickly, his body barely made any forward progress.

Laurel started out onto the ice. "Let me show you," she said.

"No, Mom!" he insisted. "I can do it myself."

"But I can teach you the way—"

"No!"

"Okay, fine," she called to him. "But glide. Try to glide!"

He nodded, his feet stepping faster, making him look, Joel thought, like one of those cartoon characters who drives a car by pushing their feet through the floor and running. He started to fall forward, but then he caught his balance and stood up straight again. A moment later he started to fall backward, and Laurel gasped. She started skating toward him, and Joel did, too. But Simon caught himself again and waved to Laurel.

"You were right!" he said. "This is the coolest thing *ever*!"

She applauded and gave him a thumbs up, and he started to move his feet more slowly and deliberately, which allowed him to cover more distance. She glanced toward Joel, and he smiled at her.

"He seems to be getting it," he said.

"I guess so. I hope he doesn't get overconfident. But it's great to be out here, isn't it? I'd forgotten how good it feels."

He nodded. "Go, Simon!" he called. It did feel great to be out here. On a gorgeous night. With Laurel Hanover and her son.

Simon pushed his glasses up higher on his nose and waved again, and then started to lose his balance once more—except this time, it didn't appear he was going to catch himself. His arms were flying and flapping, his feet thrusting out from under him, and Joel saw Laurel head out toward him. But he was faster, and he quickly reached Simon and grasped him under the arms.

"You're okay, pal," he said.

"I wasn't going to fall, you know," Simon told him. "You didn't have to catch me."

"My bad," Joel said. Simon laughed and skated away.

Laurel came up beside him, her cheeks red from the cold and her eyes twinkling from the spotlights. "He *was* going to fall," she said. "Thank you for catching him."

He shrugged. "It wasn't a big deal."

Just then another kid whizzed by, and suddenly Joel felt himself falling backward. This time it was Laurel who did the saving, grabbing him by the elbow. "You okay?" she asked.

"Yeah," he answered. "Although I think they need traffic lights around here."

He wanted her to stay, but she skated off, over to where some of her old school pals had gathered. That's when he noticed that they all had children, just like she did. Amy was with some teenagers that he assumed were hers, Chuck had a whole brood surrounding him, and Connor and Dean were both helping a circle of little kids try to skate. They were all still part of the community here, even though their lives had taken them elsewhere after high school. His life had taken him elsewhere, too—and yet he was different. He was an outsider. Just like he'd been when he helped out with the play. Until that night in the auditorium, when it was just him and Laurel.

He saw her skate away from the crowd and find a little spot of ice to herself, more dimly lit than the space where most of the people were. And then, from afar, he watched her do a twirl. It was so unexpected, but beautiful, the way she kicked out her leg and then propelled herself around, her arms moving slowly in front of her body until they were above her head, her hands gently rounded, her fingers meeting. Then she slowed down, extended her arms, and came to a stop, one knee bent and the other leg stretched out diagonally behind her, a little spray of ice dancing in the surrounding air. He was about to applaud, but then she shook her head and beat the air with her fists. She wasn't satisfied, he thought. She was always so hard on herself.

Did she ever give herself a break? Didn't she know how talented she was?

A moment later, Amy skated up alongside him. "That was amazing, wasn't it?" she said. "I didn't know she was a figure skater."

"I think she just works hard at everything she tries," he said.

He felt her look at him. "Whatever happened to you two?" she asked. "You went out for a while in high school, didn't you?"

He shook his head.

"Really? I thought you guys were a couple. You were so close."

"We got friendly when she directed the senior show," he told her. It was funny that both she and Chuck thought they'd been a couple. It was true, they'd been close. But then it had ended, so fast.

"So, anyway, I hear you've done really well for yourself," Amy said. "My mom told me about the articles they write about you. Your mom had them all hanging up in the store. She was really proud of you. I was so sorry to hear about what happened."

"Thanks," he said.

"What are you going to do about the store?" she asked.

"I'm going to close it up. And I'm heading back after that."

"Oh, that's too bad. What a beautiful store."

They both looked at Laurel, who finished her last twirl and then skated over to them. Amy asked what had brought her back to town, and Laurel explained about the inn and the teacher. "And how about you?" Laurel asked. "Do you live here now, or are you just visiting?"

"It better be a visit, if I want my kids to still love me," she explained, going on to say that she'd moved with her two teenagers from New Jersey back in with her mom, helping in her mom's linens store in town and studying for a master's in social work while trying to put her recent ugly divorce behind her.

"It's not so easy," she said. "My kids had to leave their house and their friends, and I'm back in my mom's home because I can't afford my own place. And I have an ex who can't stand me."

"But you're getting a degree," Laurel said. "That'll make a big difference."

Amy shook her head and pointed to the other aardies. "Those people," she said. "They were the nicest people in the world. We had it so great back then. If only we'd been smart enough to know it."

She sighed and skated off, and Joel looked at Laurel, who was looking down. He wondered if she was thinking what he was—that Amy was spot on; that the two of them had once had something great between them.

Then he thought about the way she'd twirled a moment ago. She appreciated praise—she'd appreciated all the accolades after the senior show—but she didn't need it. That's what he'd always admired about her. He'd grown up in a world that was all trophies and awards and speeches and prestigious college acceptances. And now newspaper articles. That's what his mother had valued. Those were the things she'd wanted for him. But Laurel had always been different. Her sisters had been the ones focused on awards and sports trophies. Laurel had a quiet strength that rose to the top, even when she was by herself on a dimly lit patch of ice. It didn't matter to her who, if anyone, was taking notice.

And Amy was right, he thought. They could have been a couple, Laurel and him. They should have been. But he had failed her. And he had ruined everything.

"You were great out there," he said, pointing to where she'd been skating. The ice was emptying off now, and there weren't many people around.

She shrugged. "Just a twirl. Anyone can do it."

"That's not true."

"I didn't even do it that well. I could do it better. If I tried harder. My sisters were much better skaters than I was."

He looked at her, and he saw her green eyes shining and her skin glistening, and he wanted to kiss her. To assure her that she didn't have to try harder at all. But he couldn't, because in her eyes, he saw confusion—and doubt. And he didn't blame her. He had failed her once a long time ago, when she was waiting for him and he didn't show. He wanted to tell her he was sorry about everything that had happened, and that she could trust him now. But why should she? Because here he was again, betraying her. He knew so much about her dad, and she knew nothing.

"Guys!" Chuck called from the shore. "Hot cocoa! Come join us!"

"I better go see if Simon's ready for cocoa," Laurel said, and she skated away.

Joel nodded and then started for the shore. Amy was right. They'd been too stupid back then to know what they had. And he couldn't shake the feeling that the same thing was going to happen now.

And he didn't know what to do about it.

TWELVE

To her great relief, Simon grew to like the winter camp very much. He reported on the Monday after ice skating that his teacher, Mrs. Pall—"although she's not really a teacher, because it's camp," he insisted—was nice, especially since she'd assigned him a seat right next to Garrett's. The camp group was smaller than his class back home, only fifteen third graders, which he thought was "kind of weird but kind of good," and the crafts and games made the school stuff easier to bear. He asked if he and Garrett could walk together to and from the program on their own, and Laurel promised to talk with Garrett's mom and see what they could arrange.

By the middle of the week, Simon had settled into a comfortable routine. Each weekday morning, Garrett would meet Simon on the driveway of the inn, and the two of them would head down the hill to the school, their backpacks strapped on and their boots stomping in the snow. In the afternoon, they'd return the same way, a little tired but happy nonetheless. If Joel was around after school, he'd often let Simon help him out with the wall, organizing the tools or hammering nails. He even taught Simon how to sand wood and use the level to make sure a plank was straight. She wasn't sure how she felt about that moment she and Joel had shared on the ice—it had been so unexpected and so intimate that it scared her a bit. She never brought it up and was glad that he didn't either. She wondered if he was as overwhelmed by it as she was.

Christopher, too, became a part of Simon's life and was always up for a game of chess or cards in the evenings. Even though he was a teacher, it seemed clear that he had never spent a lot of free time around kids, because he interacted with Simon the way others might handle a cool new kitchen gadget. But Simon didn't mind, and Laurel didn't either. Having both Joel and Christopher in his life was a good thing, Laurel thought. Simon wasn't nearly as anxious as he'd been that first night before camp, when he'd worried about how big everything around him felt.

Christopher also seemed to be taking well to life in the mountains. Every morning as she brought Simon to the driveway to meet Garrett, she'd see him head out of the inn for an early-morning run. While he didn't have a great car or boots for the snow, she was impressed that he did have good cold-weather running gear.

He'd come back an hour later and go upstairs to change, coming down just as Laurel had finished checking in with the cleaning staff, the plant lady, the heating contractor, or whatever other person was scheduled to stop by. He'd sit down for breakfast —Mavis usually had waffles, fruit and toast ready—and Laurel would have a cup of coffee with him.

Later in the morning, he'd take a walk downtown or take a drive to check out some museum or nature preserve in one of the neighboring towns, and in the afternoons, he'd head over to the school in Lyons Hill, where he taught drama. While he was gone, she'd respond to some of Joanna's emails, pay some bills, handle the reservations that were slowly trickling in for the summer, and listen to Joel working around the inn. She also made a point of sending out the Christmas gifts she'd bought for her sisters and their families and had brought with her from Queens. Occasionally, she'd read through some travel magazines and websites, and she even toyed with the idea of placing an ad. Sometimes she played around with the website her mom had created years ago; her dad had never touched it, and it needed updating.

In the evenings after Simon was asleep, she'd run back to the inn to check the thermostat, straighten up the kitchen, and survey the refrigerator to see if anything was running low. Often she would find Christopher sitting on the sofa in front of a fire, enjoying a glass of wine, and she'd stop and ask about his day. Sometimes he had a guest over, a woman, and she'd see him through the window, putting his arm around her shoulders, or stroking her back, or reaching for the wine bottle to refill her glass. On those evenings, she'd stay for a moment, watching them through the window, and then head back to the cottage, figuring she would let her chores go.

But it made her feel sad, to watch from outside in the cold. She wasn't sure why. She didn't think she was jealous—she didn't think Christopher was her type.

One morning after breakfast, she was at the reception desk answering some queries from potential guests. She was excited that the inn had guests coming this spring and proud of the changes that would be there to welcome them. Joel had fixed the closet and the upstairs hallway floor—and because Christopher's room was on the third floor, he'd been able to use the back stairs with no inconvenience.

Joel had also fixed the showers that were leaking and called in some experts to regrout the tiles in all the guest bathrooms. And Laurel had ordered new windows for rooms where they were needed. Perhaps most exciting, construction of the new wall was moving along, and she could already see how wonderful the kitchen would look with more space. It would be a welcoming country kitchen. Her mother would have loved it.

The one thing left for her to do was update the sheets and towels. Finding that slippery pillowcase on her pillow that first night had led her to discover that many rooms now had fancy sheets that weren't at all in keeping with the inn's aesthetic. It made her decide that a complete linens overhaul was needed. She liked modern luxuries, but it was strange, the choices Dad had made. The Cranberry Inn needed thick, cushy towels and soft, high-thread-count cotton bedding. And maybe bathrobes, too, to make the place feel almost like a spa. That was an addition her mother would also have loved.

She started to google images of bathrobes on her laptop, to get ideas for what she might like to buy, when Christopher came downstairs.

"You look deep in thought," he said. "What's on your mind? Some handsome, tousled schoolteacher you can't stop thinking about?"

She laughed. "If you really want to know, I'm thinking about bathrobes."

"Now, now," he said. "I thought this was a family place."

She rolled her eyes. "I'm thinking about buying bathrobes for the guest rooms. I don't know why we never did that before. Wouldn't you like a thick, terry bathrobe to welcome you home at the end of the day?

"You know what?" she said, standing up. "I'm going to go order some. My friend Amy's mother owns a nice little home store on Main Street. I'm going to go take a look right now."

"Want some company?" he asked.

She looked at him. "You want to come with me?"

"Sure," he said. "I don't have much to do this morning. You'd be lucky to have me—I have great taste. And besides, it looks like the only way I'm going to get invited to things around here is if I invite myself. I'm kind of mad at you for not telling me about the big ice-skating party."

"What?" she said. "You would have wanted to go to that? I'm sorry. I thought you wanted to be alone."

"Why on earth would you think that?"

"Because your travel agent said—"

"Well, I changed my mind," he said. "You're forgiven. Just don't let it happen again. Come on—let's get shopping."

They bundled up and headed downtown. The snow was

melting and the drips from the roof were coming down, with one hitting Christopher in the eye, and he stopped and shook his head and laughed at the risks of country living.

They reached Amy's mother's store, which was roomy and pretty, full of floor-to-ceiling shelves with towels in a range of colors, embroidered sheets and cotton and wool blankets on another wall, and bathroom accessories in the back. Amy was there, and after Laurel introduced her to Christopher, she guided them to the bathrobe section.

"I have an idea," Christopher said. "I'll be your model. I'm a pretty good size, right? Not too tall, not too skinny. I'll do a runway thing, and you two tell me what looks good."

Amy laughed. "My gosh, you're the most delightful guest the inn has ever had. At least as far as I know."

Laurel shrugged as Amy took his jacket. He was being silly, but she didn't see any point in ending his fun. She had come down here to get bathrobes, and she was pretty sure he'd help her accomplish exactly that.

Christopher tried on a few, pointing out the features of each—the wide lapel, the soft chenille construction, the thick and thirsty loops—as he did a dramatic stroll and turn. "Wait, this is hard," he said, after trying on a handful. "We need some more opinions. Anyone else we can call in?"

Amy, who was obviously charmed by the guy, offered to make a few calls, and within a few minutes, Maxine from the Grill and Stan from the smoothie shop were on their way. Both were glad to leave their stores, which tended to be relatively quiet at mid-morning in the winter. Before long, all the customers in the shop came to the back to see what all the fuss was. By that time, Stan, Amy and Maxine were also modeling styles.

"What do you think, Laur?" Christopher asked, gesturing like a game-show host.

She smiled at the nickname, then folded her arms across her chest and considered each one. "I think the thicker one is way too bulky," she said.

"But it gets cold in this town, if you haven't noticed," he said. "You need something with a little substance."

"I don't know," she said. "It's hard when you put a bathrobe on and the collar puffs up by your cheeks."

"But you can't go by you," he said. "You, my dear, are freakishly small."

"I am not," she said, hands on her waist.

"Okay, people, show of hands," he said to the crowd. "Is our friend the innkeeper freakishly tiny or not?"

"Stop," she said, batting away his hand. "This isn't about me. If you want to do something useful, take a poll about which bathrobe is best."

"Okay, people," he said, clapping his hands. "I think it feels good to put on something hefty after a shower, but Laurel wants something skimpier. So taking a poll here. What say you?" He pointed to each person, one by one, and they all weighed in.

Ultimately the majority decided on the medium-bulk one that Maxine was wearing, which came with an attached belt and breast pocket. Amy said they could embroider the pocket with the name of the inn. She gave a sample to Christopher as a gift and Laurel ordered twenty-four—two for each room.

Amy walked with her to the counter to complete the order. "Oh my gosh, he is adorable," she said.

"He's a lot to take, but he's fun," Laurel said.

"And you're so lucky—you have him for the whole month."

"I don't have him. He's a guest."

"You're not acting like he's a guest. You guys are so cute together."

"No, we're not," Laurel said.

"He seems like someone you've known for years."

"That's just the way it is with guests. My mom would have been the same way."

"This doesn't look like the way your mom would behave. I don't know, Laurel, there's definitely some chemistry. You're acting like an old married couple, bickering about bathrobes."

"You're crazy. He's just very friendly—"

"What's wrong with you? He's adorable. You've been working hard and taking care of Simon and now taking care of your family too. You've got to be lonely. You can date."

"Date? He's a guest, he's only here for a few weeks—"

"I'm telling you there's something going on between you two. Don't let him get away."

Laurel waited to sign the receipt, looking at Christopher chatting with Stan. Was there really chemistry between them? She liked Christopher and all, but she really wasn't thinking of him that way. He was silly and flirty, not the kind of guy she'd ever get serious about. At least she didn't think so. Her mom had had fun with guests too. But at the end of the day, the inn was just a fantasy, an escape for them. They all went back to their own lives, and she went back to hers.

And yet, things were different now. Her mom had been happily married. She was single. And lonely—Amy was right, she was a little lonely. Could there be something between the two of them?

Christopher was waiting for her at the door, his shopping bag with his free bathrobe in his hand. He gave a cheerful wave to the crowd inside, as though he were a celebrity leaving a personal appearance.

"What a town," he said when they were back on the sidewalk. "Everyone knows everyone here. They all talked about your dad, asked if I'd met him yet. Sounds like he's a pretty happy-go-lucky kind of guy."

Laurel stopped in her tracks. "Happy-go-lucky? Who said that?"

"A bunch of people. Someone said they noticed he was kind of bubbly lately, and everyone agreed. Maxine said that whatever he's been eating, she wants to put some of it in Gill's dinner."

"It's Gull," Laurel mumbled, barely focusing on what she was saying. "Not Gill. Gull." She couldn't believe what Christopher had just told her. She'd been starting to think her dad was struggling, maybe even depressed. How else to explain why he hadn't been keeping the inn up at all these last several months? But now, it seemed, people were finding him upbeat, even bubbly—especially lately. She remembered what Maxine had said when she and Simon were at the Grill—giddy, that's what she'd called him. What could have caused such a noticeable change in her dad just before he left town? And why didn't she know about it?

"Gill, Gull, whatever," Christopher said. "It doesn't matter. What does matter, my darling innkeeper, is that those guys with the smoothie place are working on an education-themed smoothie. In honor of me! Did you know that? Stan headed back to the shop, and he invited us to come by and taste it. Come on, let's go."

"Well... sure. Why not?" she said and followed him across the street to the smoothie shop. She decided to push thoughts of her dad out of her mind, at least for the moment. It didn't make sense to dwell on him, since evidently no one knew what was behind his new attitude. She was exactly where she'd been ever since she'd arrived home: in the dark. And with no choice but to wait until Christmas Eve when he'd finally be back and she could get her questions answered.

When they arrived at the smoothie shop, Trey had two tall cups waiting on the counter.

"Get this—it's a hot smoothie," Stan said. "A beverage innovation. Because teachers like hot coffee and hot tea, right? We're going to revolutionize the whole smoothie business."

"But there's still work to be done," Trey said. "It's kind of too dense and coffee-ish at the moment. But we're working on upping the froth factor, the airiness, if you will. And we put coffee and chocolate and sprinkles and gold sugar crystals, because we wanted a full-mouth experience with some crunch and pop, like the way kids' brains kind of explode with knowledge. Now, don't hold back. Give us your honest opinion."

Christopher took a sip, then brought his hand to his mouth. "Hey, guys, is there sand in this? It's kind of... I don't know. Sandy."

"Sand?" Stan exclaimed. "We wouldn't put sand in our drinks."

"It's kind of gravelly," Christopher said. "Don't you think so, Laur?"

She had to agree. "I'm sorry, you guys. It is a little grainy."

"Grainy—that's the word! You're brilliant!" Christopher said, raising his hands in the air. "The lady's right, I'm afraid. So sorry, fellas, but you wanted our honest opinion."

"That we did," Trey said. "Hmm. Maybe the cocoa isn't dissolving, or the sugar crystals. We'll work on it. Give us time. Before you leave this town and head back to the city life, we'll have it all worked out. Mark my words."

"Thanks, guys," Christopher said, sounding as if he'd known them forever. "Happy to come back for another taste whenever you're ready. Come on, Laur. Time to get back to the inn and dazzle me with your amenities."

She laughed and waved goodbye as he held the door open.

Back at the inn, Christopher went upstairs to get ready for work, and with a little quiet time to herself, Laurel sat down in the living room, thinking about what other improvements she might make. The way things were going with Joel's repairs, and the success she'd had with the bathrobes this morning, made her think anew about the ballroom her mother had always wanted. It was sad that her mother had never seen it built—but now Laurel thought that maybe, just maybe if she worked hard enough, she could manage a project like that.

She went to the kitchen to get her mother's notebook from the junk drawer and then sat down at the table, opened her laptop, and starting googling images of ballrooms—grand ones from huge resorts and smaller ones in boutique hotels; wedding venues from old movies and famous homes in historic cities like Boston, Charleston, and Philadelphia. She loved looking at the fabrics on chairs and wall coverings, at the drapes and the table settings, at the chandeliers and sconces. She thought about how the images touched her, how some made her feel regal, others made her feel welcome, and still others made her feel small and cold. It was something she loved to think about—how furnishings affected a person's emotions.

The coziness of the sofa in the living room, for example, had encouraged her to open up to her mom, back when they'd sit together on Saturday mornings. The breakfast room, with the sunlight streaming in and the casual bistro tables, was a place to be whimsical and playful. And the Cranberry Room, with its rich, red decor, was a place to be more subdued and introspective. That was the magic of design, she thought: It set the stage for the moments of your life.

She switched out of her browser and opened the design app on her computer, then started to sketch. She put in big bay windows, some with window seats, and elegant swag curtains in white linen. She chose a dark-walnut hardwood floor, and experimented with different styles of chairs, the cushions in lavender. She played around with lighting fixtures that resembled waterfalls.

Christopher walked in and grabbed an apple from the bowl on the counter, then came to the table. He leaned over her chair, looking at her screen. "Hey, you're good."

"It's just doodles," she said. She didn't want to tell him she was trying to design a ballroom. It seemed like such a big project, way bigger than buying bathrobes. And it wasn't as though she had a lot of experience with big projects. Working with Joel on repairs was one thing. But she still had never worked on a major project with a client of her own.

"No, this is good. I'd have a party there. If I were planning a party." He sat down in the chair next to her. "So is this the kind of thing you do at work?"

"Not really," she said. "I told you, I don't have any clients yet."

"So when are you going to stop waiting for someone to give you one? When do you get to call the shots?"

"You don't simply get to be a designer," she said. "You have to build contacts and you have to work under someone. You need to pay your dues. My boss worked for another designer in a big firm for ten years before she opened her own. And even then, she struggled a lot in those first years."

"And this is okay with you? Why don't you take your talent and do something else, something where you can make things happen? Like..." He paused a moment. "Like, have you ever thought about designing for the theater?"

"The theater? Well, no. Not professionally."

"Well, you should," he told her. "Set design is a great field. There are people who do exactly what you do—they design rooms, homes. They create a whole onstage world based on a script."

"But I don't have any experience," she said. "I haven't done anything with the theater. Not since I was in high school."

"You'd be great."

She shut her laptop. "This is ridiculous. How would I get into that? Who do I talk to? I mean, it was hard enough getting the job I have. And that's going nowhere."

"But I know people," he said. "I could help you. I hate that you're tied to what you've been doing for so long. I worry about you, Laurel."

She smirked. "You worry about me? You only met me a week ago."

"Hey, I'm a good guy. And I see you here in this little town making shopping lists and taking care of your kid. I think there should be more. So do you—I know you do. You're smart and personable and talented. You deserve to do something exciting with your life."

"You think so?" she said. It was strange and exhilarating, hearing someone who was practically a stranger describe her that way. "You know people in the theater who could help me?"

"I do. What, you don't believe me?"

"No, I believe you," she said. "I just... I just never thought about this before."

"Well, you should. I'm telling you, I know the right people. I can make it happen for you. If you're ready to make your move."

He tossed the apple in the air. "Think about it," he said as he left the kitchen.

"I will," she said, watching him leave. She didn't know if she believed him. Did he really have contacts? He had money, that was for sure—that car, his clothes, the way he could pay to have the inn to himself. Maybe he did know people. Maybe there was more to him than she knew. She hoped so.

Because it sounded amazing, to finally get the shot she'd been working for.

To finally, finally, become the person she'd been trying to be.

THIRTEEN

Joel got into his pickup that Thursday to head down to the store, hoping to get back to the inn later that afternoon. He'd gotten into a pretty good routine, going to the store in the mornings and then working at the inn in the afternoons and into the evening. But he wanted more time at the inn. And not just to build the new wall. He wanted to be around Laurel more, and Simon too. He cared for them, more than he'd expected to. And he also wanted to keep an eye on Christopher. He didn't trust the guy at all, especially since that first morning, when he'd seen Laurel having lunch with him. He couldn't forget that Meg had called him a narcissist and a flirt and a headache. He never would have offered up the inn if he'd known Laurel would be running the place. He hated that Christopher was holding the truth back from her. And he hated that he was keeping the guy's secret too.

And even more, he hated that he was keeping secrets about her dad. What a mess he'd created. But he'd promised Doug he'd stay silent. He'd caught Doug in a moment of weakness, coming out of the medical building in Ayelin Point that day, and he knew that was the only reason Doug had opened up.

"Don't tell anyone what I told you," Doug had said as they'd walked together to the parking lot. "I need you to do me that favor.

I want to tell the girls on my own. And Katie too. I'll do it my way. I need some control over this thing, you know?"

Joel had had no problem making that promise. Doug was his friend, and besides, he'd had no way of knowing he'd ever run into Laurel, let alone start to have feelings for her again. But now he was spending lots of time with her, and his feelings were as strong, or even stronger, than when he'd known her before. He was caught in a bind, stuck between keeping his word to Doug and keeping a secret from Laurel—whose trust he desperately wanted to earn. And it was getting harder to stay quiet, now that he was with her every day. What would she think when she finally found out? He would have to tell her that he'd known it all along—he would never keep the lie going. And the worst part was, he had betrayed her once in the past. Even if she was ready to look beyond that, how could he expect her to look beyond it this time?

The only positive thing about the whole fiasco, he thought, was that at least he was doing something good at the inn. He'd fixed up the floor and the closet and the plumbing, and more. And he was expanding the kitchen too. The original wall had come down easily —he'd practically been done with it before Christopher even showed up. The rest of the job wouldn't take long. It was almost too easy. He was glad there was a tarp hanging in the kitchen. He wouldn't want Laurel to know how close the project was to completion already.

He turned right onto Main Street. The truth was, he loved this kind of work. The measuring and analyzing and sanding and hammering—it felt good, working with his hands. And it was satisfying to build something better than what had been there before. Because when you came right down to it, carpentry was problem-solving. You looked at spaces, structures, and objects, and you figured out how they could be reworked, reconfigured, reimagined in a way that would make someone's life better. That would make something wrong into something so right, you wouldn't even need to pay attention to it.

It was the same way he'd felt when he'd built that revolving platform for Laurel's show all those years ago. The one that allowed her to do that quick scene change, the one she needed because she felt it important to keep the tension high, to keep the audience engaged.

Being around her these last few days had brought all those memories back to mind. He remembered how she'd sounded when she spoke to the student-council officers about her application to direct the senior play. He'd been so impressed with her that he'd fought hard in support of her. A few of the more popular girls in school had applied to be director as well, and everyone assumed one of them would be picked. That's how things always went. But he was struck by Laurel's passion, how her voice broke and how vulnerable she sounded as she finished her speech. He could hear it even now: *I truly need to do this. It's everything to me.*

And because *he* was one of the popular kids—and not only that, he was also president of the student council—he was able to convince the others to choose her. Unlikely as it had seemed when the list of applicants first came out.

He'd wanted to choose her because he understood her. And he admired her for speaking up, for asking so honestly for what she needed. He'd never spoken like that in his life. He hadn't had to. Things came easily to him—sports and academics and leadership positions. And girls. And he'd never really understood why nothing ever moved him, why nothing filled him with the intensity that Laurel had as she made her case for being named director. And why didn't it?

Because people had thought he had it all together. He was the golden boy, the one who was going to Yale on a full scholarship, the first student from Lake Summers ever to do so. The one who was destined for some huge career, the one whose name would be part of Lake Summers lore. But when he listened to Laurel speak about the play, he realized he'd never put himself out there like she had. He'd never aimed for something knowing he might not get it, as she had. And that's why he'd been so drawn to her. She was exactly what he wanted to be. She didn't know it, but she was.

He pulled into a parking spot outside the store. He would have preferred to spend the whole day working at the inn. There were lots of things that needed replacing, things that Laurel hadn't yet mentioned, although he was sure she'd noticed them by now. Chipped tiles, worn-out wood banisters, floors that needed refinishing. But he had to get started with the store. On the phone yesterday, the landlord had told him there were people interested in leasing the shop as soon as he vacated it. A camera store in Ayelin Point wanted to open a second location here in Lake Summers, and a woman who owned a shoe store in Lyons Hill thought moving next door to Lexy's dress shop would be ideal. There had also been nibbles from other merchants. The possibilities included a sandwich shop, a children's clothing boutique, a home-fragrance store, and a fix-it shop for handheld devices.

Joel wanted to be a good guy and leave the store even before the lease was up. He had no reason to give the landlord a hard time. But he didn't know how he was going to get rid of everything. There was so much stuff—all the items on display and lots of unpacked boxes, many of which Lexy had signed for while the store was closed. The answer, of course, was to have a huge liquidation sale and clear out the merchandise, and the fixtures too. But it felt wrong, to want to get rid of all the things that way. All the things people had lovingly made and his mother had bought, believing her customers would be so happy to have them in their homes.

"Knock, knock," came a familiar voice, and he turned to see Lexy walking in, holding a tray with two large cardboard cups from Pearl's, a white bakery bag folded down at the top wedged in between them. "Coffee girl, here. Well, coffee for you, hot water with a teabag on the side for me."

"Hey, Lexy," he said, taking the tray from her and putting it on the counter. It was the fourth time this week that she'd come in with coffee for him. He was grateful, but he wished she didn't feel she had to come over every day. Or stay so long.

She sat and had her tea, she talked, she rearranged things, she asked him questions about when he was going to reopen the store and whether he had spoken to any new vendors or called the newspaper to start up the ad campaign his mom had been working on, and she'd even started to unpack and display the new vases and bowls from those full shipping cartons he'd pushed into the corner. She clearly believed he was going to stay and run the place himself, and because she seemed to take such comfort in his presence, he didn't have the heart to set her straight. Why didn't she spend time with one of the other storekeepers on the block? Wasn't there someone else in town who'd be only too happy to chat?

She'd taken to putting a note on her store window letting customers know where they could find her. Often it wasn't until a customer came that she pulled herself up and finally left—and yesterday no one had come for her until noon.

"You really don't have to do this, Lexy," he said. "I already had coffee. Two cups actually."

"But did you have a fresh apple-cinnamon scone?" she said, opening the white bag and pulling out two golden-brown pastries. "I don't know how Mrs. Pearl gets them like this, so flaky and crisp on the outside and so soft and mushy on the inside. It's delicious. And the funny thing is, I never liked apples before I got pregnant, but now it's my favorite flavor. Which reminds me... your mom used to have a delicious apple-cinnamon tea. Mind if I take a look at her assortment?"

"Help yourself," he said and gestured toward the tea shop, and she headed over there, taking off her coat and tossing it on a chair as she headed to the cabinet, which made it clear she intended to stay awhile. She rubbed her belly as she opened it and looked inside.

"Um... hey, yeah, here it is. It's a good brand, and I never saw it before I met your mom. She really knew how to find the most interesting vendors. And they were all so grateful that she gave them a chance. Because she looked specifically for businesses owned by women, did you know that? Or women designers, artists. Boy, she would be so excited when she found someone new to do business with. I remember when she found the woman who makes the little bowls in the glass case. She was a single mom with six kids. And your mom had this big cocktail party for the woman when she first started carrying the line. Boy, she was a real champion for women. Single moms. I guess because she was one. Did you know she was such a champion for single women?"

"Not really," he said, a little embarrassed. But he hadn't known much at all about the store growing up. It was a girly store to him, with all the jewelry and frills and fancy-smelling stuff. He knew his mom loved looking over catalogs and trying to decide what to carry. But as a kid, he mostly wanted to steer clear of the place. And the older he'd gotten, the more involved he'd become in his own activities. Debate and lacrosse team and baseball. The fundraiser for the band trip to Mexico. His stint as student-council president, when he'd run meetings to plan prom and graduation activities, and launch petitions to demand better lunch options and freedom for seniors to leave school during free periods and less homework over vacations and all kinds of things that had seemed so important back then.

And his mom had encouraged him to do it all, because she thought he was so smart and capable, and his future was so bright. He'd been the center of her universe when he was growing up. She'd focused all her hopes and efforts on him. And he'd been fine with that. Because he'd been the center of his own universe too.

When he looked back at Lexy, he saw she was rubbing her belly more intentionally now, looking down at the front of her sweater. "Boy, this little girl is up early today," she said. "Usually she doesn't get going like this until the afternoon. I'm in for a long afternoon, I can tell already."

He smiled. "A girl, huh?"

"Yup, a little girl. Gary is so excited. He wanted a little girl. You know, your mom was the first one to guess right. Although she didn't really guess. She knew. Months ago. She was amazing, the way— Oh, here it is," she said as she reached into the cabinet.

"Apple blossom honey. So delicious. I forgot about this until just now, when I was going to drink my tea."

She walked back to where she'd left the tray. "Mind if I swap it out?" she asked. "I'll take this one and replace it with the one from Mrs. Pearl's." She picked up the teabag and started to walk it back.

"You don't have to do that," Joel said. "You can keep both teabags. You can have all the teabags."

"No. You need them for the tea shop."

"I don't think so..."

"Why not? It's one of the best parts of the store. Your mom loved seeing mothers and daughters having an elegant tea. She spent a lot of money on that space. And the new countertop and cabinets she just added."

"I know," he said, thinking of the bills he'd found downstairs. "I know."

"So anyway, my friend, when are you going to do some advertising and reopen full time?" she said. "The place was never this quiet when your mom was here. Customers are fickle. You need to start luring them back."

"Um... yeah," he said, wondering if this was an opening into the discussion he was dreading to have with her. He decided it was now or never. "The truth is, Lexy, I've been thinking about this. I think I may reopen next week with a big sale. A *big* sale. And put an ad in the paper too. Because there's all this stuff to sell. I'll need to get rid of it somehow—"

"Get rid of it?" She let go of the teabag she'd been bouncing in her cup. "You mean sell it."

"Well, no. Get rid of it. The lease is up at the end of the month, you know."

"What, the landlord's not offering you another lease? That's impossible."

"It was her store," he said.

"And now it's yours."

"No, it's not," he told her. "I need to clear it out. This was my mom's space. Not mine."

"I don't even know what that means," she said. "Her space. Your space. It's a store. It's for everyone."

"That's not what I'm saying—"

"But it's so pretty. And people love it. And it belongs in this town."

"I get that," he said. "But I'm not the kind of guy who can run a pretty store."

"You can hire someone. A manager. You won't even try?"

"I have a job. I have to get back. I didn't come here to keep the place going. I came here to close it. I'm sorry. I thought you would realize that."

"But it's your mom's store. How can you just dump it? She would want you to keep it. She loved you that much. That's why she made the tea shop and did all the other things she did here. She did it to give you something to own. She would want you to stay here."

"No, she wouldn't."

"Of course she would."

"No, she wouldn't. Lexy, you don't even know her. You think you do, but you don't. She didn't run this place to hand it down to me some day."

"What do you mean? She loved you!"

"And that's why she wanted me to leave Lake Summers. She wanted me to do something bigger with my life. I'm not saying she was right, but that's how she felt. She owned this store so that I *could* leave it behind. She thought I was successful *because* I was gone."

He sighed and ran his hand along the top of his head. He didn't know why he felt he had to justify himself. Of course he wasn't going to keep his mother's store. His mother didn't want that at all. She'd told him to leave.

He went to the drawer underneath the computer and pulled out the note he'd put there, the one his mother had left him. If this was what it took to convince Lexy he was right, then he'd do it. He hated seeing her upset. She was a sweet kid. Maybe it really was the pregnancy as she'd said, or maybe she couldn't understand how his mother would be okay with shuttering her store. Maybe she loved her own store so much, she couldn't understand any other perspective. But no matter the reason, he didn't want her to be upset. He wanted her to accept all this.

He brought the note over to her. "This is the note she left me, the one she wanted you to make sure I'd read. See? It says go back. Go back. That's exactly what she wanted. Don't stay. Go back."

He watched Lexy read the note. "But what does this part mean?" she said. "'Don't believe him'?"

"I... I don't know."

"Then how can you be sure what she meant? This store was her heart."

"The store's not her heart."

"Of course it is. Look at the name of it—The Heart of Lake Summers. This store is absolutely her heart."

"No, it's not. It's just a name. It's just a store. A building. It's a place that makes money. It's time for someone else to make money here."

Lexy started to protest, then pulled back and looked around. She spotted the stack of napkins on the counter and took one. "So what's going to be here?" she asked as she wiped her eyes.

"I don't know. A camera store maybe. A shoe store—that might be good for you. You could send customers back and forth. Or a fix-it shop for electronics..."

"A fix-it shop? She wouldn't want it to be a fix-it shop. Look," she said, pointing a finger in his direction. "Don't do any big sales yet, not right yet, okay? Give me a week. Let me try to come up with the money to take over this store. Let me try—"

"You want to own this store and your store? And have a baby? And with your husband away?"

"I can't let them turn this into a fix-it shop. I just can't..."

She shook her head and looked around for a trash bin, then tucked the napkin under her sleeve. Like his mom used to do, he thought.

"I'm sorry I'm dumping on you," she said. "I'm just..." She sat down at one of the tea tables. "I mean, I'm all alone here. And your mom was the person who was here for me. I lost my mom so long ago, and with Gary gone, and his family never even liking me because they didn't think I was good enough... I depended on her."

She leaned her elbows on the table and pressed her fingertips into her forehead. He heard her sniffling. "I'm sorry. Of course you should leave the store. It's just a building. It's only a building..."

He hated to see her cry. He walked over to the table and touched her shoulder. She got up and threw her arms around his neck and sobbed.

He didn't know what to do. Her belly was so big, but somehow she was still able to press up to him, and he put his arms around her and rubbed her back. He could feel her silky ponytail under his fingers. She was like a little girl who needed comfort, and there was no one else but him to provide it. No matter how badly equipped he was.

"It's okay," he said, the only words that felt right to say. "It's okay."

"Oh God," she said, her head buried in his neck, her words muffled. "I miss her so much."

"I know. I do too. She was an amazing mom."

"I don't know how to go on without her," Lexy said. "I'm so alone. And it's like... it's like in this space, I can still feel her. It's her space, and I can feel her here. It's why I like to be here so much."

She sniffled some more, and he shuffled over to the tea-shop counter, his arms still around her back and her arms still around his neck, and pulled another napkin off the pile. "I'm sorry, I don't even know where to begin to look for tissues," he said.

"It's okay," she said and took the napkin. Then she stepped back from him and blew her nose. "I'm so sorry. Like I said, this pregnancy makes me cry at the drop of a hat."

"It's not the drop of a hat. It's someone we both miss."

"Yeah, but I barely knew her. She's your mom."

"But I haven't been home for a long time. She saw you every day."

"But you were her baby. She raised you."

"Okay, it's a tie," he said and smiled.

She laughed and tucked the second napkin up her sleeve too and then walked to where her cup of water was. "I hope it's still hot," she said and removed the lid, then dunked the teabag into it. "Not too bad," she said and sat down.

He watched her, sitting and sipping her tea. And he felt terrible, that he had made her cry, that he had let her down, that he had said things that had upset her so badly. But he had consoled her too. And that had felt right, like something maybe he could do again.

"Lexy, is there anything you want from here that I can give you?" he said. "I'm cleaning out everything. Is there anything that might make you feel better to hang on to?"

She paused, then shook her head. "No, no, that's okay," she said. "I'll be fine. I don't mean to mess with your head. I'm not family. I just... She came into the store the day that Gary left. She saw me coming into work and she knew something was wrong. She knew I needed her. And then we just became very good friends.

"She was your mother, not mine," she added. "But I really did love her."

"Well, think about what I offered," he said. "Because if you do want something, anything... even something small. The teacups or some of the jewelry... maybe one of the mirrors..."

The door opened and a woman in a cloth coat and high-heel boots peeked in. "Oh, excuse me," she said. "I was looking for the owner of the store next door?"

"That's me," Lexy said.

"Oh. Well, there's a pretty dress in the window, dark green stripes? Does that come in any other colors?"

"Oh yes, of course," Lexy said as she rose from the chair. "Yes, that's a pretty dress. I think I have it in red and yellow. I just love it..."

She took her tea and headed out with the woman, and Joel picked up the note she'd left on the tea table. *Don't believe him. Go back.* What the hell did that mean? Who was his mom talking about, this person he shouldn't believe, the person who apparently was telling him to stay? And what if his mother was wrong, and he *should* believe this mystery person? Because how could she have meant for him to leave the store—close it up and hand the keys back to the landlord, let it become a fix-it shop? How could she have meant that, if Lexy was right—if she named the store The Heart of Lake Summers because she felt it was her heart? And the truth was, he didn't want to leave. He liked working on the inn. He liked what he was doing here in Lake Summers. He liked Laurel.

And yet how could he not go back?

After all he'd done to get out in the first place?

FOURTEEN

The following Monday, with everything going well at the inn, Laurel went to pick up Simon after camp. Garrett was away in Albany visiting his grandparents, so she'd decided that morning that it was a good day to go into town. Simon's eyeglasses were loose and were sliding down his nose all the time now, so she thought they could go to the optician to get them fixed. And then maybe they'd go to Pearl's for a treat.

"Or would you rather stop at the Sweet Shop?" she said as they started walking from the school building.

Simon shrugged. "I don't know," he said. "I don't think so."

Laurel looked at him, surprised. "Something wrong?" she asked.

He shook his head.

"Are you sure? Would you tell me if there was?"

He shrugged again.

"Are you upset because Garrett wasn't there today? He'll be back tomorrow, you know."

"Mom, forget it," he said. "I have a lot on my mind."

"Okay," she said and watched him walk ahead of her. She knew he wanted to be a grown-up; he wanted to act like he had everything under control. But she wished he'd tell her what was bugging him, so that maybe she could help.

They got to Birch Street, and he started up the hill toward the inn.

"Hey, what about your glasses?" she said. "Let's head over there, and maybe you'll change your mind about the Sweet Shop. Remember how much you liked those big chunks of white chocolate last summer? And the marshmallow with the toasted crunchies—"

"Mom!" he said with his back toward her, kicking the snow in frustration. "I said I don't want to."

"You don't even want to get your glasses fixed?" she asked. "But I thought they were annoying you."

He started to kick another mound, then changed his mind and stepped back so he could take a running start and kick harder. He stood watching for a moment, and she knew he was deciding if his revised kicking strategy had made any difference. She paused and let him study the cascading snow.

"Duh," he said.

"Duh? What does that mean?"

"It means duh, they're annoying. And duh, I don't care—I don't feel like getting them fixed!"

"Okay," she said. "We'll get your glasses tightened another day, if that's what you want."

She watched him tramp along, his head down, his arms swinging slightly beside him as he scaled the hill.

"But you know, bud, it's not easy to be the new kid, if that's what the trouble is. Or be around a group with kids who know each other so well. Or be without a friend you've come to depend on." She touched his shoulder. "But Grandpa needed us to come here to help him. And that's what you do for people you love—you help them."

He shook off her arm and took a few quick steps so he'd be in front again. She sighed and followed him. It made her heart break to think that maybe he was feeling he didn't fit in. She knew how hard that was to shake. The awful feeling of being apart.

Simon headed for the cottage, then switched directions and went toward the front door of the inn.

"Where are you going?" she called.

"I left my rocks in here," he said. "I need them."

"How about a snack?" she asked. "Mavis made those donuts again, and she dropped off some sandwiches."

"I just want my rocks," he said and stormed into the inn.

She followed him into the living room, then heard footsteps and some light hammering coming from deeper in the house. A moment later, Joel emerged from the dining room, wearing jeans and a sweatshirt, a hammer in his hand.

"Good news," he said. "I think I can put the crown moldings back on. They're in good shape. Your guest left, by the way. Said he wanted to take a walk around town and see what kind of trouble he could cause."

She nodded, only half listening, as she took off her jacket and watched Simon find his rock box on the table where he'd left it. He sat down on the sofa and scooted back, then opened the box. He didn't even bother to take off his coat or his boots, and she didn't want to annoy him by suggesting that he do so.

"Hey there, Simon," Joel said. "How was your day?"

"Bad," he muttered.

"Bad? I thought you liked it there."

"I did," he said. "But not anymore. I hate it all now. I hate my teacher, I hate the playground, and mostly I hate that they're doing a play."

"They're doing a play?" Laurel asked, her ears perking up.

"The Day... Lake Summers... Lit... up... the... World!" He kicked his foot as he spat out the words.

"The what?" she said.

"The Day Lake Summers Lit up the World!" he said. "It's that whole story you told me about when the electricity went out during Christmas and everyone got together and helped out the ones who still didn't have it. And some teacher wrote, like, a play with songs about it, and now they put it on every Christmas Eve."

"And that makes you mad because…"

"Because I'm really good at narrating and I even narrated the gymnastics show at school," he said. "And they always choose a third grader to be Narrator Number 2. But the audition is tomorrow and then the play is Christmas Eve, which is only, like, six days away. And all the other kids knew about it, and I don't even have time to get ready. And Mrs. Pall isn't going to choose me because she doesn't even know me yet, so she doesn't know how good I am."

"You want to be Narrator 2?" she asked.

"Duh."

"Can we please stop with the 'duh'?"

"Narrator 2 gets to talk about the bonfire and everything," he said. "And I'm never going to get that part because I only just got here and I'm still new and I never even heard the story until you told me."

He scooted off the sofa. "I'm going, I need quiet," he said and walked out of the inn.

She watched him, then looked back at Joel, who was leaning against the wall, twirling his hammer. "Poor kid," he said. "Not easy to be the new one, I guess. But it'll get better. In a few days, I bet he'll be fine."

"Yeah. Right," she said, hearing the edge in her voice. She turned and brushed a few flakes of snow that had fallen from Simon's coat and landed on the sofa cushion. Joel was the last one she wanted to talk to about this. He didn't know what he was talking about.

"What?" he asked, and she knew he'd heard something off in her tone. "You don't think so?"

"Of course he'll be fine," she said. "Kids like him always find a way to be fine."

"Exactly. They rise to the occasion."

She smirked. "Okay."

"You don't agree?"

"No, I agree."

"Then what's wrong?"

"What's wrong is that it's not as easy as you're making it," she said. "Kids rise to the occasion because they have to. But not before they suffer a whole lot of damage."

She started to walk toward the door, but he came over and held it closed.

"Did I say something wrong?" he asked. "Because I didn't mean to. I just wanted to say something helpful—"

"No, you didn't say anything wrong," she said, pushing his hand away. "Of course you didn't say anything wrong. Because you were one of them. The popular kids, the ones who never got what the big deal was. Only someone who never felt what Simon feels could be so flip—"

"Flip? I'm not being flip—"

"And only someone who knew how it felt would know how these things stick with— Forget it," she said, and turned to go to the kitchen.

"No, what? Stick with what?"

She turned back to him. "I'm saying that you can't know what he's going through because you were never like him. You and my sisters. I'm the one who knows how he feels. Even my dad thinks I'm not as good as they are."

"What? That's not how he feels."

"How would you know?"

"Because I know how he talks about you—"

"Yeah, and what's he going to say to you—I have two daughters I'm proud of and one other one..."

"Your dad doesn't see you that way," he said. "And nobody else ever did either. I mean, you were quiet. You kept to yourself a lot—"

She started again for the door and grasped the knob. "I'm sorry, I didn't mean to get into this. I don't mean to make you listen to all this. I guess... I don't think you know what Simon's feeling. Or how long it can last."

"Laurel, you have no idea what high school was like for me."

She let go of the doorknob and turned to face him again. "Are you kidding?" she said. "The baseball hero? The head of the student council? The guy who made all the decisions, the guy who everyone wanted to be with and be like? The guy the teachers all loved so much, they fought over who got to write his college recommendations?"

"I didn't have it that easy."

"No, no. Right. Of course not." She spotted some of Simon's rocks on the floor by the sofa and went to pick them up.

"Hey, come on," he said, following her. "I didn't mean to make it sound like what Simon is going through is easy."

"I know, I know." She dropped her hands by her sides. "I'm sorry, I shouldn't be saying all this to you. But... but being here, watching Simon living in my house, going to my school, walking home on the same roads... I mean, I love it here. I love it so much. But I have some bad memories too."

She sat down on the sofa, looking at the rocks cupped in her hand. "I remember what it feels like. I know what it is to feel like an outsider. And I also remember how it felt to finally find my place."

"The theater kids?" he said.

"It's like Amy said at the ice-skating party," she said. "Those are great people. And the stage is a place where you can feel so good. So that's why it kills me, that Simon feels he's not good enough to be in the show."

Joel sat down next to her. "I didn't mean to discount what you went through. I know how much the drama club meant to you. And that's why I loved coming backstage to help out. I don't mind saying, I had a big crush on you."

She rolled her eyes. "No you didn't."

"Yes I did. You were like... addictive. I mean, everyone in that show wanted to be around you. They loved you. That's why they brought you on stage to take a bow."

She looked down. It was funny—she had felt the same way about him. She'd thought he was addictive, if that was the right word. Intoxicating maybe. Charismatic for sure. But she couldn't believe that he'd had a crush on her too. If he had, he never would have let her down the way he did. He would have been there for her.

She looked at him. She wanted to ask him about that night after the show, to ask for an explanation of what he'd done. But she couldn't. It was still so painful.

"I didn't mean to get into all this," she said. "I didn't mean to make you feel you had to cheer me up. I'm just worried about my son."

"Maybe there's something I can do," he said. "I'm not an actor or anything..."

"That's very sweet of you," she said. "Let me talk to him. I should be going there anyway to see how he's doing."

She stood and started for the door, then turned back to him. "And I probably don't say it enough, but I'm so grateful for everything you're doing around here. I really am. Oh and hey, I don't know how long you're staying tonight, but Mavis is coming over with dinner for Christopher. If you'd like something, there should be plenty. Just try to stay out of his way, okay? That's what we promised him, privacy and quiet."

Joel stood too and put his hands in his pockets. "He doesn't seem very quiet, running around town like he's doing. He's not exactly what you think. I don't... Laurel..."

"I don't think anything about him," she said. "I'm only trying to keep everyone happy."

She left the house, closing the door firmly behind her, and headed for the cottage. She didn't want to talk to Joel anymore, because being with him was bringing her to a place she didn't want to go. She shouldn't have spoken to him like that just now. She heard herself in her head—whiny, self-centered, childish. And she'd spend the rest of the evening feeling guilty, because Joel didn't deserve to be talked to like that. He was a nice guy. And he proved it, by telling her he'd had a crush on her. By telling her what he'd liked about her.

And he'd just lost his mother, he was alone trying to close up her store. The place she'd loved. He was alone, truly alone. At least she had sisters, which sometimes could be hard, especially when she felt in competition with them for their dad's affection. But then there were times like those magical nights of the Christmas power outage, when they all came together, snug by the fireplace, the way sisters should be. Laying out sleeping bags and switching on flashlights, holding them against their chins to make their faces scary while they told ghost stories. Anyone could enjoy a ghost story. Those were the times she was so grateful for her sisters. Those were the times she wished would always last.

That night she couldn't fall asleep. She hated that Simon had been quiet and distant during the evening. And she felt ridiculous for starting an argument with Joel about what had happened years ago. She hadn't meant to snap at him and make him feel bad. Because she believed he genuinely wanted the best for her.

And that's what had made her feelings so complex, back in high school. Because she'd started out disliking him, and she didn't want to change. But he'd been the one who believed in her, who got the others to vote for her as director. That's what her friends had told her. And once he'd started helping out on stage crew, he'd started paying even more attention to her. And she hadn't known how to deal with that. She'd been so angry, so resentful, of the popular kids at school and her overachiever sisters at home. How could she fall in love with someone like that?

She hadn't meant to. There was so much else to think about. She wanted the senior play, *her* senior play, to be perfect. Because her dad was coming—for the first time, he was coming to a school play. He'd never gone to the plays when she'd been on stage crew.

"Why go to a production when all she's doing is running around backstage trying to stay out of sight?" she'd overheard him say to her mom one day, when they were fixing breakfast for the guests. Her mother came to all of the plays she worked on, but her dad didn't see the point.

Then came *her* play, the play she was directing. And that was the time her dad wanted to be there.

"Wouldn't miss it," he'd told her.

And she'd loved the play she'd chosen, the quiet musical she'd discovered after poring over collections of scripts in the town library. It had reached deep in her heart. *The Not-So Hero*, about a girl who can be a superhero, who can change the world, but only for one night, and only if nobody knows. The play had had a short, sad history. It had been performed off-Broadway for only six weeks, before the theater lost its lease and shut down. The playwright had died years ago, broken-hearted because she'd never made it to Broadway. And yet the critics had loved it, and it developed a small cult following. Performances, she learned from newspaper articles, would often pop up at high schools. The rights weren't expensive to acquire. And after reading it through once, and then again because she related to the heroine so much, she'd decided she had to get it produced. Her family had to see it. Well, maybe not Tracey—she was at Stanford by then. But the rest of the family had to see it.

Her father had to see it.

So she put in as many hours as she could, casting it, staging it, running rehearsals late into the night and coming back to the stage by 7 a.m. the next morning to paint sets or figure out new ways to block scenes before her classes began. And when the night of the performance came, it was everything she'd hoped for. The actors performed with such passion that people in the audience were crying—cast members said they could hear people sniffling from the stage.

When the show was over, the cast and crew pulled her out onto the stage and everyone applauded for her, something that had never been done before with any school production. And she'd looked out onto the darkened auditorium, knowing her father was there. Knowing that he'd realize the heroine's story was *her* story, the story of only having one night to shine. *This* night. She couldn't wait to talk to him. To finally get an apology and a promise that even though she was on the brink of leaving for college, things would get better. She wondered if he'd finally give her a nickname that mattered. Something different from "kiddo."

The lobby of the auditorium was packed with people when she came around from backstage, after the curtain had gone down for the final time. Cast members still in make-up were taking pictures with their families, holding bouquets of flowers. She spotted her mom, standing next to Deb and holding out a big bouquet of pink roses, tears running down her cheeks as she pulled Laurel close to her. "I'm so proud of you," she said. "It was glorious."

Deb hugged her too. "It was amazing," she said.

Laurel took the flowers and looked around. "Where's Daddy?" she said.

"Oh honey," her mom answered. "They put Tracey on as starting center in the game tomorrow. He had to get out to California. There was only one flight tonight that would get him there in time."

"He's not here?"

"He saw the whole play," her mom had said, her forehead wrinkled, as though she didn't want to have to tell Laurel this. "He loved it. He had to run as soon as it was over. He'll call you tonight."

"He's gone?" Laurel still couldn't believe what she was hearing.

"But he saw it. He loved it. He stayed to the end."

"He left? Before he got a chance to tell me?"

"It was the only flight he could get. He couldn't miss it. But he really loved the play. He said to tell you it was wonderful. And he'll call you tonight."

She hardly noticed what happened next, so overwhelmed had she been by the pain in her chest, the huge, miserable lump that was making it hard to take a deep breath. Her dad had left without even staying to talk to her. He couldn't put her first—not even this one time.

Somehow she'd ended up at the cast party at Chuck's house. And all she wanted to do was talk to Joel. She knew he would understand how she felt, after the talk they'd had backstage a few nights before. After he had opened up so much to her, and she had listened and stroked his head. She knew he would make her feel heard. He had trouble at home too.

But he didn't show up for her, either.

And that's when she knew she had to leave home for college. She had to go far away from her family, far away from Lake Summers. She had to get out of this town. She'd never feel at home here. If she'd ever thought she would, she'd been fooling herself.

Later that night it turned extra cold, and although the heat was on full blast, the cottage felt draftier than she'd ever remembered it. She tiptoed into Simon's room and found him curled up in a ball, his head nearly under his comforter. Gently, she put the blanket from her bed over him. Then, even though it was almost one in the morning, she put on her boots and coat and headed down to the inn to get an extra blanket for herself.

She unlocked the back door that led into the sunroom, the closest one to the downstairs linen closet, so she'd make the least amount of noise, in case Christopher was sleeping.

Opening the closet door, she pulled two wool blankets from the shelf. She started to head back, then decided to take a quick look to confirm that Mavis had dropped off fresh milk and orange juice for the morning. On her way to the kitchen, she noticed Christopher in the living room, kneeling by the fireplace, a bottle of wine and a glass on the coffee table.

She looked around to see if he had a date over, in which case she'd have tiptoed out again. But nobody was there. And she was glad. She was in the mood to make contact with someone.

"You're up late," she said, walking toward him.

"Hey, hello there," he said. "Cold tonight, boy. I thought I'd make a fire. We seem to be running low on firewood. Hope it's okay that I've been making a whole lot of fires lately."

"Of course it's okay," she said. "I'll get some more firewood tomorrow. How was dinner tonight?"

"Delicious. As always. I'm very happy here at Chez Laurel," he added with a wink. "It's everything you promised."

He watched the fire blaze for a moment, and she smiled at the way the flickering light made his face glow. He stood back up, looking rugged and charming in his jeans and a gray cardigan with a shawl collar. He pointed to the table. "Would you care to join me for a glass?"

"Um..." She hesitated, torn between wanting to stay here and feeling deep inside that it would be wrong. "Um... well, no. I should get back. Simon's asleep alone back in the house. I just came out to get these blankets."

"But there's so much we have to talk about," he said. "I do need to update you about some very essential community happenings."

She laughed. "Oh? And what would those be?"

"Let's see..." He sat down on the sofa and gestured to her to sit down too. "I was at the smoothie place again and I tasted their latest," he said. "Still not great, I'm sorry to say. How do they make a smoothie with chocolate and caramel taste so bitter? Oh, and I dropped by the bathrobe place. Amy said she'll call to put a rush on our order."

Laurel shook her head, still standing. "How do you do it?"

"Do what?"

"Make yourself so at home. You're a stranger. You just got here. But you fit in like you've lived here forever." She shrugged. "Anyway, I better go. Simon's alone."

"So where was the big Sime-ster tonight anyway?" he said. "I wanted to talk to him. I met some teachers at the store, and they were saying the winter camp is doing a play about some big power outage years ago. Sounds cute—they do this short version with songs and just a few scenes so they can rehearse and put on the whole thing on Christmas Eve. I was wondering if he was going to try out."

"You heard about that?" she asked. He was really something, getting friendly with the teachers too. She wished she knew what his formula was. "He's desperate to be in it. He wants to be Narrator 2, whatever that means. But he doesn't think they'll choose him. The auditions are tomorrow, and he says a lot of kids have been preparing for a long time."

"Well, I can help him," he said. "I teach drama, you know. Maybe I can coach him a little."

"I wouldn't ask you to do that. You're a guest."

"No, it would be fun. It's the least I can do for making you stay in this absurdly cold town all December. Standing in for your so-called complicated father."

She smiled at the way he was always teasing her. "You don't really want to coach my kid, do you?"

"Absolutely I do," he said. "We'll work on it first thing tomorrow. Bring him over early for breakfast."

She paused, then nodded and headed back to the cottage, the blankets still in her arms. It felt strange, a little wrong, to be accepting this favor from Christopher. She didn't know him very well, and she wasn't sure she trusted him. But still, she couldn't get over the fact that Simon would be coached by someone who taught drama. He'd get good tips. And feel more confident. And maybe he'd even get the part he wanted. And when the play came around, he'd have his mom in the audience. Staying the whole time to be there with him when it was over.

She wanted to make sure he'd feel good about himself. Proud of himself. Comfortable.

It was the best gift she could give her son.

FIFTEEN

Early the next morning they got right to work, with Simon practicing his audition lines in between mouthfuls of oatmeal. Sipping her coffee, Laurel watched Christopher encourage him to take a breath here or lift the tone of this voice there, to give certain words more impact, or to point his finger or stretch out his arm to add variety to his performance.

Simon imitated Christopher's voice and movements—and at one point, after Christopher said he should go "bigger, *bigger*" with his gestures, he flung his arm upward so forcefully that his glasses flew off his face and under the table. The three of them laughed so hard as Simon crouched on his knees to retrieve them that they didn't notice Joel at the doorway, cradling a stack of firewood in his arms.

"Joel," Laurel said when she realized he was there. She felt bad because he had offered to help last night. Then Christopher had offered, and he'd sounded so enthusiastic, she'd taken him up on it. Now, though, she couldn't help but notice that Joel looked disappointed that the audition preparations had started without him.

She stood and walked over to him. "Come on in. Want some coffee? Maybe you can listen too and give a little feedback. Mavis should be here in a few minutes, so there'll be waffles..."

"No, thanks anyway," he said. "I have to get to the store. I'm starting a liquidation sale today. I just thought you might want some extra firewood, with the weather getting colder this week. I didn't know if you'd called for a delivery."

"Oh, hey, big guy," Christopher said, and Laurel grimaced at the belittling nickname. "Thanks. I could use a few more logs. Laurel stopped by last night and we wanted to make a fire, but we didn't have enough. Maybe tonight. Right, Laur?"

"No," Laurel said, embarrassed. What was he saying? She didn't want Joel to think she'd come here last night to be with him. She didn't want Simon to think it either. "No, I just came over for more blankets... Anyway, Simon, finish up your cereal. Garrett will be here any second. Joel, are you sure I can't get you some coffee?"

"No, just dropping this off, it's fine," he said. "I'll be back later on. The wall's almost finished."

"I can't wait to see it done," she said, following him into the living room, where he placed the wood by the fireplace. "My dad's going to love it..."

He went back through the kitchen, and she followed him again. She didn't want him to think anything was going on between her and Christopher. And even more, she wanted to apologize again for the way she'd spoken to him yesterday. "Come on, please," she said. "Let me pour you some coffee."

"No, I'm fine. Anyway, I have to get downtown. I had the wood in my truck, so I figured I'd stop here first. Good luck with the audition, Simon."

He nodded and left, and Laurel hurried Simon into his parka and through the house out to the front step, where Garrett was waiting. She stayed outside for a moment, her arms folded over her chest, the icy wind pricking her nose and ears, as she watched Joel pull around from the back of the house and start down the driveway. She gave a wave that went unreturned.

Then she walked back into the kitchen. Mavis had just come in and was starting to cook, and Christopher was standing close to her, rubbing his hands in anticipation. Laurel motioned him to come out to the living room, so she could talk to him without Mavis hearing. He grabbed a donut from the pastry dish and followed her.

"Why did you do that?" she asked.

He took a bite and licked a spot of icing off his thumb. "Do what?" he asked, searching his fingers for more stray icing.

"Say we were going to make a fire together last night."

"I don't know. I thought it was funny. What's the big deal?"

"It wasn't an appropriate thing to say in front of my son. And it was mean to Joel."

"What? You like the guy?"

"That's not the point. I don't like anyone feeling that way."

"What way?"

"Like they weren't invited or included..."

"Included? What is he, eight?"

"No. No. He's a good guy and you were messing with him."

"I was kidding around. I'm sorry, I didn't mean to make the guy feel *excluded*," he said, articulating the word, his tone derisive. "I won't do it again, if that's what you want me to say."

He shook his head. "Jeez, listen to this. It's complicated with your father, it's complicated with Joel—is there anything that's not complicated around here? Like this whole wall thing you guys are so hysterical over, all this drama over moving the wall a few inches. It's *inches*, damn it. Who the hell has time to worry about that? There's a big world out there, Laurel, and if you want to get anywhere in it, you gotta to chill. Forget the wall. It's nothing."

He dropped the donut on the coffee table and headed upstairs, and she picked up the donut pieces and then brushed the crumbs into her hand, even though the housekeeping crew would be over in a few minutes. But she didn't like leaving things. She cared about little things. She cared about shifting the wall. Very much. She did, she couldn't help it, no matter what Christopher said.

In the kitchen, she had Mavis wrap up Christopher's breakfast to reheat later. Then she poured herself another cup of coffee and sat back down at the table. She didn't know what to make of what had just happened. Christopher had complained that her life was complicated, but he was complicated too. There was the pleasing side of him—the one that held court at Amy's mother's store and bantered with the smoothie guys and got to know the teachers at Simon's camp; and then there was the nasty side—the one that called Joel "mountain man" and "big guy," and threw his donut on the coffee table. She remembered the first day he came, when he'd helped her clear the table. And now he was tossing half-eaten food around. He did what he wanted to do, that was the point. When he felt like doing it. He owned the space, whatever space he was in. She'd noticed it before—he made himself at home, wherever he was.

She was drawn to people like that. Everyone was. They were entertaining and fun to be around. There were times she'd wished she could be more that way herself.

But the thought of being that way now left her a little cold.

Because if everywhere was home, then when did you know you really were home?

And if nowhere was home, then how could you ever be happy?

She was still thinking about Christopher later that afternoon, when she drove to do some chores in town. Now that Christmas was less than a week away, the decorations were at their most glorious, and Laurel drove slowly to let the images soak into her memory.

The 200-year-old balsam fir tree outside Village Hall was blanketed with thousands of tiny lights—breathtaking, especially at this time of day, the dusky sky a perfect backdrop. Large silver menorahs stood on either side of the entrance to the Victorian-style building, their tear-shaped electric bulbs at the ready for the first night of Chanukah later this week, while traditional Kwanzaa candleholders could be seen through the building's tall windows. Across Main Street, rows of festive wreaths with bright red bows were strung from lamp posts, the sidewalks below filled with adults and kids in parkas and snow boots dashing from store to store.

Laurel took it all in, aware of how fleeting this time of year was. Then she looked ahead and noticed a huge red sign on the storefront window: **Liquidation Sale—Everything Must Go!** She felt awful about that. She'd liked Mrs. Hutcherson's store a lot. All the girls at school did. If Mrs. Hutcherson had been a house, she'd have been the Minnie Mouse house at Disney World. Soft and pink and cushy. So welcoming. A house that people would wait in line for hours to get into, if that's what it took. Because you felt so good when you finally got inside.

Laurel stared at the liquidation sign. She couldn't imagine having to shut down a place that had been a big part of her life, the way the store had been for Joel, especially at Christmas. It was the store that allowed his mother, a single mom, to give Joel everything he had. A store could be so much more than a place you went to buy things, she thought. Just as an inn could be so much more than a place where people spent the night.

Of course, maybe not everyone felt that way. It took a certain type of person to understand how bricks and mortar could be so much more than bricks and mortar. Maybe Christopher wouldn't think that way. Maybe her sisters wouldn't either—maybe that's why they said they'd be fine if Dad decided to sell the inn. But her mother had felt that way. And she did. And Joel did too. She knew he did. Just from the things said that night they talked backstage as they built scenery for the play. Just from the way he had made the backstage area his home that night—a place where he could open his heart to her. She knew that closing his mother's store had to be killing him. And that his way of coping was to come to the inn. To drop off firewood and do odd jobs. And make a better-spaced kitchen for her father. Sometimes shifting a wall a few inches was nothing, like Christopher said. But sometimes it was everything. It was what helped you hang on.

That afternoon, Simon came home with the happy news that he was cast as Narrator 2 in the play after all. "I'm it! I'm it!" he'd exclaimed as he came tearing through the front door of the inn, hurling his backpack onto the couch and then running circles around it, stopping every few moments to thrust his arms into the air and shout "Naaaaaaaaaarrator! Naaaaaaaarator!" as Laurel, who'd been paying bills at the reception desk, stood to clap and cheer. The truth was, she wasn't all that surprised he'd been given the role. The more she thought about it, the more she'd come to expect Mrs. Pall would give him the part. What better way to help a kid make friends and grow more comfortable in a new setting than to make him a central part of a group project?

"Where's Christopher? I have to tell him! Where's Christopher?" he cried.

"I think he's still at work."

"I have to go learn my lines! Come get me as soon as he gets home! I have to go learn my lines!"

"Can I at least give you a congratulations hug?"

"No! I'm too busy!" he said and ran out the front and off to the cottage.

She paused for a moment after the door slammed shut. She understood why Simon would want to see Christopher. But she wanted to share the news with Joel. She'd been thinking a lot about that moment yesterday when he'd told her he'd had a crush on her in high school. She hadn't responded, except to basically accuse him of joking, because her mind had been on Simon. But it was a nice thing to hear. And it validated all her feelings from that night long ago, all the closeness she had sensed but they'd never talked about. And now it felt cruel, that she'd brushed him off when he'd said that. She'd been so caught up in her own frustration and worries. But he had a lot on his mind too. And she hadn't let him see that she understood what he was feeling. That she could be someone he could connect with.

Five days of intensive play rehearsals began on Wednesday for the Christmas Eve performance. Mrs. Pall had written an email to the parents of all the kids in the play, asking them to pack extra-large snacks for the week, as the rehearsals would go straight through to 7 p.m., with a break for pizza supplied by a different parent each day.

Laurel tried to stay busy without Simon around in the afternoons. There was plenty to do—the invoices from all the vendors were coming in, and she had orders to place for heating oil and beverage deliveries, and even though Christmas was just a few days away, there were still emails to send and phone calls to return for Joanna. In the back of her mind, she knew that her dad would also be arriving home on Christmas Eve. And while she was anxious to finally learn what was going on with him and why he had disappeared so suddenly, a piece of her—a large piece—was excited to show him how well she'd managed the inn in his absence. She hoped he'd be delighted with the improvements she'd made. Even now as an adult with a son of her own, she still wanted her dad to be proud of her.

She turned again to her computer screen. But it was hard to get motivated. She hoped Joel would drop by, despite the way she'd talked to him about Simon, and despite the joke Christopher had made when Joel brought in the firewood. She didn't think he'd want her to come into the store. She didn't think he'd want her to see customers going through his mom's stuff, trying to bargain him down a few cents here, a dollar there. He was proud. She just had to wait for him to return. The tarp was still up in the kitchen. And that gave her hope that he'd be back. He'd have to be.

On Saturday, it was her turn to pick up the pizza. Thinking she'd kill two birds with one stone, she grabbed Simon from rehearsal in the afternoon for a quick trip to get his glasses tightened—it wouldn't do for them to come flying off his face in the middle of his performance, the way they had in the kitchen with Christopher. Then they both went to Sal's to pick up dinner for the cast. She came home after dropping Simon and the pizza off at the school and was happy to hear footsteps in the dining room. She went in to see Joel taking down the tarp.

"All done," he said as he scrunched up the plastic and stuck it into the large trash bag.

"Oh, wow," she said, having no better way at the moment to express her surprise and amazement. The wall was complete, the chandelier was moved, the ceiling was painted, and the floor was perfectly polished.

She walked through the doorway and into the kitchen, which was also perfect, the wall also painted, and the cabinets reinstalled. It was hard to say exactly what had changed. The place just looked roomier. More welcoming, more open. It was remarkable, what he had done. How much he had transformed things with such a small change.

"It's perfect," she said.

"Not too shabby," he agreed. "It's subtle, but your dad will notice it. Every time he slides his chair back from the table."

He started back for the dining room to finish putting away his tools, and she followed him.

"Joel, I'm really glad you came by," she said. "Thanks for all your concern about Simon. I'm sorry if I sounded harsh the other night."

He shrugged. "Look, you're worried about your son. I get that. I'm in no position to tell you that he'll be fine or whatever."

He kneeled down to pack up his tool kit, and she found herself looking at his hands, so strong and so capable. His black sports watch encircled his wrist, embracing it, and it made her think of a hug, the kind that stemmed from a place of warmth and a desire for closeness. She hadn't known that looking at a watch strapped to a wrist could be so intimate, but suddenly she was both drawn to and frightened by the depth of her feelings. She wanted nothing more than to reach out and touch his wrist, hold his hand, feel his fingers on her face, her skin. She wanted to lean up against him, to feel his chest against her. It was the same way she'd felt backstage that night so many years ago, the two of them all alone. And she was mad at herself for pushing him away the other night. Because she now realized that all she'd wanted ever since she'd first seen him on the driveway a few weeks ago was to hold him as close as she could.

"No, I was wrong," she said, kneeling beside him to help. She picked up a screwdriver and put it in the box. "I shouldn't have been so defensive. Because you know what? After all that rigama-role, he got the part he wanted, and he's perfectly happy now."

"That's great. Really," he said, snapping the toolbox shut. "Do you think he'd like me to come to the show?"

"I know he would," she said, thrilled that he'd want to. "We can go together, if you'd like."

She stood and rubbed her fingers along the smooth finish of the dining-room table.

"And I'm sorry, too, about the way Christopher spoke to you the other morning," she added, her gaze focused on her fingers. She felt vulnerable and couldn't bring herself to look him in the eye. "And the stupid things he said. I didn't come here to sit by the fireplace with him. I would never have done that. Not at all. Especially not with Simon sleeping by himself in the cottage."

"I know that," he said.

She heard him come stand beside her.

"And I should have said something," she told him, still looking down. "I shouldn't have let him get away with that. Not while you were there."

"It's not your job to police him, Laurel," he said. "I can handle it. I can handle a guy who's a jerk."

"He's not a jerk," she said. "That's the thing. He can be very nice. But he sees things differently. He doesn't get us. Me—he doesn't get me. Why all this"—she pointed to the wall—"why all this, this whole place, means so much to me. Why I left New York at a moment's notice to take care of this place."

"It's because of your dad," Joel said. "You came back to do your dad a favor. There's nothing hard to understand about that. At least there shouldn't be."

"No, it was bigger than that," she said. Then she looked at him. "Are you hungry? Want something to drink? Want to sit?"

"I'm good," he said. "But sure. I'll sit. Sure."

He smiled his wide smile, and she was glad he agreed to stay. She led him into the living room, which was getting dark, the sun through the window almost below the horizon, the space lit only by a single table lamp and the glow of the lights on the Christmas tree by the fireplace. Looking outside, she could see the golden spotlights from the ground shining upward, making the blanket of snow on the lawn sparkle and showcasing the flurries dancing in the air. The wind made the slightest of whooshing sounds, sweet and soft. The inn felt hushed and still, as though it were miles and miles away from anyone or anything else. As though she and Joel were the only two people on earth.

She sat down on the sofa, and he sat close next to her. He smelled like woodwork and sawdust and balsam, a delicious blend of scents she'd known all her life.

"You're right, I came back because my dad needed me," she said. "Because he called me and told me I had to get up here. And I guess it bothered me that he just took off without any explanation. And that he leaned on me, and not my sisters. I guess I was annoyed at first."

She paused for a moment. "But when you come right down to it, I guess I'm glad he called," she said. "Because my career wasn't going anywhere. I've been working for Joanna for six years, and I finally realized she's never going to give me a client of my own. I'm never going to be anything other than an assistant in her eyes. I guess I've been fooling myself that maybe one day she would."

She looked around at the fireplace and the fresh stack of wood Joel had brought, and at the Christmas tree too—with the multicolored lights she'd found among some old decorations in the basement and put back in their rightful spot, taking down the plain white ones. "But you know something? It's felt good to be here," she said. "It's felt good to pull the place together a bit, thanks to you mostly, and to be a good host to Christopher and do everything that needs to be done to keep an inn running smoothly. And I've done it well, and I'm good at it. And I have good ideas too.

And it's turned out to be a gift, my dad calling me up here. A real gift."

He smiled at her. "Maybe your dad called you instead of your sisters because he knew you could handle it."

She tilted her head. "You think so?"

"I know so," he said. "He told me all about you and Simon, what a nice life you had made for your son, how you were working so hard for a very successful designer. He was proud of you."

She looked down, drinking in those words. "And it's been wonderful having you here," she said. "You saw in this place the same things I did, the flaws and the problems, but the beauty too. And I feel like it means something to you. I'm..." She held her breath, trying to figure out exactly what she wanted to say. "I'm glad we got to spend time together again."

"Me too," he told her.

"And I'm grateful, too, about what you did for Simon," she said. "Teaching him how to use a hammer and a level and everything." She smiled. "Catching him when he almost fell at ice skating. It's so good for him to be around a guy he can look up to. He doesn't talk much about it, but he's always had a lot to deal with. Like a dad who abandoned him before he was born."

"I didn't know that," Joel said. "I'm sorry."

"He was my professor when I went back to school for, like, half a minute to get a teaching degree," she said. "The minute I told him I was pregnant, he took off. But it's not as hard as you'd think. Simon's the best thing that ever happened to me. You know, it's funny, you see parents and kids all over the place—you'll be in a store or at the movies, and you'll see a mom walking and the kids lined up behind her, following her, because they believe she knows where they're going and they know to follow her. And I know Simon would follow me anywhere. And I want to be worthy of that trust."

She rubbed her forehead with her fingertips. "Here I go again. Talking about myself. I'm sorry. How are you doing? How's it going with the store?"

"Not bad. The sale started."

"I know. I saw the sign."

"Yeah. It's hard. Seeing people pick over all the stuff she cared so much about. She loved that place. So much more than the house, which she never really liked, because my dad built it, before he left her. I'm starting to think things will get easier when I finally leave."

"So you're leaving soon?" she said.

He nodded. "I have to. I have a job waiting for me. But it's okay. It's been hard being back, with so much I don't understand. She was so sick, why didn't she do something? She had people to live for. She had me, and she had Lexy, who really needed her. And she had your dad. They were friends too."

"Maybe she didn't realize how bad it was."

"How do you not realize you have a serious infection that needs to be treated? How do you not know that it hurts because your body is fighting an infection that's raging..." He raised his hands in surrender. "It doesn't make sense."

"No, it doesn't," she said.

"She never wanted me to come back," he told her. "That's the thing. She never wanted me here. She thought it was too limiting, that's what she said. A kid like me, I had to do bigger things. But the thing is, it's a great town. I like it here. I always did. What the hell am I supposed to do with that? When all she wanted was for me to get out." He shook his head. "It's just a store. I keep telling myself that it's just a store."

"But you know it's not," she said. "You know... that..."

She looked down into her lap. And when she looked back up, Joel was right there. And they were together in the darkened room, with only a single, tiny table lamp glowing. Just like they'd been that night backstage, next to the revolving platform he had finally finished. Except now he was looking up, not down into his hands. Now he was looking right into her eyes. Which emboldened her. She was different now, a different person than she'd been back then. She could take a risk. She could follow her heart.

She reached over and took his face into her hands. And she felt his arm move around her waist, felt his face coming closer, felt his lips find her forehead, felt his hand reach around her neck. She lifted her chin so her lips met his, warm and thick...

"I think..." she said. "I think we have to find a way to connect..."

The back door clanged open, followed by footsteps in the kitchen. The kitchen light switched on. "Honey, I'm home!" a voice called. "What's for dinner?"

Laurel pulled back from the embrace. "It's Christopher," she said. "He parks in the back and comes in through the kitchen."

"Where's the little woman?" he called again. "When I get home from work, I expect dinner on the table!"

She saw Joel's jaw tighten, and she feared she'd lose everything if she didn't convince him to ignore Christopher's antics.

"He's just fooling around," she said. "He can be very silly sometimes."

"Yeah, he's a real joker, that guy," Joel said. Then he took her hands in his. "Laurel. Laurel, I need to tell you—"

"Anyone home?" Christopher called.

Laurel stood, her hands slipping out of Joel's. "Coming!" she called. Then she turned back to him. "I'm sorry. He didn't tell us when he was coming home, so Mavis left his dinner in the fridge. I should get in there and help him. Oh, and it's late," she added, looking at the clock. "I'm going to have to get Simon from school as soon as I help Christopher..."

Joel stood and reached for his coat on her dad's armchair. "I'll let you get on with your evening."

"No, wait," she said. "Did you want to tell me something?"

"It was nothing."

"Are you sure?"

He nodded and went to the front door. "You have things to do. We'll talk another time. I have to come back anyway, for my tools and stuff. I'm glad you like the wall."

"Laur?" Christopher called.

"Coming," she repeated, more softly this time, as she stood for a moment and watched Joel step outside. And suddenly she hoped Christopher was serious about being able to help her find a theater job in New York.

Because Joel was leaving.

And she didn't want to be here in town without him.

SIXTEEN

Sunday came, and Simon could hardly contain his excitement. Since he didn't have to be at the school until ten, Laurel decided to give him a big hot breakfast at the cottage and then walked him down to the end of the driveway to meet Garrett. The cast was staying at the school through the evening performance, so she told the boys to break a leg—Garrett was playing the part of the mayor of Lake Summers—and she'd see them at the cast party in the multi-purpose room after the show.

"I'm so proud of you!" she said, giving Simon a big kiss on the cheek, despite his efforts to squirm away. "I cannot wait to see you on stage!"

She watched the boys take off, then turned around and went back to the cottage, avoiding setting foot in the inn. Even though she knew Christopher had promised Simon he'd come to the school that night to see the play, she didn't want to run into him that morning. She felt embarrassed that she'd been embracing Joel on the sofa last evening when Christopher came in. Christopher hadn't seen them together, but he could have, if he'd walked through the kitchen faster or come in through the front door. Not that she'd done anything wrong by kissing Joel. She was a grown woman and could kiss anyone she wanted. But she'd been cultivating an image of herself with him these last few weeks—independent, strong, invulnerable. And it bothered her to think that she wasn't that way at all. That she was lonely, as Amy said. That she was still capable of falling in love with Joel. And potentially being abandoned by him again.

And she was embarrassed too—no, angry—about the way Christopher had called to her when he walked into the kitchen: *Honey, I'm home! Where's the little woman?* Yes, he was making a joke about how close they'd become, how intertwined their lives were, since he arrived. But still, it wasn't respectful. He was a visitor, a customer, not some husband from a 1950s sitcom. Her mother had been right to set boundaries, to be warm and welcoming but always to keep her relationship with her guests more professional than personal. Laurel used to think this was entirely for the guest's comfort, that being deferential was how her mom made guests feel important and appreciated. But now she saw that in treating guests the way she did, her mother had been showing that she respected herself too. She was showing that she valued herself as much as she valued anyone coming to stay.

She straightened up around the cottage and checked in with Mavis and the housekeeping agency by phone, then called the woman from the plant shop to bring over some additional poinsettias, to make the place especially festive for her dad's return later that night. Next, she returned some phone calls to the inn's reservation line to confirm summer bookings, and then decided to spend the afternoon at the library researching textile ideas for her mother's ballroom—which, having seen her mom's notebook, she was increasingly determined to complete. The newly expanded kitchen provided great sunlight and a comfortable place to look at images of drapes and chair cushions and table linens on her computer, but still, she wanted to spend the whole day away from the inn. It wasn't only that she didn't want to see Christopher; she also didn't want to risk running into Joel, who would no doubt be coming back at some point to gather up his toolbox and the rest of his supplies. She didn't know how to deal with him, knowing how drawn she'd been to him last night. Knowing he'd soon be leaving town again.

She packed up her laptop and her mother's notebook—fortunately, she'd brought both to the cottage with her a few days ago—and then got in her car and headed downtown.

It was peaceful at the library, and the hours passed quickly. She loved the romantic pastels and soft floral patterns she found online, many of which reflected her mother's taste and would be so perfect for showers and weddings, a wonderful complement to the inn's vast and scenic backyard, gorgeous no matter the season. She bookmarked websites of textile designers she liked and took screenshots of her favorite fabrics, so she could see them again and continue to be inspired by how they made her feel.

She worked at the library a little while longer, stopping only to have a quick sandwich at the small coffee shop off the lobby, and at a little after four, she gathered up her things and went back to her car. She wanted to wear something nice for the play tonight, and she needed to see what Christopher's plans were—if he would make his way to the school's auditorium on his own, or if he was expecting to go with her and Joel.

On her way home, she decided to make a stop at Pearl's. It would be nice to bring back some of Pearl's famous cupcakes so they could all have a little celebration with Simon after they got home.

Inside, a group of people were gathered at a large round table. Most she didn't recognize, but Amy was there, and Stan too, along with some of her dad's pals. They were all focused on a sheet of paper on the table, and it was impossible not to hear their conversation.

"Yes, it is."

"I don't think so."

"Why would he come all the way up here?"

"He was trying to hide out. That's the whole point."

"Wait, look, there's Doug's daughter," one of her dad's friends, Russ, said. "She'll know."

Laurel stamped off her boots and went to the table. "What's up?"

"We have a question," Stan said as he rotated the screen to show her the article they were all examining. "Russ's niece in New York emailed this."

"She writes for *The Daily News*, and it seems there's a Broadway actor who's gone missing," Russ said. "And rumor has it he's somewhere here in the Adirondacks. My niece found this little piece and is determined to break the story wide open, and she asked if I'd seen any interesting strangers lately. And then I remembered the guy who's staying at the inn."

"And I think that's ridiculous," Stan said. "Why would he pick Lake Summers?"

"Why not?" Russ said. "If it could be any town, why wouldn't it be this one?"

"And he does kind of look like the guy who's staying with you," another of her dad's friends, Mickey, said. "Even though this picture is kind of hard to make out. Maybe your guy is just pretending to be a teacher over in Lyons Hills."

"So we've got some friendly bets riding on it," Stan said. "You must know. Is this the guy?"

Laurel looked at the article and the picture, and she knew right away—it was definitely Christopher. There it was, everything she'd seen the moment he'd walked into the inn: his thin nose, his narrow eyes, that straight posture. The guy in the photo had a full beard, while Christopher was clean-shaven, and he was wearing a cap in the photo, so his golden-brown hair wasn't visible. But even so, she recognized him immediately.

And then she moved the page closer, so she could skim the article.

Leading Man in *Orange Nightsongs* Reportedly Hiding Out

Christopher Rhodes, rumored to have been cast as the lead in the upcoming Broadway musical *Orange Nightsongs*, is in hiding, according to industry insiders.

The future star was linked previously to model Carolina Messey, but that relationship is believed to have ended. Producers are reportedly concerned about the disappearance, although some believe that he has squirreled himself away deep the Adirondacks in the hope that he can get some real-life experience that will help him with his upcoming role.

A relative unknown, Rhodes is expected to originate the role of Maxwell, a young man who leaves the city and begins teaching at a rural school following the murder of his sister. Producers decided to tap him for the role when they saw him in *Sweeney Todd* at Berkshire Rep in Lee, Mass., last summer, according to theater insiders.

"He's quite charismatic," one person familiar with the production said. "He's definitely got star quality."

At least one West Coast agent, who asked not to be identified, mentioned that Rhodes is already under consideration for several upcoming Hollywood projects.

Rhodes did not return calls made to his New York City apartment.

Keeping her face expressionless, Laurel stared at the page. She could hardly believe what she was reading. So this was who Christopher really was? And he'd been lying to her all this time? She bit her bottom lip, trying to stay calm. She'd grown to like him; they'd become friends, at least up until recently. And it had all been an act?

And yet, a part of her wondered if she had any right to be angry. He'd made it clear all along that he wanted some peace and quiet. He'd asked her about her life, he'd admired her sketches of the ballroom, and he'd encouraged her to aim for a job where she could display her true talents. She supposed he deserved a chance to explain. She thought the only right thing to do now was to guard his secret. And to give him the opportunity to tell her the truth.

"Wow, a real Broadway star," a woman in the crowd said. "I wish I had known when I saw him at the store with the bathrobes."

"Not just Broadway," someone else added. "Hollywood too."

"Think if we keep his secret, he'll get us all tickets to the premiere?" Russ said. "Or maybe introduce me to Carolina Messey?"

The others laughed, but Laurel shook her head. "I hate to disappoint you all," she said, "but that's not the guy staying at my inn."

"It isn't?" Mickey said. "Are you sure? It looks an awful lot like him. His name's Christopher too."

"There are a lot of Christophers in the world," she said. "And his last name is different. Sorry, everyone."

The people shrugged and sighed and started going about their business. Her dad's pals gathered at another table to finish their coffee, while some other customers went up to the counter to place their orders. Laurel followed them. She wanted to speak to Christopher right away, but she didn't want to attract attention by rushing out.

When it was her turn, she ordered a half-dozen cupcakes and a small decaf coffee, then took her time pouring in some milk and sugar. She stirred the coffee, looking around the shop as she did. Everything was looking normal, so she thought it was safe to leave. She was confident that she'd helped Christopher dodge a bullet. Now she wanted to go home and find out exactly what was going on.

She left the shop and made her way back to her car. She didn't like lying to people—not strangers, not her dad's friends, and not her own friends, like Stan and Amy. But she thought it was the right thing to do, for now. Maybe Christopher had a good reason for hiding out. And maybe she could convince him to come clean, so she wouldn't have to lie for him any longer. But how would he justify what he'd done, winning her trust the way he had? It was crazy, how often she'd been betrayed or disappointed by men she thought cared about her—Joel in high school, Simon's dad, her own dad, and now Christopher. Why was she always putting herself in the path of someone who would let her down? What was she doing wrong?

She went down the street and started to get into her car when she felt a tug on her elbow. She turned around to see Stan and Amy. She could tell by their expressions that they knew the truth. They knew she'd been covering for Christopher.

Stan was holding the article out, and he shoved it into her hand.

"They're going to start looking at social media," he said. "Nobody's going to believe this for long."

Amy nodded. "I don't know what his story is. But if he really needs to hide out, he'd better leave. And soon."

Back at the inn, Laurel parked the car and went inside. Christopher wasn't home, so she put the article Russ had found on the coffee table, then brought the cupcakes into the kitchen. She took her computer and her mother's notebook out of her bag and put both on the counter. Then she changed her mind—there'd be people around tonight and some messy cupcakes being eaten, and she didn't want anything to happen to the notebook.

She brought it over to the junk drawer and started to slip it inside. But then she noticed a business card for a jewelry store in Lyons Hill, which had evidently been beneath her mother's notebook. It was a beautiful card, a tea-stain color, with a romantic, slender vine of pink roses curving down one side and along the bottom. The typeface was an ornate script, full of generous swirls and curlicues.

But it was the handwriting along the top of the card, rough but familiar from as far back as high school, that most stood out to her:

This is the place with the engagement rings. Congratulations to you and Katie! Looking forward to the wedding!

Joel

Laurel read the note again and again, six or seven times at least. It didn't make any sense. But then, suddenly, it did. Her dad and Katie were together... and they were getting married. There was no other explanation. And they were probably away together right now—hadn't Mavis said that Katie was away this month too? But why hadn't her dad told her? Why did he have to keep it a secret? Didn't he think she deserved to know?

That's when another realization hit her—one that felt even worse. There it was, Joel's named signed to the note. Joel had known about the engagement this whole time! Her father had confided in him about buying Katie an engagement ring—and Joel had recommended a jewelry store. And yet he'd stayed quiet all these weeks, while she'd taken over for her dad at the inn. And wondered why he had brought her here. And what on earth he was hiding.

Now Christopher's deception paled in comparison. Because Christopher was a stranger, someone she'd just met. Joel was someone she'd known forever. And he'd been so kind and generous —helping out at the inn, taking so much interest in Simon, telling her he'd liked her in high school, making her put aside all the hurt he'd caused her so long ago. She'd started to care for him again, she'd started to trust him. Not just that—she'd started to fall in love with him. Just like she had in high school. Before he let her down.

She walked into the living room and sat on the sofa, her back straight and her arms crossed over her chest, to wait for him to show up to head to Simon's play.

So she could tell him, once and for all, to get the hell out of her life.

SEVENTEEN

"I want him gone," Joel said into the phone, standing in the center of his store, surrounded by bright red signs that said **75 percent off!** and **Everything must go!** He kicked an empty shipping box out of his way as he paced to and from the window, the street growing empty in the late-afternoon light. It had taken him all day and several messages to get Meg to call him back, and he was nearly out of his mind. He couldn't shake Christopher's smug tone from last night out of his head: *Honey, I'm home! What's for dinner?*

"I'll drive him anywhere you want," he added. "I'll pay for a hotel. But he has to leave."

"What?" Meg said. "What on earth are you talking about?"

"You heard me," he answered. "I want him gone. Find him a new place. He's got to get out."

"Are you crazy? He's happy," she said. "He likes it there. He's not going anywhere. What's wrong with you?"

"He's making trouble. And someone's going to get hurt."

"Who's going to get hurt?"

"The innkeeper. The one he's staying with."

"Your old school friend? The daughter of the owner? He says

they're getting along fine. He likes the kid. He said he's helping the kid with some play."

"Exactly. He's pretending he's someone he's not. He doesn't belong in a small town getting involved with the people. Look, she's being nice to him. It's not right that he's deceiving her." He stood still for a moment, hearing his words again. It killed him that he was deceiving Laurel too. But he was doing it for her father, and he had every intention of apologizing and explaining his behavior as soon Doug returned. Christopher had no such intentions.

"Joel, you're acting like a child," Meg said. "What is it? Do you like this girl or something?"

"It's not that—"

"You're like a little boy who's worried his girlfriend's going to prom with someone else. Look, this is between them. It has nothing to do with you."

"Yes, it does. I'm watching him lie to her."

"Technically, he's not lying. He never claimed not to be an actor."

"What? That's ridiculous."

"Well, maybe it is. But he asked me to find him a quiet place to hang his hat, and you're the one who suggested Lake Summers. And I spoke to him last week, and he's feeling much better about his break-up with that model and much less stressed about the new show. Look, he's been a major headache in my life, so I'm not going to risk sending him into a tailspin again. They're going to make the announcement on New Year's. There's already been some leaks in the New York papers. Cousin, take it easy. It's Christmas Eve already. This is only going on for another week."

"Meg, I'm not letting you off the phone until you tell me—"

"Look, I know you're upset," she said. "I know it's hard having to liquidate your mother's store. Just leave it all for now. Come to St. Thomas for a few days."

"I don't have time for that. I have to be back in Singapore soon. Look, I'm just telling you, it's not right, what he's doing to her—"

"Nobody cares about him or his deceptions except you! He'll

be out of there soon, and she won't even remember him. Now take it easy. If you're in love with your friend, then tell her. Don't let Christopher get in the way—"

"No, it's not that. I'm not in love with— Okay, look, just let it go. Forget it. I'll talk to you before I head out of the country."

"But Joel—"

"You're right, okay? You're right. It'll all work out. Say hi to Reed and the kids. I'll call you soon."

He hung up, staring at the phone for a few moments. Then he sighed and looked around the store. It was far emptier than it had been earlier in the week. The sale had worked, and while the store had been packed yesterday and the day before, it was quieter today, with so little merchandise left. He was glad that things had moved fast. The landlord had called last night to complain that the liquidation sign was unsightly and cheapened the look of the building. He'd asked Joel to take it down, and Joel had agreed. He could only imagine how crushed his mom would be if she could see the way her store looked now, with red sale signs all over the place, and her carefully chosen and arranged vases and bracelets and pillows strewn all over the countertop and along the shelves. And on Christmas Eve, of all days. But he had no choice. The lease was up and he was leaving soon.

And so was Laurel. It was asinine, that they'd allowed themselves to get close last night, and it was good that they'd been interrupted, even if it was Christopher who'd done the interrupting. Because Laurel was leaving too. She was heading back to New York. They'd both just returned home to take responsibility for places their parents had built up and loved once upon a time. This had always been a temporary stop for both of them. And at least they both had something positive to show for it, he thought. Laurel had fixed up the inn, and he'd built her father a new wall.

And that's what was killing him now, he thought. He wasn't meant to break things down, tear them apart. Not stores. Not inns. Not even companies, the way he'd been doing all his adult life, the way he'd be helping to do again once he returned to Singapore. He was meant to build things. He was a builder.

He was a builder. And Laurel was too. They made things, they built things, they designed things. It was who they'd always been. They were meant to be here together, creating things. That's why it bothered him so much to be going. He wanted to stay and build something meaningful—maybe even a life with her. Maybe that's what he'd been working toward from the moment he first saw her on the driveway with Simon. But he was leaving, and he needed everything to be out in the open before he left. He needed Doug to come home and tell Laurel everything, so that he could explain why he'd hidden her father's secrets. And apologize for it before he took off.

It was starting to snow when he heard the door open and a jingle ring out. He looked up to see Lexy walking in, wearing her beanie hat and carrying a bag from the Sweet Shop.

"I'm going to crush that damn bell," he muttered.

"Why? It's sweet," she said as she stamped her feet on the mat. "I like that sound. Your mom also usually had a candle going. So the place sounded nice and smelled nice too. Anyway, I'm ready to dig into some chocolate, and I'm hoping you'll join me so I don't scarf them all down..."

"Thanks, no," he said. "Look, you really don't have to come by anymore. I'm almost done here."

"It's okay, I left a note on my door like always. Boy, if I hadn't had your mom to speak to last fall, I'd have been plenty worried. But she warned me that sales slow in the winter, so I didn't need to worry at all. Because I had a great season last summer. It's so funny, how mostly in retail they tell you that you have to make all your money at Christmas, right? But for me, the seasons are opposite. We did a crazy big business all summer. Fall was good too. Not as good as summer, but very good—"

"Lexy, what do you need?"

"Nothing. I just want to help. Try a chocolate. There's caramels and almond clusters." She pulled out a piece and popped it into her mouth. "Wow. So good. So anyway— Hey, look at this," she said, picking up a small, mirrored box from one of the display shelves. "A make-up kit. I helped her choose these. She bought a dozen, I think—and wow, there's only one left? They sold well. So anyway, what can I do? Anything you want me to unpack—"

"No. There are no more boxes left. You should go—"

"But don't you see?" she said. "I feel better when I'm here. It wasn't just her heart, this store. It was my heart too. Because she was here.

"And it's Christmas Eve," she said. "Can't I stay and help you?"

He walked over to the tea corner and sank down in a chair. Of course Lexy wanted to stay, of course she wanted to help. She was alone. And it was Christmas Eve. And she was looking for a home. The feeling of home that she'd lost with the loss of his mother.

"Yeah, okay," he said. "Look, I'm still trying to make sure I've found all her invoice records and bills. I know she didn't do it all electronically. Could you maybe go downstairs and see if you can find any other paperwork in that cabinet downstairs? Can you handle the steps?"

"Can I handle the steps? Of course. I'm pregnant, I'm not lazy. I'm on it, boss!"

She headed downstairs, and Joel leaned back, his elbow on the armrest of the chair. He would be sorry to leave this place. He liked what he'd been doing these past few weeks—not the liquidation sales but the rest. He liked Lexy—she was sweet and funny and so willing to show how much she needed connection. And he cared about the people in town—the old-timers like Doug and his pals, and Maxine and Gull, and the newer ones, like the smoothie guys, who'd moved in just before he'd visited town six years ago.

And he cared about Laurel. Most of all, he cared about Laurel.

He pushed his feet on the floor, making his chair swivel a little in one direction, a little in the other. How different his life would have been if he had stayed in town all these years, instead of living in fancy houses and luxury apartments in some of the most exciting cities in the world. And never finding a home in any of them. Not like the inn that was always home to Laurel. Or this shop, which had become such a loving home to Lexy. He might have liked to build a life here for himself.

He got up from the chair and went back to the counter to look again at the note his mother had left for him. *Go back. Don't believe him.* Would he ever know what that meant?

He started to put it down—but then he looked back again. The handwriting was really jagged. He looked closer at the message. *Don't believe him.* And he could see now there was something very strange about that word "believe." It didn't really look like believe at all. The first "e" wasn't attached to the rest of the word. And there was something strange about the "ev" at the end. The "e" was more of a smudge than a letter, and the "v" was the wrong size, too tall. He lifted the note closer to his eyes. And then he saw it. The note didn't say "Don't believe him"; it said "Don't be like him."

"Don't be like him." Now it all made sense. She didn't want him to be a builder. Like his dad. Because his dad had been cruel to her. His dad had left her.

But how could she think that he'd be like his dad simply if he had the same job? Didn't she realize? No matter what he chose to do with his life, he could never be like his dad. Because *she* had raised him. She had taught him everything he knew. The most important lessons he knew. With the way she'd devoted her life to him. She had taught him all about love.

Just then the bell over the doorway jingled again, and he looked up to see the last person in the world he wanted to see.

"Hey, look who's here?" Christopher said, walking toward him. "I didn't know you worked here. Look at you, a man of many talents."

"What are you doing here, Chris?" Joel said.

"It's Christopher. And I came here because I heard there was a sale. I want to get Simon something. A little gift to congratulate him on the show."

Two women had walked into the store after Christopher, and he went over to them at the pottery display.

"Ladies, hi," he said. "I could use some advice. I'm a teacher, so I don't know much about these things, but I'm looking for a little gift for one of the kids who's in the play at school tonight. I know there's not a whole lot for a little boy here. But what do you think he'd like? Maybe the set of colored pencils? Or the corkboard? Or maybe that fun little clock with the wizard hat? What do you think?

"Ladies, ladies," he called over to two more women who had just come in. "I'm conducting a little poll. Show of hands, which is the better gift?"

Joel watched him carry on. It was the same schtick he'd heard about at the linens store when he and Laurel were shopping for bathrobes. Why did he get such a kick out of being the center of attention? Whatever the reason, it didn't matter, Joel thought. Because he was going over the line. By lying to everyone. By lying to Laurel. He was no teacher. He was taking all of these people for fools.

He watched Christopher finish his little show, then thank the women and head over to the counter. "Looks like the wizard clock is the big winner," he said. He put it down on the counter. "How much?"

"Just take it," Joel said. "Okay? Take it and leave."

"What? Why?" Christopher said. "I want to pay. How much is it?"

"Forget it, I said. Just take it."

"What the hell's wrong with you?" he said. "What did I ever do to you? Why are you such a dick all the time?"

Joel knew he should keep his mouth shut. If he spoke up, he'd be asking for trouble. But he couldn't help it. The guy needed to be put in his place. "It's because I'm sick of you scamming everyone in town," he said. "A teacher, huh? We both know that's bullshit."

"What are you talking about? I am a teacher."

"No you're not. I've got your number, pal."

"And how exactly is it that you've got my number?"

"Because I happen to have a cousin named Meg," he said.

Christopher's back stiffened and he pursed his lips. "Your cousin?"

"That's right," Joel said. "So, look. I'll keep your secret, okay? If you back off until the big announcement about your Broadway debut is made. Back off with Laurel and back off with the rest of the people in town. Nobody likes being lied to. You wanted a quiet place, right? So be quiet already. Don't make it any worse than it is."

Christopher folded his hands across his chest, his body looking even narrower than usual in that position. "No, I've got a better idea," he said. "You tell your cousin she's fired. And if anyone else in town learns the truth, I'm going to sue her sorry ass. Let's see how quiet *she* stays then."

He turned around and marched to the door, pulling it open with such force that the bell overhead fell off the hook and the customers in the store all gasped in surprise.

Joel rubbed his chin. There was going to be hell to pay for what he'd just done. Meg would probably never forgive him. But he couldn't deal with the guy any longer. And he couldn't keep lying to Laurel. Even if she got mad at him for lying this long. He had to tell her what he'd done.

Just then Lexy came up beside him, holding a stack of invoices, her mouth and her eyes wide open.

"What's the matter with you?" he said.

"Oh my God," she said. "Isn't that the big star everyone's been taking about? That's the guy, isn't it? Right here in our store."

She put the invoices down and shook her head. "Oh my God, that's him. They were right. He's here."

EIGHTEEN

The door of the inn opened, and Laurel caught her breath, waiting to see Joel come in. But it turned out to be Christopher who arrived first.

"Hello there," he said as he took off his jacket. "Big show tonight, right? I tried to get Simon a gift, but it didn't quite work out. I'll figure something out. So when do we have to leave? Do we have time for a little dinner? That steak Mavis made last night was really good."

"Sure, we have time," she said, and he started for the kitchen. "Unless you want to prepare a little performance yourself. I bet all the kids would be happy to sing with a Broadway star, *Mr. Rhodes.*"

He stopped and turned to her. "How did you find out? Did Joel tell you?"

"What? Joel? No—this." She picked up the article on the coffee table and held it toward him. "Someone in town has a niece who sent this to him. A lot of people saw it. A lot of people recognized you."

He took the article and studied it. Then he came to the sofa and sat down next to her. "I never meant for you to know," he said.

"Clearly."

"No, I mean I never meant for it to turn out like this. When I first came, I figured I'd get through December this way. And then maybe I'd get in touch one day and tell you. And we'd have a good laugh over it."

"A good laugh?" she said. "How is this funny? We talked about our lives together. And I let you get close to my son. And you were lying the whole time."

"No," he said. "Not the whole time. I mean, I have been working as a part-time teacher in Lyons Hill. That's true. And I am dealing with a lot of pressure. And I did want to get away and de-stress. That all was true."

"Oh, come on. You were using us to test out this role you're playing. Not just me, everyone—"

"I didn't mean it."

"You had to. You did it."

"But it wasn't how I intended all this to go. Laurel, listen. Please let me explain—"

"Do you really expect me to believe anything you say now?"

"But I came here because I was under pressure. That was all true. I didn't mean to deceive you—"

"We're back to that?" She started to get up.

"Laurel, just listen for a second. Okay?"

He looked so sincere, so distraught, that she couldn't help but sit back down.

"I don't blame you for being mad," he said. "But maybe you can see it my way for a minute. Here I was, coming to this inn to get away. I didn't come here expecting to get to know you. And to become friendly with you. And to like it here. I never meant to get involved with you or Simon. But you made it impossible not to. From the moment I walked in the door."

"That's how we are," she said. "That's how my mom always was. This isn't some impersonal hotel. It's our home."

"I know. I get that now. You made this a nice place for me. And I guess I got a little too comfortable, a little too arrogant maybe. It's a fault of mine, I know. But we had a good time, didn't we? It's not that terrible, is it? I can understand you being annoyed with me, but this furious? Is there something else going on?"

She let out a breath. "I don't know," she said, looking down. "Maybe." He was onto something. Her real anger was toward Joel. And her dad. And Christopher was bearing the brunt of it. Because he'd had the bad luck to show up first.

"And by the way, the stuff I said about your sketches? I meant every word of that. They were great, and the way you talked about design, it really impressed me. And this is the good thing about my not being a schoolteacher. Because I do know a lot of people in the theater, and with my show coming up, I know I can make something happen for you. I can help you with your career. I owe you this, for what I put you through."

He looked at the clock on the wall, then jumped up from the sofa. "Jeez, I better get going. Come on—come help me pack."

She followed him and grabbed his arm. "Wait! Where are you going?"

"You told me that people are recognizing me," he said, pulling away and heading for the stairs. "I can't have that. I have to go."

"But why? Why can't you just be honest now?"

"Because I can't. I can't," he said, looking down at her from the middle of the stairway. "That article is a problem. I can't have people knowing that I ran off, that I was stressed and upset over Carolina. I'm on the brink of my breakout role. I can't look weak. I'll destroy my career."

"But you're human. Everyone needs to get away once in a while."

"I can't have people thinking they discovered me. I can't have them taking my picture tonight and posting it on their Instagram. I can't have people asking me why I'm here."

"But Simon's expecting you."

"You'll explain it to him."

"You have to be there. You promised him. I know what it's like when someone doesn't show up. You can't not be there when he's counting on you—"

Just then the front door opened, and Laurel turned to see Joel dash inside. He looked past her and up toward Christopher.

"They're talking about you," he said. "The whole town knows."

There was silence for a moment, and then Laurel turned away from both men and walked back to the sofa. She faintly heard Joel talking about Lexy and how Joel had rushed the customers out of his store so he could run right here. She faintly heard Christopher insist he had to leave. But she couldn't process much of it. All she could think about was that Joel was here, and that Joel knew her dad's secret. And evidently he knew Christopher's secret too. He knew everything. And had kept it all from her.

It was true. He had betrayed her. Once again. And it was worse, far worse, than the first time. Because now they were adults. Now they were even more responsible for their actions. And now she had really been falling in love with him.

She sat down, pressing her fingertips against her mouth. Joel came over to her, and she looked up at him.

"You know who he is," she said.

He nodded.

"You let me introduce him to you. You acted like you'd never met him before."

"I hadn't. My cousin, Meg, is his agent. She was looking for a place for him to hide out in secret. She's the one who made the reservation. I didn't even know you'd be here when all this started. I did it to help your dad."

Laurel looked up at him. "And tell me, why did you want to do that? Because you thought he might need money? Because you knew he was getting married to Katie?"

He looked at her, and she could tell he was stunned.

"Yes, I know about my dad's engagement," she said. "I found the business card for the jeweler where he bought the engagement ring. And I saw your note to him. Congratulating him and Katie."

He sighed and sat down, and that's when she stood up.

"How could you not tell me any of this?" she said, her voice cracking. She put her hands on her waist, feeling more secure, less likely to fall apart, in that position. "How could you say you were my friend, you cared about me, that you once had a crush on me? How could you spend all that time with me the other night, letting me open up to you about everything, all my deepest feelings about the inn and my father and my son? I trusted you! I knew I shouldn't, I knew I was making a mistake, because of what happened before between us. But I let myself believe that all didn't matter. And here you were, betraying me."

"I wasn't betraying you, Laurel. It all happened before I could stop it."

"You knew he was engaged to Katie. You knew he was traveling with Katie. You knew they were going away together. And that's why he was bringing me here."

"No, no, I didn't know all that at all. I didn't know he went away with Katie. I'm not even sure he did, although I guess it makes sense now. I thought Katie was going away for the holidays herself, and your dad was staying back to run the inn. That's why I told Meg to have Christopher come here. I thought your dad could use a guest. I knew he had a lot on his mind. I was worried about him."

"Worried about him? Why would you worry about him?"

"Because..." He paused. "Because... because I ran into him coming out of the medical building when I was in Ayelin Point renting my pickup. And he looked pretty shaken. He said something about getting bad news. So I guess maybe I thought he could use some company or the distraction. That's really why I had Meg call."

Laurel sank back down on the sofa. "What?" she said. "My dad?"

"Oh, Laurel," he said. "I don't want to be the one telling you this. And he looked okay, I promise. And he wasn't very specific. And he asked me not to say anything to anyone, and I wanted to respect that. I thought that he'd feel better with Christopher here and the inn busy, and that I could convince him to tell Katie and you and your sisters what the doctors said."

He leaned forward, his head down, his clasped hands between his knees. "It was so soon after my mom died, and she didn't tell anyone she was sick. Believe me, Laurel, I wouldn't want that to happen to anyone else. I intended to spend the whole month, all of December if I had to, trying to convince him to get you and your sisters here for Christmas, so he could tell you everything. Because if anyone could have convinced my mom to call me—well, I'd sure have wanted them to.

"I had no idea he was going to take off like that," he said. "I tried to call him, but he didn't answer his cell phone."

"I know. I couldn't get him on the phone either," she said. Then she looked at him. "Do you... Is it serious?"

"I don't know. I only know I never meant it to come out this way. But I desperately wanted you to know. I felt awful about what I was doing."

She looked away. "Is that why you kept coming back?" she asked. "Is that why you built the wall? Because you pitied me?"

"No, not at all. I felt guilty, yeah. But that wasn't the whole reason. I liked coming here each day. I liked that I was fixing the place and moving the wall, making the kitchen better. That was the bigger reason I kept coming back. It felt good, seeing you and Simon every day, and—"

"Oh my God, Simon!" she said, jumping up. "His show is soon. I can't even think about any of this now—I have to get over there. Where's Christopher?" She called for him up the stairway as she pulled her coat on. "Christopher?" She ran to the kitchen and looked out the window.

"Where's his car?" she asked as she came back to the living room. "Where is he?"

"He left. Didn't you hear him say that?"

"Yes, but... but..."

"He left because people know about him. He said he'd get Meg to send someone to pick up his stuff after Christmas."

"What? No. He can't leave. He has to come to Simon's show.

How am I going to explain this to Simon? He needed Christopher there at the end, to tell him he did a great job."

"But he just met the guy. Why does it matter?"

"Because it does," she said. "I know what it's like when someone's not there. I was waiting after my show for my dad, and he'd left. And it was awful."

"But this isn't your dad."

"That's not the point."

"Of course it's the point."

"No it's not." She picked up her phone from the coffee table to try to call Christopher but then felt Joel take her by the shoulders. He held her gently and looked straight into her eyes.

"Laurel, this is your issue, not Simon's," he said. "Christopher is nobody to him. It doesn't matter to Simon if Christopher is there to congratulate him when it's over, or if I'm there or Maxine is there or Stan and Trey are there, or anyone in the world. The whole theater could be empty. As long as you're there."

She looked at him. And realized that of course he was right. What had happened between her and her dad was between them. There was history there, a lot of history, that probably needed to be cleaned up. But despite her dad's absence after that show long ago, she had never failed Simon. All by herself, she had made a nice home for him—first in Queens and, more recently, here at the inn. She had brought people into his life who'd made it better—Maxine and Gull, Garrett, Joel, and yes, even Christopher. It was a very nice home. Her mother would have been proud.

"You're right," she said. "Come on, it's time to go."

They arrived shortly before the show started and were lucky to find two seats together, as the auditorium was packed. Simon did a beautiful job as Narrator 2, using gestures and speaking slowly, just as Christopher had taught him. He described exactly how the Lake Summers community had come together around a bonfire by the lake on that Christmas Eve so many years ago, after a week without power, when the electricity finally went back on. Garrett was a perfect mayor, encouraging everyone to go back home and gather all the food they could fit in the cars, and extra presents too, to make sure the people without power would still have a wonderful Christmas.

The play ended with a medley of holiday songs, and the cast came out to take their bows. Laurel loved watching Simon line up with the other kids to raise their arms and then bend at the waist. He'd made lots of friends these last few weeks, and his classmates liked him a lot. She was so happy for him.

Afterwards, everyone proceeded to the multi-purpose room, which had been decked out with garlands and lights. Tables around the perimeter were piled high with snacks and treats from Mrs. Pearl's, the Grill, and the Sweet Shop. Along the far wall, Stan and Trey had set up a special table for parents and kids to sample their newest concoction, the Schoolhouse Smoothie. Joel offered to go get them a sample as the cast members entered the room.

Simon came over to her, and she hugged him and kissed his sweaty, make-up-covered face. She wasn't surprised that he never asked where Christopher was. Maybe he'd ask later, she thought, and then she'd explain. But for now, Joel was right. All that mattered was that she was there.

Her phone buzzed, and she took it out of her bag and read the text. It was from Christopher. "Sorry I had to take off," he wrote. "But the offer still stands about the job. Let me know when you're back in New York."

Before she could process the message, Joel came up beside her with a sample cup of the new smoothie, and she put her phone away and took it. She was glad to discover the drink was far better than what she and Christopher had sampled in the store. It was warm and frothy and chocolatey, with peaks of whipped cream and swizzles of caramel. She couldn't figure out how it related to school, but she didn't think that mattered, given how good it tasted.

She tossed the cup in a nearby trash can and then turned back to Joel. "I understand why you hid everything from me," she said. "And I'm sorry my dad put you in such an impossible situation. And I'm grateful for how worried you were about him. He's lucky to have a friend like you."

"You know Lexy over there?" he said, pointing to the pregnant woman by the smoothie table. "She owns the store next to my mom's. She was closer to my mom than I'd been for years. I guess being close to your dad was my way of making up for not coming home as much as I should have."

He put his hands in his jeans pockets. "So, what do you think you'll do now?" he asked. "Since your stint as an innkeeper is coming to an end?"

"I don't know. My dad's coming back tonight, then and Simon and I are sprung. I guess I'll go back to New York. Christopher said the other day he can help me start a whole new career in set design. He just texted me to say the offer still stands. Despite his quick exit."

"No kidding," Joel said. "That's great. Are you going to do it?"

"I don't know," she repeated. "I mean, the news about my dad changes everything. If he's sick, he may need me. And besides, I'm not in such a rush to leave. I like it here. And Simon's pretty happy here too."

She clasped her hands together in front of her chest. "How about you?" she said. "Everything all set with the store? When exactly do you leave for Singapore?"

"I don't," he said.

Her eyes widened. "You don't? You're not going back?"

He shook his head. "I know it's crazy, but I liked working on the inn. That's the kind of thing I always wanted to do. I never liked what I was doing overseas.

"You know," he added, "I realized today why my mom never wanted me to follow my heart and build things. It's because my dad was a carpenter, and she didn't want me to be like him. Because he left her. She didn't realize I could build houses and rooms and homes without turning into the kind of guy he was."

"She must have been so hurt all those years," Laurel said.

He nodded. "She hated when I did anything that resembled what he did for a living. She even hated when I worked on the senior play with you. She surprised me after that show with a trip to New York to visit Meg and spend the whole weekend watching the Yankees. We left right after the play was over."

"You did?" Laurel said, remembering how angry she'd been at him. "So that's why you didn't come to the cast party?"

"I tried to explain it to you," he said. "But you wouldn't let me. I couldn't tell my mom no. She was so excited about that trip. And I was excited too. I mean the Yankees, wow. And besides, I didn't always feel comfortable around you theater types. You all knew so much, and you were so good at what you did. I felt like a dumb jock around all of you. Especially you."

She looked sideways at him. "I don't believe it. You had everything going for you. How could you feel out of place?"

"Hey," he said. "I don't think anyone has a monopoly on feeling out of place in high school."

She felt a pull on her arm and looked down to see Simon beside her. He pressed his face against her elbow. "I'm tired," he said. "I want to go home."

"Me too," she said. "It's been a long day. Why don't you go over and tell Mrs. Pall thank you? I'll wait here."

He nodded and trotted off.

She looked at Joel. "Are you ready to leave? I can drop you off at your house."

"No, that's okay," he said. "Simon's tired, you should go straight home. I'll get a ride with Lexy."

"Are you sure?"

He nodded.

"What are you going to do for Christmas tomorrow?" she asked.

"Haven't give it much thought."

"You should come by," she told him.

"We'll see. You have a lot of catching up to do with your dad. And Katie too, I guess. I don't want to get in the way."

He took her hand and leaned down to kiss her cheek. The kiss felt good, and she closed her eyes as he lingered there a moment.

"So long, Laurel," he said. "I wish you luck, no matter what you decide. I hope you stay in Lake Summers, I really do. But if you decide to see what Christopher has to offer... just make sure to say goodbye."

She watched him disappear into the crowd and then looked over to Simon, who was talking animatedly to Mrs. Pall. It made her think about what Joel had just said, how he had come to terms with what his mom had wanted and was now going to do what he wanted to do with his life. Looking at Simon, she felt glad about how the evening had turned out. Not only had she been here to congratulate him, but she had finally resolved everything with Joel. It felt as though she had finally made right what had gone so wrong for her that night in high school when her father hadn't been there. It felt like she'd found closure.

And now, finally, she'd be able to move on.

NINETEEN

The sun was starting to drift down toward the horizon the next afternoon, orange and glowing through the tall windows of the inn. The harpist started to play a tuneful classical piece, and Laurel walked down the stairway of the inn, the bannister festooned with white ribbon and bows, her sister Tracey in front of her and Deb behind. She was grasping a small bouquet of white roses, the petals looking especially bright as she held them close to her lacy blush-toned sheath dress that matched Tracey's and Deb's, all of them sporting sprigs of baby's breath in their buns.

This had been the Christmas surprise her dad had hinted about in the note she'd found the morning she and Simon had arrived in town—a Christmas wedding.

He and Katie had made all the plans, although she suspected that Katie had been in charge of most of the planning. The two of them had arrived home late last night, and Katie's management skill was evident in how seamlessly the inn had been transformed that morning, with the florist, bartenders, a photographer, hairdresser, and waitstaff showing up at eight to get ready for the celebration.

A short time later, her sisters and their husbands and kids had arrived, having been alerted recently by their dad about the

Christmas surprise as well. Yes, Laurel and her sisters had had their problems growing up, but it was good to know that, in the end, they were all family and were together at the most important times of their lives.

Of course, since it was a last-minute wedding, and on Christmas no less, the guest list was small, but everyone who mattered was there, sitting on the white folding chairs decorated with ribbons and bows. Mrs. Pearl and Jake, her assistant. Stan and Trey. Maxine and Gull. All of the cooks and servers on Katie's staff, including Mavis, who had been sworn to secrecy in the last week as they prepared the special wedding feast that was now waiting in the kitchen. Amy and her mother. Chuck and his wife, and the other aardies; Russ, Mickey, and the rest of her dad's pals. And Lexy, who looked radiant in a form-fitting blue dress that showed off her pregnant belly. It was thanks to Lexy that Laurel and her sisters had their beautiful dresses. Lexy had secretly ordered all the clothes—with directions from Katie on style, color, and probable sizes—and had come over early this morning to do a fitting and some last-minute alterations.

And, of course, there was Joel, looking so handsome in a suit and tie, sitting by the aisle, smiling at her as she passed him. She smiled back, so glad to see him. Their discussion at the play last night had spurred a lot of soul-searching for her, as she took in the news that he was giving up his high-powered job overseas and staying in Lake Summers. That he had decided he wanted to be here. That it was, in fact, where he'd always wanted to be.

Then the music changed, and all eyes turned toward the staircase. Katie came downstairs looking elegant and beautiful in a stunning champagne-colored chiffon dress with a flared skirt and beaded bodice, her platinum, shoulder-length hair pulled back from her face. There were sweet tears in her eyes as she reached out and took Doug's hand.

Laurel had always known that Katie was lovely and had sophisticated tastes. Which had made her realize last night that it was probably Katie who'd decided on the all-white twinkling lights on the Christmas trees and those slippery sheets and pillowcases in the guest rooms. Katie's choices were stylish, the same way Joanna's modern kitchen in the Samposiera showroom was. But Laurel much preferred her mother's way of decorating. The Cranberry Inn was a warm, homey place, and its furnishings and accessories should reflect that. She imagined that at some point she'd talk to Katie, and she was confident the two of them would agree on what the inn should look like going forward.

Because she was going to be around next Christmas, and for many Christmases after that. Late last night, she and Simon had decided that, like Joel, they were staying in Lake Summers. She was going to help her dad run the inn.

She had planned to speak with her dad about it last night, but they'd all been so tired that they'd barely gotten past the subject of the wedding before they all decided they couldn't keep their eyes open any longer. So she'd gone downstairs early this morning, before all the vendors started arriving for the wedding, to talk to him about it. He'd always been an early riser, and she'd smelled the coffee brewing while she was still in bed. She'd enjoyed being in charge all these weeks, but still, it was nice for a change that someone else had gotten up and started the coffee.

Still in pajamas and slippers, she padded into the kitchen, where he was sitting at the table, reading the most recent issue of the *Lake Summers Press*. He looked great, she'd thought, especially for a man who hadn't had more than a few hours of sleep last night. And yet, she had to admit, he looked a bit thinner than she'd remembered from last summer.

"Hey, kiddo," he'd said, smiling.

"Hi, Dad," she'd said, giving him a hug. "Can I join you?"

"Wouldn't mind a bit," he answered, starting to get up to pull her chair out. He was old-fashioned that way. Still, she put her hand up. She had lived on her own for a long time, and she preferred showing him that she could pull her own chairs out. He sat back down and motioned to the new wall. "Nice surprise," he said.

"I'm glad you like it. Joel did the work."

"But you had the idea, I suspect," he said and then took a sip of coffee. "I'm glad you came down. I wanted to talk to you."

"Oh?" She sat down, surprised by his remark. She'd expected she'd be the one to open the conversation.

He smiled. "You really love it here, don't you?"

"Of course. We all do."

"But you most of all," he insisted. "Your sisters feel at home in their own homes now. But this place has never stopped being home to you, has it? Just like your mom."

There was a time she would have resented this kind of talk. It would have made her back stiffen and her jaw clench. That was another frequent topic, when she'd talk with her mother on those Saturday mornings—how she always felt different, like an outsider. *Especially in my own house,* she'd often thought, although she never said it directly. But somehow it didn't bother her that morning. He was right, and there was no reason to deny it. She did love the inn more than her sisters. And there was nothing wrong with that.

He put his elbows on the table and rubbed his hands together. "You know, when we were just starting out, your mom and me, I never dreamed of owning this place so long. But your mom adored it. And it all worked out. For as long as we had together."

"And now you're getting married again," Laurel said. "And the truth is, Dad, I knew even before you got back. I found the business card Joel gave you, the jeweler you went to for Katie's ring. And it was a huge shock. And I wish... I wish you'd told me about you and Katie before. I don't know why you felt you needed to hide that. We all love Katie, you know that."

"I do," he said, nodding slightly as he turned his head to the side. She'd always known her father to be confident, making decisions and never looking back. But now he seemed regretful.

"But you've got to understand, kiddo, that I didn't expect this to happen," he continued. "I didn't even realize it was happening. Or maybe I didn't want to think about it happening. She was a friend and... then she was more. And it all felt so strange, after all these years. I suppose I was scared that you and your sisters would think I was betraying your mom. I guess I should have had more faith in you. I feel bad about that."

Laurel looked down, thinking of how much she loved her mother, how much she missed her still. Had she given Dad the impression she could never accept him falling in love again? She hadn't meant to. But families were complicated. Misunderstandings happened all the time. And then, thankfully, there were moments like this. When everyone finally had clarity. And the future looked bright again.

"I feel bad too," she said. "I'm sorry if I did something to make you feel you couldn't be honest. I know you loved Mom. You were great together. And I'm glad you're with Katie now."

He squeezed her hand. "She saved me, you know," he said. "She gave me a new lease on life. I was pretty lonely these last few years. Which brings me to what I want to talk to you about."

He went on to tell her about his visit to the medical building in Ayelin Point. Joel had been right—her dad had been given some bad news. It turned out there was a worrisome spot on his liver. By that point, Dad and Katie were engaged, and they decided before the wedding to go out to San Francisco for Dad to see a specialist Katie knew. That's why they had left town so suddenly, he said, and why he had called her to come take care of the inn. And why he had avoided all her phone calls while he was away—he didn't want to discuss anything until he had answers. Fortunately, his illness was treatable, and his prognosis was excellent. It looked like he and Katie had many happy years ahead of them—and this little health scare had only brought them closer.

"I'll tell your sisters about this after the wedding," he said. "But because it impacted you the most, I thought I owed you an explanation first."

"I'm so glad you're okay," she said. She decided not to tell him that she already knew some of it. It didn't matter. The only thing that mattered was that everything was fine.

"So what about you?" he said. "Will you stay a few days after the wedding? Maybe through New Year's?"

That's when she told him that she and Simon had had a long talk last night after the play, and they'd both agreed they wanted to stay.

"Yeah?" he said, a smile spreading across his face. "I'm happy to hear this, kiddo. It's exactly what I hoped you'd say. What I always wanted for you."

She chuckled. "Come on, be honest. It's not what you always wanted for me. Maybe now you do, but not always. You wanted your daughters to leave Lake Summers. You wanted us all to do bigger things than stay around the inn. You made us all go to college in big cities. You made it clear we shouldn't stay."

"Now, wait a minute," he said. "That's not exactly how it was. I wanted you to get a taste of what your options were. I never wanted you to stay here and regret it someday. I wanted you to choose this life after considering everything else that was possible for you."

He looked at her. "I knew that if you really wanted to run the inn, you'd be back to do it. You were so strong. The strongest of the three of you. Just like your mom. I never had to worry about you. Which was a good thing, since it was your sisters who needed me more."

"But I needed you," she said. "I needed you too."

"You had your mom. You two were so close."

"But I needed you too," she repeated. "You never seemed to see that."

"That's not true. I always cared. But I didn't think I had much to give you. I didn't understand what you were involved with—the plays, the make-believe, the way you liked to help your mom choose curtains and dishes and things. And you were so determined to do what you wanted, even as a little girl. I had to beg you to even let me teach you to ice skate."

"I wanted to go skating with you," she said. "I was so glad when you took me that day. I loved that day. I loved having you all to myself." She put her hand to her mouth, feeling the tears stream down her cheeks. "I never wanted that day to end."

"So I messed things up with you, did I?" he said.

He reached over and squeezed her hand again and then looked out the window, as though he couldn't bring himself to watch her crying. Or to look at her while he thought back on those long-ago years.

"I don't know, kiddo," he said. "I thought I did my best. Your mom and I, we had three daughters and an inn to run and bills and guests and things that needed to be repaired or replaced all the time. And it felt like we were always juggling. But I thought I usually got it right. Maybe every parent feels that way. Maybe we have to feel that way to make it from one day to the next. Maybe we're all always fooling ourselves."

He paused. "You know something, Laurel? One day you're going to sit in your kitchen with Simon, and he's going to tell you something you did wrong. Something you messed up that you had no idea about. Something he's been stewing over all his life. And you're going to tell him the only thing you can say. That you tried to make good decisions. And you did your best. And you know you weren't perfect, but there was one thing you did perfectly. You loved him with all your heart.

"So kiddo," he said, finishing his coffee and taking the mug to the sink. "Things are about to get busy. We have a wedding to get ready for."

She hugged him and then went upstairs to get dressed.

It was a quick ceremony, just a few words from the judge followed by the vows. The kiss was long and sweet, and the guests applauded, and Laurel was so moved at the affection Katie and her dad had for each other, she felt her eyes water. Then a waiter came down the aisle serving glasses of champagne.

Doug held up his glass, thanked everyone for giving up their Christmas plans and being with them, and then gave a special thanks to his three daughters and their families for being part of the day. He ended by putting his arm around Katie and thanking her for opening a new chapter in his life.

"And I have other news too," he added. "I'm proud to announce that my middle daughter, Laurel, and her son, Simon, have decided to stay here in Lake Summers to help me run the inn. So here's to all my three daughters and, especially today, to Laurel. The next generation to be continuing the family legacy.

"Right, kiddo?" he said, calling over to where she was standing by the fireplace. She nodded and everyone raised their glasses and drank.

A band started playing from deeper in the inn, and people made their way toward the improvised bar in the dining room, as servers with trays started passing hors d'oeuvres. Joel had been right—the room didn't look the tiniest bit smaller, even though it had lost eight inches.

Laurel watched the guests for a moment, and then wandered over to the sunroom and looked out onto the backyard, to take in all that had happened. She had come back to Lake Summers stressed and confused, concerned that she'd never be the interior designer she wanted to be. And here she was with a whole new wonderful direction for her life. Starting a new career in the theater would have been glamorous and exciting, but last night, it had become clear that this was where she belonged.

Suddenly she heard Joel's voice next to her. "So you're not leaving? To be with Christopher?" he asked.

She shook her head.

"Why not?" he asked. "Isn't it what you wanted? A new career?"

"I thought it was. For about a minute. And then I heard you last night. And I realized you were right. That you were following your heart and doing exactly what you wanted, and I needed to do the same. You set us straight, Simon and me. You fixed everything."

He smiled. "Laurel, I fix things for a living. Companies. Business mistakes. And now walls and floors. And because I fix things, there's one thing I can tell you for sure. You are someone who never needed fixing."

She waited a moment, then threw her arms around his neck. And as she hugged him, her gaze landed on the backyard, the place where her mom's ballroom was supposed to have been built. She wanted to see it through. Sure, it would have been nice if it could have been completed for her dad's wedding. But there was no way she could have built it in three weeks. Still, she'd get it done. And by next Christmas it would be ready.

It would be ready to host its first wedding, she thought. And maybe, if things went the way she hoped, that wedding would be hers.

Smiling at the thought, she hugged Joel tighter. That's when he pressed his lips to her ear. "Laurel," he whispered. "I love you."

TWENTY

ONE YEAR LATER

It was December first, a year to the day after her dad had called with that mysterious request to come quick to the inn, and, as usual, New York City was packed. Especially, it seemed, in the theater district. Outside the theater where the Saturday matinee of *Orange Nightsongs* had just ended, a bundled-up crowd gathered by the stage door. Laurel stood a little to the side, listening to the conversations of people who were pressed up against the red velvet rope, hoping to snag an autograph from the star.

"He is so cute," one woman said.

"I know. I'm in love with him," another fan responded. "I've seen this show three times now."

"You know, he's leaving the cast next month," the first one said. "I heard he's starting to film a movie."

"I heard that too. This play will never be as good once he's gone."

Just then the door opened, and Christopher came out, waving as the crowd applauded and cheered. He moved along the line of people, signing programs and posing for selfies, until his eyes locked onto Laurel's. She waved, and he reached through the crowd and hugged her, and she sensed a gazillion pairs of eyes on her, a gazillion people wondering who she was and why she was the one getting the hug.

Christopher pulled back, holding her by the shoulders. "Hey. Why didn't you tell me you were coming?"

"I wanted it to be a surprise."

"Did you see the show?"

She nodded. "You were incredible."

"Got time for a cup of coffee? Just give me a few more minutes here."

"I'd love to. I'll wait here."

She stepped aside to watch him continue to sign autographs. He looked great, his open jacket revealing a sweater and jeans, the same type of outfit he'd worn as he'd made his way around Lake Summers last winter. His hair looked a little lighter and his face a little softer than the last time she'd seen him. He was still incredibly handsome, but he seemed more relaxed, less manic than he'd been at Amy's mother's store last winter, where he'd also been the center of attention.

, She looked at her phone to check the time. She didn't want to drive home too late. She wanted to get back in time to say goodnight to Simon, although she would probably have to settle for a kiss on his sleeping head and then breakfast with him tomorrow morning. She'd missed him so much this week, being down here in New York, visiting furniture showrooms and the big design center on Lexington Avenue to check out some ideas for redecorating the living room and the guest rooms at the inn. It was an expensive project, but it was necessary. The Cranberry Inn was as busy as it had been when her mother was alive, and running it with her dad felt right. The ads she'd placed last winter and the work she'd done on the website had paid off—but she knew the change in the inn's fortunes was mainly due to Christopher, who mentioned it in every interview he'd given since he'd opened to rave reviews last May.

He'd also published a letter that month in the *Lake Summers Press,* admitting that he'd spent all of December at the Cranberry

Inn and thanking the town for its hospitality. He credited the community with seeing him through a period of time when his confidence was suffering, and for helping him return to New York ready to take on the challenge of a Broadway musical debut. And he'd apologized for lying about who he was—to her, to Joel, and to the whole community.

Everyone in town had been tickled to read about Christopher's affection for Lake Summers—and, of course, everyone had forgiven him. Not only that, but they were happy to celebrate him. The historical society was considering adding his picture and bio to their year-end wrap-up exhibition, while Stan and Trey had gotten right to work inventing a Great White Way smoothie, with tons of glittery candies, to commemorate Christopher's visit.

Christopher finished autographing programs, and the two of them walked over to the nearby Midtown Diner, where they peeled off their coats and ordered coffees and a plate of mini donuts. Christopher pointed out that they weren't nearly as good as the ones Mavis had made.

He circled his mug with his hand and took a sip of coffee. "So, how's Simon?"

"He's fine. The Christmas Eve play is coming up. He's hoping to be Narrator Number 1 this year since he's in fourth grade. He said if I saw you, I should ask if he can call you for some more tips."

"Absolutely," Christopher said. "Anytime." He picked up a donut and popped the whole thing in his mouth. "And how about mountain man?"

"*Joel* is fine," she said, feeling her cheeks warm. "His construction business has really taken off." He'd started up Hutcherson Builders soon after Christopher had left town, and he was so busy with projects after just a few months, he'd already hired two employees. He had gone ahead and sold his mother's house—but had decided to renew his lease on the store. He'd also convinced the landlord to let him cut out a doorway between his store and Lexy's, so that Lexy could oversee his store as well as her own.

"She understands my mom's business almost as well as my

mom did," he'd said.

Lexy had hired a couple of sales assistants and was enjoying her new management role. Laurel loved going downtown to see Lexy running both operations, with her baby girl, Jamie, entertaining customers from her playpen.

"So why does the mention of Joel make you blush?" Christopher said. "Anything I should know about?"

"As a matter of fact, yes," she said. "We're getting married."

"For real? Hey, that's great news!" Christopher exclaimed. "Congratulations. I'm happy for you guys. I always knew there was something between you. I was always a little jealous."

"No, you weren't," she said. "But I think we have you to thank. It never would have happened if you hadn't come to town."

And that was the truth. If Christopher hadn't come to the inn, Joel wouldn't have been around her so much, and she'd never have had the chance to fall in love with him all over again.

And she had waited to schedule the wedding until she could do it at the inn, in the ballroom her mother had always envisioned. It was finally a reality, exactly as her mom had wanted, according to the notes she'd left in the floral notebook. Joel had taken those notes and the sketches she'd made and had transformed them into a beautiful space. Watching him work, she'd often remembered the story about how her parents met—how her dad had changed his whole life for her mom and proposed on the porch overlooking the woods and the path to the lake, and had promised to build her a ballroom. Joel had changed his life too when he'd fallen in love with her. And he'd proposed to her last summer, in the same spot her dad had proposed to her mom.

She remembered standing on the porch last winter, doubting that anyone would ever love her the way her dad had loved her mom. But she'd been wrong. Joel loved her just as much. And she loved him too.

"So when's the big day?" Christopher asked.

"Christmas." Just like her father's wedding. In the ballroom that was now finished and would remind her of her mother every day. "We'd love you to come. I know it's kind of late notice. And Christmas. So don't worry if—"

"Are you kidding?" he said. "I wouldn't miss it. I'll be there. I have a show the day before and another the day after. But I'll get up there for sure, to see the two of you tie the knot."

He finished his coffee and looked at his watch. "I hate to cut this short, but I should get going. I go on again in a few hours."

She nodded. "I should get going too. I have a long drive ahead."

"Oh man, I remember that drive. And all I can say is, better you than me." He motioned for a check. "It was great to see you, Laurel. And thanks for everything. I know I hid it well by being kind of a jerk, but I was really a mess when I went up there last winter. And you showed me such kindness, right up until the end. Thanks for getting me back on my feet."

"Thank you," she said. "For making me see the inn through fresh eyes. And for helping me realize it's where I belonged. And for those gorgeous bathrobes in every guest room."

They hugged goodbye on the street a little while later, and as she braced herself against the brisk wind and walked to get her car, she gave a quick call home to tell Joel she was on her way. She couldn't wait to get back. A week was way too long to be away from her boys.

She fetched her car from the garage and started up Eighth Avenue. To the east, on her right, was the route to her old apartment in Queens, and to the west, on her left, was the Samposiera showroom, where Joanna had designed that model kitchen last winter, and where Laurel had stood, helping the photographer while she wondered who would live in such a sophisticated kitchen, and what kinds of food they'd serve on Christmas.

Now she didn't have to wonder about things like that anymore. Because now she didn't deal in empty rooms. Now, finally, she had made a home for herself. With people she loved. In a place she'd never want to leave.

She pressed a tiny bit harder on the gas. She couldn't wait to get there.

A LETTER FROM BARBARA

I want to say a huge thank you for choosing to read *The Cranberry Inn*. If you did enjoy it and want to keep up to date with all my latest releases, just sign up at the following link. Your email address will never be shared, and you can unsubscribe at any time.

www.bookouture.com/barbara-josselsohn

A few years ago, I saw a performance of *She Kills Monsters*, a stunning and incredibly moving by play Qui Nguyen. It was written in 2011 and is based largely on *Dungeons & Dragons*, the fantasy role-playing game that was so popular back then. The play explores how easy it is to feel like an outcast, even in your own family, without anyone even knowing, and how essential it is for everyone—especially a young person—to feel seen and acknowledged. *She Kills Monsters* was the inspiration for *The Not-So Hero*, the play that Laurel discovers and directs in *The Cranberry Inn* and the launching point for the novel's exploration of what it means to feel at home.

Writing this novel about a family inn at holiday time became, for me, an act of discovery about the ways we look for home and—if we're lucky—the places where we ultimately find it. Laurel, Joel, Doug, Lexy, and even Simon are all searching for home. And I love how in their own ways, they each gradually learn that home is both a place and a state of mind.

I hope you loved *The Cranberry Inn*, and if you did I would be very grateful if you could write a review. I'd love to hear what you think, and it makes such a difference helping new readers to discover one of my books for the first time.

I love hearing from my readers—you can get in touch on my Facebook page or through Twitter, Goodreads, or my website.

Thanks,

Barbara

www.BarbaraSolomonJosselsohn.com

 facebook.com/BarbaraSolomonJosselsohnAuthor

 twitter.com/BarbaraJoss

ACKNOWLEDGMENTS

Writing *The Cranberry Inn* was both a deeply emotional and an immensely joyful undertaking. As with every book, I relied on so many amazing people, whose support, insight, feedback, and encouragement proved invaluable. I'm very happy for the opportunity to thank them here from the bottom of my heart.

As always, it's hard to express the extent of my gratitude to my agent, Cynthia Manson. As she's done for many years now, Cynthia provided me with the wisest advice, the most generous guidance, and unwavering friendship. Although she's one of the busiest and most in-demand people I've ever met, she still always makes me feel as though I'm her top priority!

I am also grateful beyond words to my brilliant editor, Jennifer Hunt, who blends the most incredible insight and vision with an uncanny ability to connect with authors on such a warm, thoughtful and crystal-clear level. It's beyond me how she can spot the essential story that lies deep within the drafts I send her, and how she can strategize the best route forward to make that story emerge triumphant! I truly love working with her.

Thanks, too, to the incredible publishing, marketing, editorial and PR teams at Bookouture. I am overwhelmed by your talent, knowledge, professionalism, and generosity. And a big shout-out to my fellow Bookouture authors—I'm truly in awe of your talent.

I'm excited, too, to recognize a new and wonderful friend, Kerry Schafer. Kerry's a genius at social media and a wonderful human being to boot. And if that wasn't enough, she is also an amazing novelist!

I am privileged to have a truly spectacular community of author-friends, some of whom I've known for over a decade now. Thanks with all my heart to Jimin Han, Patricia Dunn, Jennifer Manocherian, Marcia Bradley, Victoria Cowal, Veera Hiranandani, Diane Cohen Schneider, Patty Friedrich, Maggie Smith, and Susan Schild. I appreciate each and every one of you.

Thanks, too, to the talented writers and professionals who make up the Women's Fiction Writers Association, the Writing Institute at Sarah Lawrence College, and the Scarsdale Library Writers Center. And a super-big virtual hug to the amazing book bloggers and reviewers I've come to know. Although our interactions have been online, I feel so close and connected to you, and I'm so glad to call you all my friends.

In writing Laurel's story, I found myself going back in my mind to my own high-school experiences, as well as to the parties and chance meetings I've had with many classmates in the ensuing years. Laurel's delight in discovering her high school "family" and her deep affection for the "aardies" was based on my own memories. I am a proud graduate of Syosset High School on Long Island, New York—and I'm deeply grateful to the alumni who run our Facebook groups and plan our reunions, so we can all still connect.

Finally, as always, my deepest and most heartfelt thanks to my husband, Bennett, and our kids, David, Rachel, and Alyssa. You guys are my everything, and I couldn't love you more!

Made in the USA
Las Vegas, NV
18 December 2021